STEPHEN GILBERT was born in Newcastle, County Down in 1912. He was sent to England for boarding school from age 10 to 13 and afterwards to a Scottish public school, which he left without passing any exams or obtaining a leaving certificate. He returned to Belfast, where he worked briefly as a journalist before joining his father's tea and seed business. In 1931, just before his nineteenth birthday, Gilbert met novelist Forrest Reid, by that time in his mid-fifties. Reid's works reflect his lifelong fascination with teenage boys, and he was quickly drawn to Gilbert; the two commenced a sometimes turbulent friendship that lasted until Reid's death in 1947. Reid acted as mentor to Gilbert, who had literary aspirations, and ultimately depicted an idealized version of their relationship in the novel *Brian Westby* (1934), also available from Valancourt Books.

Gilbert's first published novel, *The Landslide* (1943), a fantasy involving prehistoric creatures which appear in a remote part of Ireland after being uncovered by a landslide, appeared to generally positive reviews and was dedicated to Reid. A realistic novel, *Bombardier* (1944), followed, based on Gilbert's experiences in the Second World War. Gilbert's third novel, *Monkeyface* (1948), concerns what seems to be an ape, called "Bimbo," discovered in South America and brought back to Belfast, where it learns to talk. *The Burnaby Experiments* appeared in 1952, five years after Reid's death, and is a thinly disguised portrayal of their relationship from Gilbert's point of view and a belated response to *Brian Westby*. His final novel, *Ratman's Notebooks* (1968), the story of a loner who learns he can train rats to kill, would become his most famous, being twice filmed as *Willard* (1971, 2003).

Gilbert married Kathleen Stevenson in 1945; the two had four children, and Gilbert devoted most of his time from the 1950s onward to family life and his seed business. He died in Northern Ireland in 2010 at age 97.

ANDREW DOYLE is a playwright and stand-up comedian. His plays include *Borderland* (national tour for 7:84 Theatre Company, Scotland), *Jimmy Murphy Makes Amends* (BBC Radio 4) and *The Second Mr Bailey* (BBC Radio 4). His most recent solo stand-up show was *Whatever It Takes* at the Soho Theatre, London. He has a doctorate in English Renaissance Literature from the University of Oxford where he also worked as a lecturer.

By Stephen Gilbert

The Landslide (1943)*

Bombardier (1944)*

Monkeyface (1948)*

The Burnaby Experiments (1952)*

Ratman's Notebooks (1968)*

* Available or forthcoming from Valancourt Books

STEPHEN GILBERT

THE LANDSLIDE

With a new introduction by
ANDREW DOYLE

VALANCOURT BOOKS

The Landslide by Stephen Gilbert
First published London: Faber & Faber, 1943
First Valancourt Books edition 2013

Published by Valancourt Books, Richmond, Virginia
Publisher & Editor: JAMES D. JENKINS
20th Century Series Editor: SIMON STERN, University of Toronto
http://www.valancourtbooks.com

ISBN 978-1-939140-78-4
Also available as an electronic book.

All Valancourt Books publications are printed on acid free paper
that meets all ANSI standards for archival quality paper.

Cover by M. S. Corley
Set in Dante MT 11/13.2

PREFACE

At various points throughout this year I have spent time in Belfast undertaking research for new editions of novels by Stephen Gilbert (1912-2010) and his mentor Forrest Reid (1875-1947). The Special Collections department of the McClay Library at Queen's University holds a wealth of material from the personal archives of both writers, acquired and catalogued in the summer of 2007.

I recently had the pleasure of meeting Diarmuid Kennedy, one of the members of the project team who had originally archived the Gilbert and Reid collections. During the course of our conversation, he alerted me to the existence of five large boxes of unread and uncatalogued material, formerly in the possession of Stephen Gilbert. The university had acquired these boxes in March 2011, almost a year after the author's death. Naturally, I was eager to examine the contents.

Beneath all the dust and the desiccated spiders I was astonished to find an array of unpublished work by Gilbert, spanning a period of at least sixty-five years. The material includes fourteen unpublished novels in various drafts, numerous short stories, plays, poems, and other miscellanea. It had been commonly supposed that the sixteen-year hiatus between Gilbert's novels *The Burnaby Experiments* (1952) and *Ratman's Notebooks* (1968) was indicative of an extended period of writer's block. In actuality, Gilbert never stopped writing at all.

Given the intimate nature of some of the documents, it is clear why Gilbert might have wished to hold on to them. Most revealing are the accounts of Gilbert's own life: a journal written between October 1998 and November 2000; an undated fragment which includes some of Gilbert's memories of Reid; and an extensive four-volume pseudonymous autobiography, also undated, remarkable for both its detail and its candour. Scholars interested in Gilbert's relationship with Forrest Reid will find these typescripts particularly enlightening. I have discussed the complexities of Gilbert and Reid's relationship elsewhere (in my introduction

to Reid's *Brian Westby*, published this year by Valancourt Books),
but these recently uncovered documents have proved invaluable
for this present edition of *The Landslide*.

As will be seen, I have quoted from these sources at length in
my introduction. The material is due to be archived by Queen's
University in the near future, at which point reference numbers
will be assigned. For now, I have simply identified these as "uncatalogued" in the endnotes.

I am extremely grateful to Diarmuid Kennedy for pointing me
in the direction of these documents. Deirdre Wildy and her team
at Special Collections have been as helpful as ever. I would also like
to thank Tom Gilbert, who has been hugely supportive and has
clarified a number of details about his father and his work. Tom's
son Matthew Gilbert has been likewise patient with my numerous requests for biographical information. Thanks also to James D.
Jenkins at Valancourt Books for republishing these long-neglected
novels.

ANDREW DOYLE

October 1, 2013

INTRODUCTION

For a long while it looked as though *The Landslide* would never be published. We can date its composition to the exact hour, thanks to Stephen Gilbert's handwritten note on his first draft indicating that it was "begun at about 10 p.m. on 6th October 1936" and "finished at about 9 p.m. on Friday 9th April, 1937".[1] Such specificity tells us something about the importance of this manuscript to the young writer, who had suffered from bouts of depression after having failed to secure a publisher for his first novel *The Assailants* (c. 1936), a school story with a murderous twist based on his time at Loretto in Musselburgh, Scotland, between the years of 1925 and 1930.[2] In his unpublished autobiography, Gilbert considers the possibility that his new novel will likewise be consigned to oblivion:

> Will my poor book ever be read by anyone? It is about a dragon and a sea serpent, and a kind of prehistoric dog and an old man and a boy and a priest. I sent it to a publisher last July and it has been lost ever since. I know it is good and so does Webster. It is unlike any story that has ever been written before.[3]

"Webster" is Forrest Reid, Belfast's foremost novelist, who met Gilbert by chance in 1931 at a party at the Belmont Tennis Club and soon became his mentor.[4] The novel went astray when it was sent to a publisher in early 1940, although it would seem that the original draft had been retained by Reid: "the manuscript was lost," Reid wrote to his friend J. N. Hart in March of that year, "though fortunately I had a copy".[5] In spite of these difficulties, *The Landslide* was eventually published by Faber & Faber in 1943.

In spite of Gilbert's innate creativity and his desire to be a writer, as a young adult he lacked the discipline and technical skill to produce anything of literary value. This can be confirmed from even a cursory reading of his first attempt at a novel entitled *Nature Suppressed*, which was mercifully abandoned during its third chapter.[6] Under the auspices of Reid his skills developed rapidly.

Gilbert had only recently left school when he met the older writer and was highly self-conscious about what he perceived to be his own academic shortcomings. Indeed, his reports from the time reveal an erratic approach to his studies; he tended to fare better in the humanities subjects and was identified as having "distinct literary ability", although phrases such as "evidently rather backward" and "lazy young monkey" are hardly indicative of the model pupil.[7] His father, William Gilbert, had urged him to complete the matriculation examinations, in spite of the reservations expressed by the Headmaster, James Greenlees.

> Stephen will have to make a very big effort if he is to get through in March and I really am in a difficulty to know what to advise you to do or what would be best for the boy. He has undoubted ability along his own lines, but his lines are not those of the everyday school boy . . . He has no real interest in games or any of the ordinary boys' pursuits. On the other hand he is infinitely better read than the average boy and along lines that interest him does a great deal more thinking.[8]

Of course, British public schools have never been particularly well regarded for nurturing those of a free-thinking or individual temperament, and Gilbert was evidently not best served by an atmosphere dominated by team sports and enforced conformity. Public school had left Gilbert with an English accent, a diminished capacity for empathy, and a profound sense of guilt for the financial cost to his parents. He was simply not the kind of boy who could possibly thrive in such an environment. As Greenlees later wrote after Gilbert had failed matriculation: "I think it more than probable that he will eventually do something quite out of the ordinary, as he has an original way of looking at things".[9] In *The Landslide*, Gilbert was to prove Greenlees right.

The Landslide is a fantastical tale set in an unspecified rural location in pre-industrialized Northern Ireland. The narrator is Wolfe Emmet, a sensitive boy with a love of nature and a fertile imagination. The story begins with a landslide on the "Far Shore", caused by a sustained period of heavy rainfall, which uncovers a number of eggs and hibernating creatures from the remote past. Before

Photograph of Stephen Gilbert taken by Forrest Reid, c. 1932 (Special Collections, Queen's University Belfast, MS44/7/5/2)

long the district is alive with primeval flora and fauna. Wolfe and
his grandfather (known throughout as "Gran'papa") soon estab-
lish contact with these antediluvian species, initially through the
reptilian Procyon—named after the brightest star in the constel-
lation *Canis Minor* due to his affectionate, dog-like qualities—and
thereafter through more enduring relationships with a dragon
and a sea serpent. Whisperings of devilry and witchcraft spread in
the community, and before long the villagers have turned against
Wolfe and Gran'papa in the belief that they are agents of Satan.

When Oscar Wilde's father wrote of the Celtic race that they
have a "deep-rooted belief in the supernatural", an "unconquer-
able reverence for ancient customs, and an extensive superstitious
creed", his generalizations were well-founded.[10] Irish literary history is testimony enough to the pronounced susceptibility to
superstition that has been so commonplace amongst rural com-
munities. Forrest Reid maintained that this was an ineradicable
faith, "absolute, uncompromising; we may deplore it, or sympa-
thize with it, but it is there, a living factor in everyday life".[11] One
need only consult Lady Gregory's *Visions and Beliefs in the West of
Ireland* (1920), which Reid had been reviewing, to appreciate the
extent and variety of such beliefs, in spite of their apparent incom-
patibility with Christianity.[12] Many of the traditions described by
Lady Gregory are based on the notion of evil as an insidious and
tangible force, forever seeking a foothold in reality. Like religious
sectarianism, this has led to much mutual distrust and internecine
feuding throughout Ireland's history, most memorably illustrated
in the writings of William Carleton (1794-1869).

As a product of his environment, Wolfe is inevitably predis-
posed to folkloric beliefs. When confronted with a vista of new
trees in the valley of Neencroom, Wolfe assumes that "the fairies"
are responsible. As a young child, his mother tells him that thun-
derstorms are created by angels "rolling big stones in heaven",
resulting in Wolfe's fear that "they might fall through on top of
us". His Gran'papa tells him that toads "are magic creatures, and
have jewels in their heads". The myth of the toadstone dates back
to the writings of Pliny the Elder, and Gilbert drew on this tradition for his poem "The Toad":

Toad with the jewel in your head,
Do you sleep easy in your bed?
Do you not fear that some dark night
A magpie with one sudden bite
Will snatch the jewel for her store,
And leave you dead upon the floor?[13]

Like many children, Wolfe finds a certain appeal in stories of the supernatural. For Wolfe, there is a ghost in the rafters of his home who watches his every move, and when he plays with his toy boat he visualizes a crew of "fifty men . . . bringing a cargo of silk from China to Arabia". Yet *The Landslide* is not a novel about the transformative power of perception, or the porous distinctions between fantasy and reality that exist in the mind of a child. Wolfe's telepathic conversations with animals are a reality, and he shares the skill with his Gran'papa and, later, the local parish priest Father Binyon. It was this feature of the novel that prompted E.M. Forster to recommend *The Landslide* to his two pet cats. "They replied that they had read it many years ago, and then fell into a still profounder sleep," Forster wrote in a letter to Gilbert. "Cats are so bad at discussing literature."[14]

Like his hero Wolfe, Gilbert was repeatedly drawn to supernatural and fantastical themes, as evinced throughout his body of work. "I need something out of the ordinary to work round," he wrote in his journal on 29 October 1999, "which is what has taken me to Fantasy".[15] Of his five published novels only one, *Bombardier* (1944), is based on a realistic premise, that of his own experiences as a gunner in the 3rd Ulster Searchlight Regiment during the Second World War. *Monkeyface* (1948) tells the story of Bimbo, an ape-boy who learns how to speak and is integrated into human society. *The Burnaby Experiments* (1952) concerns a sinister recluse (based on Forrest Reid) who attempts to teach his protégé the esoteric powers of psychic translocation. In *Ratman's Notebooks* (1968), a young man learns how to train rats to commit crimes on his behalf, including vandalism, theft and, eventually, murder. In the genre of fantasy, Gilbert was able to find his authentic voice. It is perhaps no coincidence that of the numerous realistic novels he produced in his lifetime, only *Bombardier* ever made it to print, and only then with the endorsement of a "rather reluctant" publisher.[16]

The story of *The Landslide* represents a kind of inversion of the legend of Saint Patrick, the fifth century missionary who is credited with Christianizing the nation and, as Gran'papa explains, driving away "not only the dragons, but all the snakes and toads and lizards that were in Ireland". Gilbert's tale sees the triumphant return of these banished reptiles, and with them the reintroduction of pagan sensibilities. The motif is present in the opening chapter, when Wolfe and his Gran'papa discuss the creatures and their possible origins. Gran'papa explains that they are unlikely to be dragons as "Saint Patrick chased them away", but he agrees with Wolfe that they may now have returned. Later, as Gran'papa becomes an established member of the animal community, he is represented as a kind of anti-Patrick. "Gran'papa sat down," says Wolfe, and "all the creatures clambered over him and the snakes curled away in his pockets".

Gilbert's own fascination with the supernatural stemmed from his Presbyterian upbringing. His parents, William Gilbert and Evelyn Helen Haig (known as Helen), were devoutly religious, and had hopes that Stephen would be ordained as a minister on leaving Loretto. They had not counted on his instinctive agnosticism, a feature that he held in common with Forrest Reid and which, no doubt, helped the two writers to forge their bond in the first place. If Gilbert's autobiography is to be believed, his earliest memories are of his maternal grandmother reading aloud passages from the Book of Revelation, specifically the account of Satan being cast into the abyss.[17] Rather than inspire fear, the story only fired the young boy's imagination:

> I know what that bottomless pit is like, because I have seen pictures of it. Satan I know too. He is a man with a green face and pointy ears. I know what he looks like as a serpent, which is a kind of big snake . . . I know too what dragons look like. I see a golden beast with a scaly, curly tail, a body like a huge scorpion, a mouth like a crocodile, nostrils like a horse, with a great, brass chain round its neck being thrust into a world which fills all the space below our world.[18]

In *The Landslide*, the dragon and the serpent are reimagined as essentially benevolent creatures, misinterpreted as demonic by the villagers thanks to their concurrent and yet contradictory belief systems of folklore and Catholicism. When Michael the fisherman encounters the sea serpent he assumes that he is the Devil, and that he is to blame for the paucity of fish. It is Father Binyon who takes a more balanced view, suggesting that it is merely the hot weather that has encouraged the fish to swim deeper. Needless to say, such a rational approach is not accepted.

From the outset, it is clear that in this society the presumption of diabolism and magic is commonplace. Local opinion is divided on Wolfe's innocuous new pet Procyon, who is deemed to be either "a devil" or "a fairy dog, who would disappear when the clock struck midnight". As a result of Gran'papa's affinity for the dragon, he is denounced as a "wizard", and Wolfe as his naïve stooge. It is Gilbert's intention to show that the tenets of Christianity are indistinguishable from the beliefs of folkloric tradition. This is clear in the conversation that ensues in the kitchen of Wolfe's house after the dragon has trespassed across the family farm:

> "Perhaps it's a unicorn," my father suggested, and after that they began to talk of all sorts of strange creatures—dragons and unicorns and sphinxes and cockatrices.
> Father Binyon spoke about Saint George and Saint Patrick, and Gran'papa told of Hercules and the Hydra; and also of the Minotaur of Crete. After that Father Binyon began again—Saint Anthony and his temptations I think it was—and then I fell asleep.

The sheer range of superstitions makes Father Binyon's interjections seem equally fanciful. Both Christianity and folklore are represented as irrational responses to the unknown. This association is confirmed when Father Binyon's early scepticism is overcome by a sudden conviction that his mind has been possessed by the "evil . . . spirits of paganism". Ironically, it is the dragon and all his fantastical allies who represent truth and rationality against the superstitions of lore and religion.

The Landslide is a threnody to a bygone era. When the narrator recalls the landscape of his childhood, "before the introduction of railways", he sees it as "a last forgotten fragment of the golden age". This notion of a utopian society that preceded the advent of modern technology would have appealed to Gilbert's mentor. During the Second World War, Forrest Reid wrote of his conviction that "the rush and noise and all the horrible perfecting of machines during the past twenty years is in part at least responsible for the present insane upheaval of ferocity and barbarism".[19] Wolfe's Gran'papa has a similar philosophy. His excitement at the discovery of Procyon and his friends elicits some wistful musings on a lost world:

> What *is* round that corner? Something as strange as the Sirens. It may be a Gorgon or a Cyclops. When we go round there we shall return to the age of adventure—the age of Scylla and Charybdis. Ever since that age there has been nothing strange, or mysterious, or inexplicable, in the whole world. Everything has been cleared up and solved and explained, and now, by just going round a corner, we can step back thousands and thousands and thousands of years.

Gilbert's invocation of Greek mythology is doubtless a gesture towards Reid's Hellenistic sympathies. Like Reid, Wolfe's Gran'papa has a tendency to romanticize the past. As far as he is concerned, the creatures who have emerged in the wake of the landslide are morally and spiritually superior, having escaped the ravages of the modern times, the "wear and tear" and "gradual deterioration of the ages". Moreover, the golden age envisaged by Gran'papa is specifically prelapsarian. Theirs was "an age of innocence and simplicity", and he considers the possibility that "every animal had its Adam and Eve, its temptation and its fall". Along with their innocence and moral rectitude, Gran'papa posits that previously human beings were able, like the animals, to communicate telepathically, and have "abandoned it" in favour of speech, "the much inferior method". In essence, this is degeneration theory. "Every new period seems worse than the last", Gran'papa tells Wolfe. It is his belief that humankind has regressed to a state of mindlessness and malevolence. They have become "the dumb animals", whilst the dragon and his kind represent a higher way of life; an epoch of intellect and purity, now re-established.

However, Gran'papa's idealizations are too simplistic. *The Landslide* is no fairytale, in spite of initial appearances. The dragon is a

Forrest Reid in Newcastle, County Down, July 1931. Photograph taken by
Stephen Gilbert (Special Collections, Queen's University Belfast, MS44/7/4).

morally ambiguous figure, melancholy and introspective but at the same time haughty and obstinate. Furthermore, he has the capacity to be ruthless. When Wolfe learns how to read the dragon's mind, he sees an image of him pursuing the villagers and "trampling down the cottages", and taking a sadistic pleasure in doing so. The sea serpent is similarly problematic, an embodiment of the belief that pleasure is the only intrinsic value. This is most clearly expressed when he attempts to coax Wolfe into leaving with him in search of warmer climes:

> "Think, Wolfe," he told me, "how happy we'd be—sunshine all day long, lovely fruits for you to eat, warm water where you could bathe and never grow cold. I would give you rides too, whenever you wanted; and brown native boys would teach you to dive for pearls and ride upon the surf."

Such rhetoric makes no apologies for its appeal to hedonistic principles. In response, Wolfe accuses him of behaving "just like the Serpent in the Bible, who tempted Adam and Eve". Wolfe's analogy is a little unfair, of course, given that the sea serpent could hardly be said to be guilty of duplicity. Gilbert's depiction of the conflict between the past and the present is never reduced to the dichotomy of good and evil that underpins the Christian faith. There are no moral certainties, and for all Gran'papa's pining for a lost "golden age", Wolfe understands that such ideals can never be anything other than a fiction. After all, it is no accident that "utopia" derives from the Greek for "no place".

Reid was fully aware that he was the model for the Gran'papa character. In the archives at Queen's University, Belfast, there is an undated Christmas card which was sent from Reid to Gilbert which is signed "with love from Wolf [sic], Procyon, & Gran'papa".[20] Reid was an avowed pagan, and his animistic belief in the power of nature is reflected in Gran'papa's observation that the local landscape has "a spirit and a soul". The sentiment is strongly reminiscent of a moment in Gilbert's autobiography in which he describes walking with his mentor in a forest and happening upon a rocky glade through which runs a "completely silent stream".[21] Impressed by the atmosphere, Reid (or "Webster Moore" in Gilbert's account), decides that they should offer a sacrifice "to propitiate the gods of the wood".[22] They assemble a makeshift altar from rocks and flowers and call on the god Pan. Gilbert's discomfort is palpable:

> I place the flowers on the topmost stones. The atmosphere is heavier than ever. The whole air is full of gods and spirits. "Oh Lord," I whisper feverishly below my breath, "this means nothing. I am not really sacrificing to Pan or any other heathen false gods. I know there are no such things." Just in time I stop myself saying, "I know there is no other god, but you." That would be lying. I don't really believe in him either. I am trying to be both honest and prudent.
>
> "Oh Great God Pan show yourself to your worshippers," Mr Moore calls. "Show that you are still alive and powerful. Show that you are not dead."
>
> There seems to be a shiver in the air. The leaves rustle. The branches stir. "Don't come. Don't show yourself," I pray feverishly. "Oh Lord Jesus, don't let him."
>
> There is a sudden flash of lightning followed after a few seconds by a roll of thunder. Zeus about to hurl a thunderbolt? Pan dissatisfied with the flowers? Jehovah about to scorch us up with fire from heaven? I don't know. I only know I am very frightened and want to get away. "We shouldn't be among trees in a thunderstorm," I point out to Mr. Moore.
>
> "It's going to pour," he replies. "Maybe we'd better get back to the bus-stop.["]][23]

It is a curiosity of Gilbert's autobiography that he repeatedly calls upon the god of his upbringing, in spite of his view that such a god does not exist. Later in life, Gilbert re-embraced Christianity, but was apparently never fully able to shed his inherent agnosticism.[24]

The conflict between paganism and Christianity, so prominent in The Landslide, is confirmation of Reid's influence in Gilbert's early writing. We are told that the men of the dragon's time performed sacrificial rites to appease the gods of nature. According to the dragon, they "bowed down to the sun, to the moon, and to the stars. They killed animals, or sometimes one of themselves: they were always killing." Whilst Reid would have balked at any form of bloodshed, the animistic tradition is in keeping with his philosophical outlook. Towards the end of the novel the connection between Gran'papa and Reid becomes explicit, when Gran'papa suggests paganism as a valid alternative to Christianity. "Before the church there were other gods," he says to Wolfe, "spirits of the earth and the rocks, of the streams and the trees. Maybe we should call *them* to our aid".

The collision of faith and reason, of the old world and the new, the pagan and the Christian, is reified most memorably in Chapter XI, in which the dragon is found sleeping in the local church. The image is at once comical and potent, a heightened variation on the elephant in the room, and Father Binyon is even compelled to attempt a spontaneous exorcism. Gran'papa is blamed for summoning the dragon and, when he refuses to remove him, is branded a "sorcerer" by Wolfe's mother. Gran'papa's reaction is an accurate summation of Reid's own views on the blinkered attitudes of the religious when confronted with those of an alternative mindset: "Anything they don't understand they think is wrong—and there's very little they *do* understand".

Reid was delighted with *The Landslide* and Gilbert's decision to dedicate the novel to him. He wrote a glowing review for *The Northern Whig and Belfast Post* in which he described the book as "the most enticing romance I have read for a long time".[25] This was no doubt a professionally dubious act given his close association with the author, which explains why he wrote under the name of his friend Knox Cunningham. But the publication of *The Landslide* was one of the great consolations of the last few painful years of Reid's life. After all, he cared dearly about Gilbert's writing and reputation, and had worked tirelessly to support his literary ambitions. He not only corrected Gilbert's drafts, he also set him deadlines for rewrites, diligently typed out his manuscripts, and introduced him to potential publishers. In their many evenings together at Reid's house in Ormiston Crescent he would read novels to his protégé and discuss them at length. Reid was effectively providing the equivalent of a university education, and it is certain that without Reid's devotion *The Landslide* could never have been produced. The title was Reid's invention, and his fascinations and preferred themes—childhood, the superiority of the past, the transcendence of time, the conflict between Christianity

Stephen Gilbert and Forrest Reid, c. 1932 (Special Collections, Queen's
University Belfast, MS44/7/2).

and paganism, the animistic power of nature—are more prominent in this novel than in anything else that Gilbert ever wrote.[26]

Reid made no secret of the fact that he was deeply in love with
Gilbert, regularly sending him handwritten declarations of his
feelings, and writing poems lauding the young man's beauty.[27] The
extent of his devotion meant that he was frequently possessive and
overbearing. In August 1937 Gilbert was engaged to be married,
and Reid reacted with the truculence of a scorned lover. Under-
standably, Gilbert was often tempted to terminate the friendship,
but was all too aware of the value of Reid's knowledge and literary contacts. His autobiography makes this clear: "I don't really
care for him at all. He entertains me, and is useful to me in my

writing."[28] There is a fascinating ambivalence here. There are moments of genuine affection between the two men in the extant correspondence, and Gilbert clearly respected Reid and valued his guidance and encouragement. At the same time, he saw Reid as an "incubus" who had stolen his youth.[29] Gilbert had dedicated *The Landslide* to Reid "gratefully and affectionately", although this was a hollow gesture. As he later wrote, "the dedication to *The Landslide* is not sincere. I put in the word *affectionately* to please him. I don't mean he asked for it, but I knew it would please him; and it did please him a great deal."[30] The intensity of Reid's desire had blinded him to the opportunistic motives of his beloved, a familiar enough scenario in the annals of unrequited love. One is reminded of Father Binyon's words of caution to Wolfe about his new reptilian friends: "They may be good; they may be evil. They seem beautiful; they seem pleasant: but their beauty may be a false beauty, and the pleasure of their companionship a false pleasure".

Indeed, a prominent theme of *The Landslide* is the inevitable misapprehensions that underpin all human interaction. Through the disintegration of Wolfe's family, and the community at large, we see the unpalatable ramifications of moral absolutism; Gilbert exposes the limitations of human judgements, and the dubious sense of security such judgements provide. One particularly revealing episode takes place in Father Binyon's garden, and involves his pet cat Polyphemus. Having rejected Wolfe's lap in favour of his master's, Father Binyon puts this down to the cat's innate wisdom. Almost immediately the priest is punished for his confidence. Polyphemus pushes his claws into Father Binyon's legs and abandons him for Wolfe.

"It just means he's not so wise as I thought," he said. "If he had been really wise he would have stayed where he was."
"Don't you think he was wise enough to know I was all right?"
"No one is wise enough to know that anyone is all right," Father Binyon answered. I looked down and stroked Polyphemus, and wondered if this were true.

This short episode has the succinct and instructive qualities of a parable. It gets right to the crux of *The Landslide*, a novel which serves as a powerful reminder of the ephemeral nature of loyalty, the fragility of human bonds in the face of ignorance and fear, and the uncomfortable truth that, to borrow the words of Philip Roth, "our understanding of people must always be at best slightly wrong".[31]

ANDREW DOYLE

October 1, 2013

NOTES

1   Stephen Gilbert, original manuscript draft of *The Landslide* (Special Collections, Queen's University Belfast, MS45/2/5/1).

2   Stephen Gilbert, *The Assailants*, unpublished manuscript (Special Collections, Queen's University Belfast, MS45/2/1).

3   Stephen Gilbert, unpublished autobiography, undated typescript (Special Collections, Queen's University Belfast, uncatalogued), vol. III, p. 256.

4   Gilbert has concealed all identities throughout his autobiography. The practice extends even to the titles of his books. *The Landslide*, for instance, is referred to as *The Cataclysm*.

5   Letter from Forrest Reid to J. N. Hart dated 14 March 1940 (Public Record Office of Northern Ireland, Belfast, T2121/1/52).

6   A full transcript of *Nature Suppressed* is reprinted in Forrest Reid, *Brian Westby* (Richmond, Va.: Valancourt Books, 2013), pp. 209-226.

7   English report, Summer Term 1928 (Special Collections, Queen's University Belfast, MS45/7/2/9); Headmaster's report, Summer Term 1926 (Special Collections, Queen's University Belfast, MS45/7/2/3); Modern Languages report, Summer Term 1928 (Special Collections, Queen's University Belfast, MS45/7/2/9).

8   Letter from James Greenlees to William Gilbert dated 8 January 1930 (Special Collections, Queen's University Belfast, MS45/1/10/6).

9   Letter from James Greenlees to William Gilbert dated 1 April 1930 (Special Collections, Queen's University Belfast, MS45/1/10/8).

10   W. R. Wilde, *Irish Popular Superstitions* (Dublin: James McGlashan, 1852), p. v.

11   Forrest Reid, "The Host of the Air", *Retrospective Adventures* (London: Faber & Faber, 1940), pp. 156-160. See p. 156.

12   *Visions and Beliefs in the West of Ireland. Collected and Arranged by*

Lady Gregory with Two Essays and Notes by W. B. Yeats (New York and London: G. P. Putnam's Sons, 1920), 2 vols. Reid's essay "The Host of the Air" is a review of this text.

13 Stephen Gilbert, "The Toad", typescript poem dated 18 December 1943 (Special Collections, Queen's University Belfast, uncatalogued). Famously, the toadstone myth appears in Shakespeare's *As You Like It*, in the Duke's remark that "the toad, ugly and venomous, / wears yet a precious jewel in his head" (2:1, 15-16).

14 Letter from E. M. Forster to Stephen Gilbert dated 24 February 1943 (Special Collections, Queen's University Belfast, MS45/1/18/2).

15 Stephen Gilbert, unpublished journal, typescript (Special Collections, Queen's University Belfast, uncatalogued), p. 4.

16 Ibid.

17 See Revelation, chapter XX. Gilbert's maternal grandmother was Margaretta Annie Cafel Cope Browne (c.1846-1924).

18 Autobiography, op. cit., vol. I, p. 5.

19 Letter from Forrest Reid to J. N. Hart dated 21 May 1940 (Harry Ransom Center, Texas).

20 Undated Christmas card from Reid to Gilbert (Special Collections, Queen's University Belfast, MS45/1/14/71).

21 Autobiography, op. cit., vol. II, p. 33.

22 Ibid., p. 34.

23 Ibid., p. 36.

24 For an account of Gilbert's apparent conversion to Christianity see his autobiography, op. cit., vol. IV, pp. 202-219.

25 "An original, individual story", review of *The Landslide* signed "S.K.C.", *The Northern Whig and Belfast Post* (13 February 1943). A hand-written note next to Forrest Reid's copy of this article indicates that he was the author (Special Collections, Queen's University Belfast, MS44/4/1/6).

26 Reid's title was not favoured by the publisher, as Reid explained in a letter to Knox Cunningham: "Faber has written an extremely nice letter accepting *The Landslide*, though he wants the title changed. One in the eye for me! since the title was my humble contribution. But Faber says it won't do at all, and S., who brought me the good tidings before breakfast this morning, has probably thought of a dozen others in the meantime". Letter from Forrest Reid to Knox Cunningham dated 16 March 1942 (Public Record Office of Northern Ireland, Belfast, MIC/45/1).

27 See for example Reid's letter to Gilbert dated 16 August 1931: "I can't help it, Stephen dear, if I seem horribly soppy, but the fact is that I

would rather you loved me a little than anything else in the world . . .
I am writing this in a storm of wind & rain, & somehow I feel you
very close to me. I love you. I love you in three different ways & yet
they are all mixed up together. I wish you were here now" (Special
Collections, Queen's University Belfast, MS45/1/14/3). See also Reid's
poems "For a Birthday" and "S.G.", reprinted in Forrest Reid, *Brian
Westby* (Richmond, Va.: Valancourt Books, 2013), pp. 228-229.

28 Autobiography, op. cit., vol. II, p. 291.

29 See Stephen Gilbert's essay "A Successful Man" in *Threshold* 28 (Spring
1977), pp. 104-114: "Time and again I wished he would take himself
out of my life. I felt bitterly that he had stolen my youth. I knew that
he had given me a great deal in exchange. I carry these gifts with
me yet. And for good or bad he influenced my writing. For good or
bad . . ." (p. 106). Gilbert refers to Reid as an "incubus" on two occasions in his autobiography, op. cit., vol. III, p. 116a and p. 363.

30 Stephen Gilbert, autobiographical fragment, undated typescript (Special Collections, Queen's University Belfast, uncatalogued), p. 6.

31 Philip Roth, *The Human Stain* (London: Vintage, 2001), p. 22.

THE LANDSLIDE

*The events described in the following pages took place in a remote
district before the introduction of railways.*

CHAPTER I

Till I was twelve years old I lived in a big cottage with several
rooms, overlooking a long inlet of the sea. Our cottage was
high up on the hillside and down below were the village and the
harbour. It was a very remote place in the west of Ireland, and
during all the time that I lived there no stranger ever came to the
village.

The cottage and the little farm belonged to my grandfather, but
my father and mother lived there also, and it was they who did the
work. Our name was Emmet, and my father was called David and
my mother Rebecca. My name was Wolfe.

It was when my father married, that my grandfather bought
the farm and added the extra rooms to the cottage, but he did
not come to live there himself till I was ten years old. Before that
he had lived in the school at the village, for he had been a schoolmaster all his life.

He had chosen the cottage because it was very lonely, and he
could look out over the sea. Yet my father and mother often complained that the land was bare and unfruitful and brought poor
return for their labour. There were only a few fields, and in many
places the hard, grey rock jutted through the soil. Whins grew
here and there, and in the marshy places were rushes and bog-
cotton. Nearly all round us was the sea, for we were close to the
headland, and on the other side of the hill were the Far Bay, and
the open Atlantic.

One night in spring, just before my twelfth birthday, a strange
thing happened. For over a week there had been continuous heavy
rain and I had gone to sleep that night listening to its steady thud,
half-wondering if it were ever going to stop. Suddenly I was awakened by a loud rumbling sound, and at the same time I felt my bed

trembling. It was like thunder, but I knew it wasn't thunder. I was very frightened because I thought it was the end of the world. It lasted perhaps a minute; then it died away and I noticed that the rain had stopped.

Presently a light shone under the door. I heard the others talking in the kitchen, and Mother came in to see that I hadn't been frightened.

Very soon I went to sleep again, but I didn't forget about the noise, and in the morning everybody was talking about it. Nobody really knew what had caused it, but there were a great many suggestions as to what it might have been.

The rain did not come on again: instead the days became extraordinarily hot, and though it was not yet really summer the men found it difficult to do their work in the fields.

One evening, about a week after the rumbling in the night, when Gran'papa had gone down to the village to see Father Binyon, I lay alone in the heather. On our side of the hill the sun had already set. It was dusk, and I watched the movements of the water, and the steep shadowy land which rose so abruptly on either side of the inlet.

The colour of the sea was grey, a thin, translucent grey, lined faintly by the many currents of the changing tide. The colours of the land were darker and more varied, though gradually they were being toned down, turning to an ever deepening purple. But for the narrow strip of sea, and the sky, which still seemed unnaturally bright, the whole landscape was composed of hills and mountains. They stretched away to the east in a jumbled confusion, and from this dark mass, like faint, flat eyes, there gleamed three lakes.

Even in those days I found a particular fascination in the gradual approach of evening, the gradual change to night. I had lain there for a long time in a sort of dream, but little by little, as it grew more dusky, I began to shiver and feel cold. At last I got up, and turning round, I saw that the skyline was illumined by a long halo from the setting sun. So I decided to go to the hilltop and look down on the Far Bay.

I followed a narrow path, sometimes running, sometimes walking, but soon the path ceased and the ground became bare and gravelly. There was no vegetation here, but odd tufts of heather, and the shrivelled lichens and mosses which existed somehow in the cracks and crevices of the grey rocks and boulders. When I reached this bald expanse, I found myself quite suddenly in brilliant sunlight. For a moment I was dazzled; then I saw a sight so strange, that I forgot everything else.

Down on the shore were two beasts: both were green, one a light clear green, like the sea over sand; the other darker, with a tinge of brown. They gambolled on the shore like young calves. They were very big, and when they rushed into the water the waves broke against them, and not over them. As I watched, I thought how beautiful they looked, and wondered if they were dragons. Suddenly they left the edge of the sea and came quickly up the shore. The greenish brown monster bounded over the sand, and the sea-green creature followed him, with swift, undulating movements. They disappeared below the cliff.

I waited for a little, and then I became frightened, fearing that they would come up the hillside and catch me. So I ran down our side of the hill to look for Gran'papa.

Soon I came to the cottage and peeped carefully through the window, because I didn't want Mother to see me. It was nearly milking time, and I was afraid she would send me to bring home the cows. But she wasn't there, nor Gran'papa either, and I knew he must still be with the priest. So I went out into the heather once more, and lay down on a little hillock. The heather covered me up; I was hidden, but I could see. I wasn't frightened either, because I could run to Mother and Father if the dragons came. I thought of telling them about the dragons, but I knew they wouldn't believe me; instead they would make me help with the milking. But Gran'papa would be interested; *he* would come.

I saw Mother come out, and when she called me I did not answer, though I knew this was very wrong. So she had to go herself to bring in the cows.

Presently I saw Gran'papa, climbing up the lane to the house, and when he got near I called to him. He heard me, but though I stood up he could not see me, for by this time it was nearly dark.

I went to meet him. He was walking very slowly, but when I told him there were dragons on the Far Shore, he came with me at

once. As we went up the hill he took my hand, because I could see
the path much better than he could.

At last we reached the top, but when we looked at the shore,
and all round, there was nothing there. So I said to Gran'papa,
"Wait and you'll see them." And we waited.

Before us was a long slope of heather, then the shore and the
sea. Between the heather and the shore there was a more abrupt
slope, and a few sandhills, invisible from where we stood. Now I
could not see either of the monsters, though I looked carefully
from end to end of the wide sandy bay, which stretched between
two headlands. These headlands were entirely different, that on
the right being steep, with a dark high cliff: the other was lower;
its colours were green and grey, its slopes more gentle. At the end
it was cracked and broken; and beyond it, half-submerged in the
water, were the tumbled and battered fragments, which had once
formed part of it.

To every natural colour in this landscape there was added a
tinge of gold. To the sea in particular this gave a peculiar, magical
effect.

That evening, it is true, my mind was too full of what I had seen
for me to think much of the landscape. Now, when I look back on
it from far away, in time as well as space, it seems to me that that
remote western spot was a last forgotten fragment of the golden
age.

I don't know how long we watched there, but gradually the
colour faded. The green of the sea became fainter, and the light
vanished from the sky. The shore was a black streak: the darkness
spread upwards over the heather. And now the sea was grey, a faint
and silvery grey: the rocks seemed to move like boats.

Suddenly, like two green streaks, the monsters reappeared. It
was impossible to distinguish their actual outlines: they were two
long phosphorescent shapes, but one was longer than the other. At
the edge of the water they stopped for a moment, quite still. Then
the longer creature slid gradually into the sea, and we saw him
moving quickly, a long shimmering greenness, till he disappeared
round the point. As I watched him swimming, so beautifully and
so smoothly, and all glowing with light, illumining the grey waters
as he passed, I forgot all about the other creature.

Presently Gran'papa grasped my arm, "Come, Wolfe," he said, "quickly." I saw then that the shorter beast, or one very like it, had appeared at the top of the slope and was coming towards us. It must have been nearly a mile away, but it glowed like a dark green beacon, and seemed very large.

We hurried up the hill, for, half-unconsciously I think, we had wandered a little way from the summit. When we reached the top we looked back for a moment, and were glad to see that the dragon had stopped, and seemed to be looking after his playmate.

"Are they dragons?" I asked, as we came down the hill again towards home.

"There are no such things as dragons," Gran'papa answered hesitatingly. So I wondered what they could be. I hoped to see them another time, but I didn't want them to catch me in case they were like lions and tigers.

Presently Gran'papa went on as if he had never stopped speaking, ". . . not nowadays at least. There may have been—long ago."

"What happened to them all?" I asked.

"Saint Patrick chased them away."

But I thought perhaps Gran'papa was making fun, though I'd heard something like it before. So I said, "Where did he chase them to?" and he said he didn't know.

So I said, "Maybe they've come back," and he said, "Maybe they have."

After that I kept quiet because I knew he was thinking and didn't want to talk.

When we reached the lane I happened to look up at the sky, and then I could keep quiet no longer. "Look, Gran'papa"—and I shouted, though he was close beside me; at the same time I tugged his sleeve.

In the sky there was one cloud. In the middle of that, rather dim and misty, but nevertheless distinct, there was reflected a faint green light.

Just before we reached the cottage door Gran'papa bent down and whispered to me. "Don't tell anyone," he said, "not even your father and mother."

CHAPTER II

Though Bran and Rory were barking as we came to the cottage, I entered with a feeling of mystery. The sheep-dogs, father and son, followed us stealthily. Sometimes, when Gran'papa wasn't there, they were shut outside—and poor Bran was old, and his coat was matted and dusty.

Our kitchen was big and bare, with whitewashed walls, and a floor of grey stone slabs. The hearth was so wide and open that you could walk into it and look up the chimney at the stars. That was when the fire was small. But it was unlucky to let the fire go out completely, and this only happened once that I know of. Now there was a huge turf fire which lighted the room as well as heated it, and round the fire were figures, seeming vague after the darkness without. The floor, because of its unevenness and the flickering of the flames, was covered with rippling shadows like a pool of water. If I looked up I saw neither ceiling nor roof, only a vague darkness, with a suggestion of something there, but when, from time to time, there was the flare of a brighter flame, I could see the black oak of the rafters and catch a glimpse of an old spade or a fishing rod, or the barrel of an antique gun. But beyond the rafters, and the lumber that lay stretched across them, there was thicker darkness still, heavy and impenetrable. Up there, where the bats slept in the daytime, was our ghost, watching over us. I saw the wink of his eye, from the blackness, and looked away again fearfully.

I heard Gran'papa's clock which repeated again and again, as it slowly swung its pendulum, "Tock, tock." I couldn't see it because it was a dark old clock, and always stood in the duskiest corner of the kitchen, but I could see the white scrubbed wood of the table and the chairs. The chairs were pushed back now and I saw the stout figure of Father Binyon get up from one of them—and when everyone was talking the two dogs crept close to the fire.

"Come, Wolfe," Father Binyon said. "Sit beside *me* and tell me what you've been doing."

8

"He's been doing nothing at all," Mother cried sharply. "He's been hiding somewhere, when he should have been bringing in the cows."

"You should always help your mother," my father said weakly, but that only got *him* into trouble.

"A lot of help I get from you, don't I?" she snapped. "Where were you all afternoon—fishing?—and what did you catch?"

"Now, now," the priest interposed. "Sure you'd have been pleased enough if he'd brought you two or three trout, big ones—and Wolfe's a good boy. We all forgot our duty sometimes when we were his age."

This was more than I deserved; nevertheless I felt quite virtuous.

"It wasn't in the stream I was fishing," Father said; "it was off the herring rocks."

"You ought to know it's no good there," Gran'papa told him, "except at low tide."

"Good enough for him," Mother sniffed. "It was sleep he was after, not fish."

Father Binyon frowned, and she stopped. The priest was a heavy man, with a red face and black eyebrows, and when he frowned he looked very fierce indeed.

After this they all began to talk about fishing, and only half listening to them, I leaned my head against Gran'papa's knee and grew sleepy. For instead of going to the priest, I had sat down beside Gran'papa on a little stool which he had given to me once, because I liked to sit there. I saw a brown stream with big stones in it, all fringed with moss, and the swirl of the water caused the moss to move. There were trout in the stream, and then there was only one trout, which was me. And I was swimming in and out among the stones, and presently I saw a bait—a worm hanging on the end of a line, and I swam up, and looked at it, and pressed against it with my nose. Then I found that I'd been caught, and that it was Gran'papa who had caught me. I sat on the bank beside him and he pushed his fingers through my hair. I half awoke and found that he was really doing that, and it was very pleasant. So again I dozed: but this time Mother noticed.

"It's in your bed you should be—away you go now, and no complaints."

"But, Mother . . ."

"Go on now: no dawdling." So I kissed Gran'papa good night, and went.

My room was just off the kitchen, and if I stood near the door I could hear all that they said. Father Binyon was telling a story about some young curates who went out to fish in a river in Italy, when Mother came in suddenly and nearly knocked me down.

"Not in bed yet!" she exclaimed. "Be quick: I'll count twenty."

I was in just after nineteen, and she was stooping over me to kiss me good night, when the dogs in the next room growled.

"Quiet, Rory, quiet, Bran," I heard Father say, and I knew that the dogs were sniffing under the door. Then I heard someone, and Rory gave a short bark.

"Who can it be at this hour?" Mother muttered, and instead of blowing out the candle she took it in her hand, and went to the threshold of my room. *I* went too, and peeped out from behind her into the kitchen.

The footsteps came nearer, and going to the door, Father opened it, and leaned over the lower half.

"It will be someone for you, Father," Mother said to the priest. "There'll be somebody dead, or dying perhaps."

"Is Father Binyon here?" It was the voice of Michael Rymple the fisherman, and at once I thought it must be Peter, his son, who was dying. Peter was my friend; and he was all Michael had, for his wife had died before I could remember. But Peter was with him, and they stood together at the door, both fair-haired and blue-eyed and sun-burned. They both wore blue jerseys, and long blue trousers. I envied those trousers of Peter's, because he was younger than I; yet mine were short. Peter was very small and light; his father was big-boned and spare. They were often out together in the boat, but if it were rough, or the boats were going to be out all night, Peter was left at home, and then he spent most of his time with us.

Peter's skin was smooth and brown, and I can still remember him, just as he stood at our door that evening, while his father asked for the priest.

"He's here, to be sure," Gran'papa said. "Will you take a seat?"

"I will, thank you. I didn't see his Reverence, there in the darkness."

"Did you not then?" said Father Binyon. "Indeed I've got so insignificant of late you *would* hardly see me. What's your trouble?"

"Och, no trouble at all, Father—only the fishing's bad."

"And isn't it always bad?" the priest asked, a little testily, "like farming, and everything else."

Mother allowed me to get up again because of Peter, and I came into the kitchen with a blanket round my shoulders. Peter and I sat on a rug on the floor, because there were only five chairs.

"I'll play you at marlies," I said, but he shook his head.

"Ssh—Da's got something to tell."

"What?"

"You'll hear if you wait. He'll tell it himself."

So I waited, but Michael said nothing. Nobody said anything while they were settling down. Then my father asked, "What's wrong with the fishing, Michael? What's making it so bad?"

"It's the Devil," Peter whispered to me.

"It's the hot weather," Father Binyon said. "Sure you never catch fish in hot weather. They go away where it's deep to get out of the sun."

"It's not the hot weather at all," Michael answered. "I know myself what it is."

"He saw him," Peter whispered again, "out near the point."

"The Devil?"

"Yes, but ssh: I was to let *him* tell."

We listened again to the grown-ups. "Then what is it?" Father Binyon was asking in a very sharp voice. "Can you tell me that?"

"I can indeed."

"What?"

"It's the Devil."

They all got a bit of a start, and Father Binyon frowned. "Nonsense, man," he exclaimed, "you've been drinking."

Michael looked angry, for everyone knew he didn't drink, but Father Binyon smiled. "Let's hear about him," he said, "for it's not often he honours us."

Then Michael smiled too, and I remembered that the Devil was to blame for everything, and wondered if that was what he meant.

"The Devil," my father said, in a pondering tone, as if he wasn't quite sure of what he had heard.

"Yes," Michael answered. "He was in the sea. I saw him. It was near the point he was—swimmin'—an' his tail all out behind him ripplin' over the water."

"Didn't I tell you?" Peter murmured, but I made no reply. That was what *we'd* seen, I thought—and it wasn't the Devil. Besides we had seen *two* things, and there was only *one* Devil. I very nearly said what we'd seen, but I stopped myself in time.

I felt sure that Michael hadn't seen the Devil, only one of our dragons, and when he described it I found that I was right.

"The Devil doesn't swim in the sea," Father Binyon declared. "He was never one for a bath. What was this creature like? Had he horns on him?"

"He had not."

"Had he cloven hooves?"

"Sure he hadn't feet at all. He was just a great big tail, with a head at one end; nothing else."

"Then it wasn't the Devil," Father Binyon said very decidedly.

"Faith then, who was it?"

We all looked at Father Binyon as if he would tell us, and my father repeated, "Yes, who was it?"

"The man was dreaming," began the priest, "it was only . . . ."

THUMP THUMP THUMP

It wasn't very loud, but it was heavy, and it seemed to come along the ground.

THUMP THUMP THUMP

The fire had died down a little, and the kitchen had grown darker. Now, slowly, it began to glow with a new light, green and strange, which came not from the fire, but from the window. Gradually the light grew stronger and we caught sight of a dim, glowing bulk. Something brushed against the back wall and slithered past the door. We heard it at the chimney, and at the front, and once, when it knocked against a corner, the whole house shook. Still we heard the thump of its feet and we knew that it was close to us. Not one of us spoke.

Then there came a splash and a perfect turmoil of quacking.

"Duck for his supper," Father Binyon said, but nobody dared to reply. We could hear the ducks tearing off down the hillside, and then there was another noise—a splintering crash—and fresh squawking. It was the hen-house, of course, and off they all went, hard after the ducks.

That was more than Mother could bear. "Away you go, David," she exclaimed, "drive the brute away; he'll be at the cows next." But my father never answered. He just sat there as if he were too frightened even to hear her. Then I noticed Gran'papa: he was sitting quite still like the rest of us, but on his face there was the slightest little flicker of a smile. He was amused, but why? I wondered.

The thumping grew fainter and it sounded as if the creature were going up, and back over the hill.

"That was *him*," Michael said; and nobody said it wasn't. Nevertheless I felt sure it was the beast *we* had seen, the one that had stayed on the shore.

"Has he gone?" asked my father in a whisper, and every minute or two someone would wonder if he'd *really* gone, and if it would be safe to go out. Presently Father thought it would be, but he wouldn't go himself to see what the damage was, and I knew that the others were afraid to go home.

So Gran'papa asked them to stay the night, and Mother said she could put them up easily. At first Michael said he'd go on, and risk it, but Peter begged him not to, and in the end they all stayed.

After that everyone began to discuss what it *could* have been. Michael still thought it was the Devil, but Father Binyon said it wasn't.

"Perhaps it's a unicorn," my father suggested, and after that they began to talk of all sorts of strange creatures—dragons and unicorns and sphinxes and cockatrices.

Father Binyon spoke about Saint George and Saint Patrick, and Gran'papa told of Hercules and the Hydra; and also of the Minotaur of Crete. After that Father Binyon began again—Saint Anthony and his temptations I think it was—and then I fell asleep.

When I awoke it was very late. I shared my bed with Peter, but where the others slept I don't remember.

CHAPTER III

When I opened my eyes next morning they looked straight into Peter's. His eyes were half-sleepy, half-alert, and his face was flushed. He was leaning over me, and staring steadily. "It's true," he said, without altering his gaze the littlest bit.

"What is?"

"If you stare hard at someone who's asleep, it wakes them up."

"It was the draught that woke me," I murmured sleepily. "Lie down; you're making the bed cold."

"I'm not, and it wasn't the draught," but he lay down all the same, and pulled the clothes around him. "It's queer, isn't it—just staring, and it woke you up."

"Who told you about it?"

"I don't remember—I just know about it. Would *you* like to do it?"

"How can I?"

"I'll go to sleep; then you can try."

"You won't be able to."

"I will," and he closed his eyes. I watched him and he began to breathe very deeply. Then he began to snore, at least he pretended to.

"You're not asleep," I told him.

He gave one more snore. "How could I be?" he said. "I could feel you staring at me—and that's what wakes you up. So how could I go to sleep?"

"I *said* you couldn't."

"Well, it proves that it *is* staring wakes you. I could feel it, feel you staring."

"It's late," I said. "We ought to get up."

"Nobody else has," he replied, but at that moment we heard noises from the next room.

"It *is* late," I repeated, "I know it is. Come on," and I threw off the bedclothes.

We got up, and when we were dressed we went into the kitchen, where Mother was making breakfast.

"Don't go out," she said, and I noticed that the door was still shut.

"Is it there?" I lowered my voice involuntarily.

"No; it's gone."

"How do you know?" asked Father, coming in from another room.

"I went out to fetch an egg for his Reverence, but there's not one there—nor a hen either. The fowl-house is upside down, and I don't know where the ducks are."

"Sure they'll come back," Father said, with a sort of easy unconcern.

"If *you* fetch them," Mother told him sharply, "and it'll take you most of the day too."

Father mumbled and grumbled at this, and I wasn't surprised when after the others had gone he told *me* I'd have to find them. I didn't mind, but it would have been more fun if Peter had stayed to help me.

I started on the lower part of the hill and searched all day, but in the evening three hens and one duck were still missing. The next morning I decided to try the top of the hill, and at the same time I hoped to see the dragons again. So as soon as breakfast was over I slipped out quietly, because if Mother had known where I was going, she would certainly have stopped me.

It was rather misty and the heather was soaked with dew, but I knew that later on, when the sun came out, it would be very hot. I went up by the same path as two nights before, but when I got there I forgot about the hens and the ducks; I remembered, instead, a lake Gran'papa had spoken of, away out to the south, among the hills. It was a long distance off, I knew, but he had said that it was lonely and mysterious, and I liked lonely things. I would have to cross, too, the strange glen of Neencroom, where I had been only once before. I remembered it, peaceful and quiet, with a little stream running between grassy banks. There were many flowers there, and a few small trees and bushes, but no people. It was very fresh, and green, and solitary—some said it had a curse on it, and others that it was a playground for the fairies.

Now *I* wasn't afraid of fairies, like the other boys in the village, because Gran'papa had told me many wonderful tales about them, and I wished they would carry me away to Fairyland. So I set off to Neencroom, and I thought that perhaps the fairies might be dancing in a ring.

The sun had come out, and the last trailing clouds of mist were vanishing before it. I was still high enough up to look at both seas, the huge ocean—deep, blue and profound—and the greener blue of the moving waters in the bays and creeks of the great inlet.

Then, because I had gone beyond the summit, the inlet was hidden from me, and when I was passing through hollows, the Atlantic was invisible also. Everywhere the ground was wet. Here and there were tufts of bog-cotton. Rainbow-coloured rivulets oozed from the black, peaty soil, and the emerald-green moss was moist and sparkling.

Before me and around me was a huge tract of heather-covered country. In the far distance the heather was sombre and purplish; nearer, it was a dark, greyish brown; but when I looked at it closely I saw its small green leaves, the faded flowers of last year, and the new flowers, which had already begun to form.

But it was not all heather. The ditches and hollows were covered with grass of many kinds—long, dank grasses soaked with grey dew, short, spiky grass, which thrust up through the moss, like young reeds. There were purple orchids, and flat, yellow mayflowers. There were a few late primroses also, and violets, hidden deep among the grass.

Gradually I was descending into a long, narrow valley, which extended to the sea; it was the valley of Neencroom. Up on the hilltops there had been a cool breeze, but now it grew warmer, oppressive; I had the feeling of being shut in.

Of course the weather *had* been hotter recently. The old people were talking about it: they recalled warm spells in previous springs, and yet admitted that this was even warmer. I did not realize then how unusual was that admission.

Here it was dreadfully hot—and what was wrong? I felt the first slight haunting of fear. Was this the glen; was this the valley of Neencroom? I looked down and saw neither stream nor grassy banks. Instead there was a confusion, a dark green tangle of flow-

ers and plants and trees—and I went on. I was frightened in a peculiar way, with a fear I did not understand, and yet I was drawn on
by some strange magnetism.

Half-reluctant, curious, a little dazed, I wandered into the
middle of it all. I went from one thing to another, down, down,
down the steep sides of the valley. What strange creepers there
were! how strong! they were almost muscular in their thickness
and vigour. Then I caught sight of some scarlet things and ran to
them. They were huge flowers, growing flat on the ground like
begonias. I had never seen begonias then, but none that I have seen
since has been a quarter that size. Their leaves were not dark, but
a bright lizard green—and as I watched, one of the leaves moved
quickly: it *was* a lizard.

But a lizard was a reptile, and Gran'papa had said that Saint
Patrick had driven away or killed not only the dragons, but all the
snakes and toads and lizards that were in Ireland, and that they
could never come back. But perhaps one had escaped. Perhaps one
tiny lizard had hidden away in some rocky fissure, so that Saint
Patrick had overlooked it, or been unable to reach it, and now,
after all these years—hundreds of years—*I* had found it. But it was
lost again, and I began to search for it.

I searched under stones and plants, and when I looked up again
I was still further into the valley. What a quantity of young trees!
Everything was young here, and everything seemed to be growing
so fast. I couldn't understand; I wondered if I were lost: this was not
the valley I knew. *There* everything had been green or grey. Here I
could see neither grass, nor old crumbling rock, nor stream. . . .

Suddenly I knew what had happened—it was the fairies after
all: no wonder they were feared. They had changed the landmarks,
and raised up new trees. I might wander and wander and wander,
but I would never find home again. If I turned to go up the hill,
it would turn too, and I would plunge deeper into the jungle. . . .
And then, faintly, I thought I heard the sound of the stream. I
determined to go to it, because once it was found I should be able
to follow it to the sea.

Would the shore be altered too, and the sea; would it be a hard
blue sea, with white monotonous surf, a strip of yellow sand, and
a belt of waving palms?

I looked at the sky, to see if it had changed also. I don't know what I expected, or hoped, or feared, but, though cloudless, the sky was the same soft, summer blue that I had always known. This comforted me somehow, and listening carefully I searched for the stream.

As I went on it grew hotter and closer; the undergrowth became thicker and the flowers more profuse. Everything was coloured brightly: all the leaves on the trees were young leaves; buds were bursting and I could almost see the new, vigorous shoots forcing their way upwards through the tangle in their effort to reach the light and the air.

At last I came to the bottom. The choked murmur of the stream was nearer now, and I wished for a drink. If only I could see it. I came into a little glade where six or seven rowan-trees grew, but round them there were twining huge creepers, strange, choking parasites. And what was that, that amber-coloured thing, which swayed slowly at the far end of the glade? It was a flower, with a long, straight stalk, about eight feet high. I took a cautious step forward to look at it more closely, for something large and blue was moving lazily in one of the petals. Then its movement stopped and it looked at *me*: it was a silly, stupid, staring eye.

I stared back, unable to move, my mouth half open. A drowsy, enervating scent floated to my nostrils, and ever so slowly the flower bent towards me. And suddenly, as in a nightmare, I turned and ran. Creepers caught round my feet, branches hit me in the face, thorns scratched my hands, and the heavy scent hung round me and made me weary. But I ran, on and on, and up and up. Gradually the air grew clearer, and I felt at last the fresh breeze from the sea. I was on heather again, and I knew that it was neither necessary nor possible to go further. I sank down in utter exhaustion, and closed my eyes. The breeze blew on my forehead and ruffled my hair. I smelt the faint smell of the heather, and sank, unresisting, into a great peacefulness.

I was lying under a waterfall, while the water splashed, cool and pleasant, round my face. Close to me were steep, green rocks, and the water dripped from hanging mosses.

It was very refreshing, and Bran bounded up and began to lick my face. I forgot about the waterfall, and it couldn't be Bran, for I was too far from home for him to have come. It must be Rory who had found me. Or perhaps, I pretended, it was a lion. What a cool tongue he had! Was Rory's tongue as cool as that? Slowly I opened my eyes and looked.

A green animal, similar in colour to a cabbage caterpillar, and of about the same size as an ordinary sheep-dog, was staring at me with the most friendly expression on its face. I was not in the least frightened: I couldn't have been. It had a rounded body like a puppy's, at the far end of which was a little, ridiculous, curled-up tail. Its neck was long; its head broad and almost the size of a bull-dog's, though of a different shape, for there was more snout and a wider mouth.

Thinking it was a dog of some sort I sat up and patted it, and like a dog it responded by licking again my face and hands and coat. "Good dog," I said. "Whose dog are you? You'll be my dog, won't you?" But really it wasn't like a dog: it had no hair for one thing; and its skin was quite smooth.

Suddenly I felt very empty and sat up. It must be very late, long after dinner-time. I jumped up and looked round at the mountains; they were familiar, placid, and beautiful in the afternoon sun. Their colours were rich and dark, but I could see valleys with the bright green of young corn and growing grass.

And fifty yards below me was something extraordinary—a monstrous jungle growing where once had been a pleasant valley, part of the full harmony of the landscape. I looked down at this seething blot: the green was quite different from the natural colours I knew; it was a huge stain, dropped upon the countryside.

Till this moment I had felt that once I was out of the jungle I was safe. Now I had a horrible thought; perhaps this was not the only place where a jungle was springing up; perhaps there was more jungle between me and home; perhaps I should be surrounded and captured by it; perhaps it would spring up on this very spot.

I must get home as quickly as I could, if it were still possible. The green creature, I realized clearly, wanted me to go in the opposite direction—back into the valley or down to the sea. But eventually it came with me, running in front sometimes, or circling round in a wide curve. It was lithe and energetic, and in its erratic course it went three times as far as I did; yet it was always waiting for me, though I ran more than walked, because I was frightened.

At last I saw Gran'papa in the distance, and knew that when I reached him I should be safe.

CHAPTER IV

Naturally there was a lot of talk about the strange creature who had come home with me, and half the village came to the cottage that evening to see him and to hear of my adventure. Some said he was a fairy dog, who would disappear when the clock struck midnight; others that he was a devil and that we ought to cast him out: but Gran'papa said that he was an angel, who had been sent to save me, and that we must cherish him and feed him. So he called him Procyon, because, he said, he was a dog from heaven.

Of course he didn't disappear at midnight, and next morning we took him with us when we went, with a great many of the villagers, to show them the jungle. But the villagers were frightened, and after gazing at it for a little from the top of the hill, they decided to go home. So far I wasn't frightened, for I had a good deal of confidence in Gran'papa's protection, and he wanted to stay and to explore. Therefore we stayed, and the others left us, with many warnings and shakings of their heads.

"They are stupid," Gran'papa said, "always frightened, distrustful and hostile when they meet anything new, anything which they don't understand. The uneducated are always the same."

"Would you not be frightened, Gran'papa, even if we met the Dragon?"

"Why should I be?" he asked. "Has he harmed anyone, or hurt anyone?"

"No," I answered doubtfully. "But you went away the other night when we saw him from the hill."

"I know I did, but that was only caution—and if you hadn't been there I should have stayed."

"He frightened the ducks and the hens," I persisted.

"Now, Wolfe," Gran'papa said, "surely we've more sense than

the poultry. *They* were frightened of him undoubtedly, because they had never seen him before: there is little difference between them and the rest of the village."

"I didn't mean we *should* be frightened," I explained, though of course I had been, "but he was doing harm—chasing the ducks and hens—and he knocked over the fowl-house."

"That was an accident. I have been thinking a good deal about it. He is lonely and he was attracted by our light: perhaps, even, he thought it was another dragon, phosphorescent like himself. I am looking forward to meeting him, and Procyon, I hope, is showing us the way."

I hoped *not*, though, running ahead, and pausing to wait, Procyon was obviously taking us somewhere—and it was in the direction of the Far Shore and the open Atlantic.

We kept along the top of the valley for a while, but presently, because it was the easiest way, we turned into a little hollow, which should have brought us out again close to the mouth of the stream. As we went through this dip we were out of sight of the jungle. There were a few small trees, and the flowers which grew among the grass were speedwell and vetches. Simple, delicate, and half-hidden, they were flowers with which we had always been familiar, and now, by comparison with the fleshy, vigorous growths of the forest, we found them more beautiful still.

Before, we had been accustomed, when we came out of the dip, to find ourselves at the top of a sort of gorge, looking down on the last turn of the valley, and the last stretch of the stream. The shore had been reached by a narrow path, which wound down precipitously, and was used more by animals than people.

"There will be changes here too," Gran'papa said, and I ran on to look. He was right. There had been rocks and shrubs; ferns and grass and heather. Now the surface had been torn away to a considerable depth, leaving a raw stratum of mould and clay and stones. The rocks which remained were different. They were scarred and jagged; and they lay on a mass of gravel, or jutted out from the earth at awkward angles. At the bottom of the valley there was a grey confusion. The roots of one tree lay close to the broken top of another, and there were many battered branches among the loose stones and boulders. All this had blocked the stream, and formed a new, still lake, which looked artificial and out of place. At one side were some bushes half in and half out of the water.

"The abomination of desolation," I heard Gran'papa murmur, but really it wasn't that. There was a green tinge in the grey, and I knew that here too the fleshy plants would grow, and cover this naked wilderness.

Procyon was out of sight; he had bounded away over a heap of boulders. With a noise to which I was well accustomed, partly a grunt, partly a sigh, Gran'papa sat down on a little grassy bank, which, somehow or other, had escaped the general catastrophe.

"We'll wait here for a little, till he comes back," he said, referring to Procyon.

I waited, but I was far too excited to sit down. I was slightly nervous too. I felt that there was something very strange just round the corner—yet I didn't want to go on without Gran'papa. "Can I go down to the lake?" I asked instead, but the question was more an expression of impatience than of a real wish.

"No," Gran'papa said. "Don't be in such a hurry. Sit down and rest for a while."

"I'm not tired," I replied, but I sat down all the same. He put his hand on my shoulder, and it seemed as if something of his own calmness flowed into me.

"I do want to know what it all is," he said. "Do I seem old to you, Wolfe?"

"Oh yes, Gran'papa; of course you're old."

"Antediluvian, I suppose—and yet I have seen more strange things in the last few days than in all those years."

"Yes," I answered, but I didn't quite understand.

"And you," he went on, "have, I hope, as many years before you as I had at your age. So, with all that time on our hands, it doesn't matter very much, does it, if we space it out a little now?"

"Gran'papa," I said, "you're teasing me, aren't you?"

He smiled. "You always think I'm teasing you."

"You always *are*."

"No. This is serious. It's partly because I want to rest, of course, but it does add to a pleasure, if you think about it and wonder. What *is* round that corner? Something as strange as the Sirens. It may be a Gorgon or a Cyclops. When we go round there we shall return to the age of adventure—the age of Scylla and Charybdis. Ever since that age there has been nothing strange, or mysterious, or inexplicable, in the whole world. Everything has been cleared up and solved and explained, and now, by just going round a corner, we can step back thousands and thousands and thousands of years."

He spoke very softly and dreamily and I could only just hear him—and then I noticed a low noise. At once I felt cold inside, and frightened. It was so faint—scraping, or rustling, or slithering. I looked at the rocks over which Procyon had I gone, and Gran'papa looked too.

First of all came a head—flat and smooth like a snake's. It was lifted, and the angular, blinking eyes looked round lazily: but they didn't seem to see us, and with a slow undulating movement, wave after wave of the body appeared over the boulders. It wasn't a snake actually, for it had a great many tiny legs like a caterpillar's: its skin was smooth and glossy.

This huge creature was about thirty feet long: it passed close to us, slowly and deliberately, its questing head moving from side to side, on its way to the lake. We remained absolutely still and silent, bound by a sort of tension. It rippled over the gravel and the rocks, with an unhesitating persistence. When it reached the lake it did not pause; it went straight down into it, until it was entirely hidden.

Then, a few feet away, close to where the huge creature had passed, a grey lizard turned its head, just half a turn, and blinked one eye. Gran'papa laughed, and I had a feeling of relief—and immediately we noticed a great many other grey lizards, who lifted their sleepy eyelids for a moment. Their eyes were so different: some were sharp and alert, others grey and lethargic, revealing a sort of contentment in the steeping, sleepy rays of the sun. One after the other the eyelids were lowered again, and the lizards became stones and rock, so that it was difficult to distinguish them. Yet I watched the one who was so close, and I could see the quick movement of his fragile body, expanding and contracting as he breathed.

I was so interested in this that I forgot about Procyon until Gran'papa called him. He was standing just where he had disappeared about a quarter of an hour before. He did not move, but stood waiting, with an expectant look on his face. "Procyon," I shouted, but it was no use.

"Now we shall see round the corner," Gran'papa said. "Our guide has returned."

"Yes, Gran'papa," I answered, though since I had seen the giant caterpillar, I was less anxious to explore than I had been.

Gran'papa got up and I stayed close to him. As soon as he saw that we were going to follow him, Procyon came half-way to meet us, though he immediately went on again.

We made our way over the ridge very slowly, for Gran'papa found it difficult. "If we could only go like *him*," he said, for Procyon was bounding backwards and forwards, to the left and to the right, above and below, but always in front.

"*I* could," I said.

"Oh! Wolfe!" Gran'papa had a way of saying that, as if he were shocked—and I always thought he was at first. So I was quite indignant.

"I *could*," I told him, and I rushed after Procyon. At first he waited for me, and I thought I should overtake him, but then he ran on, harder than ever. I tried to catch him. He went up a very steep place and I followed. All of a sudden I slipped, and earth and stones came with me. I rolled quite a distance, and I was bruised and sore when I picked myself up.

Gran'papa took my hand and brushed the earth from my clothes. "Are you hurt?" he asked.

I shook my head.

"Are you sure?"

I nodded and we walked on for a little in silence. Then he smiled. "And what do you think now?"

"I think you're right, Gran'papa."

We went on over the ridge and saw below us a new, shale-like slope. At the bottom of the slope were a few sandhills, and beyond them the wide curve of the bay, with the waves breaking on the shore.

"Look at the sea," Gran'papa said, but there was nothing unusual about the sea, and my eyes came back quickly to the peculiar round objects, some quite small, some very large, which were scattered on the shale.

"Look at the sea," Gran'papa repeated. "It is always different and always the same."

I looked again, but I was too young, or too vital perhaps, to understand what he felt. I think I understand now. To me at any rate, at many times and in many places, that sea comes back, and the long stretch of the beach. I remember how, time after time, I have seen the waves sweep in, in just the same way, from the dark immensity that stretches to the horizon. I know that whatever happens on land, whatever people do, whatever animals do, whatever plants do, the sea will remain the same, breaking summer day after summer day on that long, quiet shore.

I know that now, but I didn't then, for I'd always had it and been accustomed to it; I had never longed for it in vain. So instead of looking at it, I was more interested in those round things, and I pointed them out to Gran'papa.

One or two were half buried in the ground. A number of others, mostly the smaller ones, were broken. They were hollow, and we could see that inside they were smooth and white.

"They look like eggs," I suggested.

"They *are* eggs," Gran'papa replied—"abandoned eggs. Procyon probably hatched from one of them."

"What do you think sat on him?" I asked. "A dragon?"

"Nothing—just the heat of the sun. Listen to that."

From the nearest egg came a slight noise—click, click—and it rolled over a little on one side. We stared at it curiously. It was of medium size, not any bigger than the black, three-legged pot which we used at home to boil the food for the pigs. On the outside it was very rough, encrusted with earth and rock. There was actually, growing on the underneath curve, a small hart's-tongue fern.

"It's going to burst," Gran'papa said, and almost immediately it did. There was a movement from inside, and a thin, stretching, cracking noise; then came a sudden pop, and a limp, sleepy-looking creature, blinked out at *us*, and at the sunlight. It lay in flabby inertia, while the sun beat down upon it and dried it. Then slowly it gathered strength.

Its first movement was back to its shell, and it began to lick the white, sticky substance which had been inside; but Procyon had been there first, and there wasn't much left. A disappointed, almost bitter expression came over its face, and it turned away without a second look at us, and waddled off up the valley in the direction of the lake and the jungle.

"It wasn't fair of Procyon," I said.

"No, it wasn't," Gran'papa agreed. "It was stealing, but I think the alligator'll be all right, even if he is a bit hungry."

"Is that an alligator?"

"Yes, I think so—an alligator or a crocodile—I'm afraid I don't know the difference."

"What size will he be when he's grown-up?"

"I don't know, but I imagine they grow to ten or twelve feet."

"D'you think there are more alligators in these big eggs?" I asked, "bigger ones?"

"I shouldn't think so," Gran'papa replied. "I expect all alligators' eggs are about the same size."

"Then maybe they're dragon's eggs," I said. "Are they, Gran'-papa?"

"My dear child! I don't know everything—and nothing about this. Do dragons lay eggs at all?"

"Let's wait and listen, Gran'papa. Maybe another one will burst, and we'll see what'll come out."

"I don't believe they'll all burst," he said. "Indeed I'm surprised that so many *have*. Now sit down," he added, "and we'll have something to eat."

We had brought some bread and butter with us, and Gran'papa made me sit down and eat my share. But I was very excited, and as soon as I had finished I jumped up again. I pressed my ear against all the biggest eggs in turn, but there was no sound, and Procyon, once more, seemed impatient: so again we followed him. He led us over the white, dry sand, above the high-water mark. He chose a way through the low dunes, and the sharp spiky bents brushed against my bare legs and scratched them. Soon we came to a little hollow, and a new and stranger sight.

To me it seemed very warm in that hollow, in which there was no shadow and no wind.

Lying there, between the little clumps of marram grass, were nearly a dozen creatures. There were two snakes, coloured a vivid green, with scarlet spots: neither was very big, but they both raised their heads and hissed menacingly. Procyon hissed back, a gentle soothing hiss, and they lowered their heads on to their smooth coils.

Then came a crimson scorpion, with a curved, spiky tail; it darted forward at us, but Procyon murmured a low sound, and it ran back.

Next a huge hornet, nearly as big as a squirrel, flew at us, with whirring wings. Procyon called to it, in a high, trilling voice, and it glided down again to the sand.

Last of all, two creatures similar to Procyon, but different in colouring, came forward like suspicious dogs; one was speckled, a dark, leafy green, and the other was a sandy brindle. Gran'papa bent down and patted the green one, and I stroked the brindle.

They lay down at our feet, and rolled lazily on their backs. Procyon tugged at Gran'papa's coat: so *we* sat down too. Then all the animals began to move towards us in little, short journeys. First came two toads; they hopped two or three hops, and stopped and blinked—and when I looked away from *them* the snakes had glided closer. I saw a crimson movement, as the scorpion darted a few short steps: and even the hornet was crawling across the sand. It was to Gran'papa they came, though they allowed me to stroke them too. The snakes wriggled into his pockets: the scorpion snuggled under his coat: the hornet crawled on to his hand. He lay back and closed his eyes; the two toads hopped on to his chest.

I was lying on my front, with my elbows on the ground, and my chin on my hands. I watched him. There was a very peaceful expression on his face: he wasn't exactly smiling, but he looked happy. The hot sun beat down on us.

"Gran'papa," I asked presently, "don't snakes bite?"

"Not if you make friends with them," he said. "If you make friends with them 'snakes don't bite nor scorpions sting.'"

"What do toads do?"

"They don't do anything to *us*, because they're friends with us too."

"What do they do to other people?" I questioned curiously.

"Oh they are magic creatures, and have jewels in their heads."

"Jewels!" I said, staring at the twins on his chest.

"Yes, jewels," he repeated, but he was thinking of something else.

I waited, and after a time he said, "Wolfe, do you like this?"

"Oh yes, Gran'papa," I told him. "It's been so exciting, and very interesting."

"I know, I know," he replied, "but do you not feel something else?"

"No . . . not . . ." I murmured doubtfully, and he went on.

"As if everything were right—everything here I mean. I do. I feel, somehow, as if all my life I had been wandering—a little homesick, without knowing it, and without knowing the way home. It's impossible to explain, if you don't feel it. *Do* you feel it?"

"I think I'm beginning to," I told him. "Go on talking about it, Gran'papa. I can feel things when you talk about them."

"It's a feeling of completeness," he said, "a feeling that *every*-thing is perfectly right. You and I have always liked this bay. There is something about it; it has a spirit and a soul. Isn't that true?"

"Yes, Gran'papa: I feel it now."

"These animals feel it too: they more than feel it; they have it. Perhaps, even, they *are* the spirit and the soul. They must have lain buried here for many thousands of years, preserved in some way or other, neither alive nor dead, till the land slipped. . . . Do you remember that night when it was raining so hard—and we heard a great rumbling noise like thunder?"

I nodded. "It made my bed shake."

"That must have been the beginning of it all. Most of the top soil of the valley must have been washed away that night, and the hot weather since has hatched the eggs and germinated the seeds."

He thought over this for a moment or two and then went on, "But it's because of the animals I feel so peaceful. Before, when we came here, we got a faint scent of all this; and we liked it and came back. Now the earth and the stones and the rocks have rolled away and the real thing is exposed. When one has no more need to strive, or search, when one has found everything, *then* one is peaceful."

"But we haven't found everything yet, Gran'papa: we haven't found the dragon and the sea serpent."

"No," he said, "nor the Sphinx, nor the Hydra, nor a unicorn; yet they too belong to it all more than we do. This is not a place;

it is a time, an era. All these animals are new as well as old. They come straight from the farthest past. They have not suffered for generations from wear and tear, from the gradual deterioration of the ages."

I listened because I was interested, though perhaps I did not really understand him. But he was talking more to himself than to me. Behind us I could hear the sound of the waves—low, monotonous and peaceful—and his voice seemed to rise and fall in time with it. I felt that these animals whom I had thought so strange were not strange at all, but part of a primeval world which had taken root in me too, and was growing up like the green things in the jungle, and softly entwining my heart.

"They are simple and innocent," Gran'papa said. "There must have been an age of innocence and simplicity. Our animals aren't like this—cows, dogs, horses, and even cats I used to think innocent enough; but they're not like this. Perhaps they have suffered, and been tainted, because of their contact with humanity—or has every animal had its Adam and its Eve, its temptation and its fall? Probably in their age of innocence they didn't quarrel with each other, or prey upon each other. Then, in each race, some malefactor came, bringing retribution a thousand-fold to millions of descendants."

"It doesn't seem fair, Gran'papa."

"It isn't fair; but now you and I have gone back, back to the age before the unfair things began."

I looked round and saw the changing colours of the cliffs and of the mountains. It was growing late, and even in this sheltered spot it was no longer warm. One of the toads shivered; it hopped from Gran'papa's chest and made its way across the hollow; it came to two or three stones, and suddenly I couldn't see it.

Procyon and his brothers pressed closer against Gran'papa; a breeze came from the sea and stirred the dry powdery sand: and from the marram grass there trailed long, pointed shadows.

"Gran'papa," I asked, "do you not feel hungry?"

"No," he said, "not yet; but do you want to go home?"

"It's not that," I answered, "but we'd very little dinner."

"All right: I'll come." After a moment he raised himself slightly. "I'll have to put you down, toad," he said. Then he got up, and instantly the inquiring heads of the snakes peered out of his pockets. He lifted them out, and put them down on the sand, and stroked them. We both stroked all the creatures and patted some of them as well.

After we had spent a considerable time petting them, we turned our backs resolutely, and set off for home. We heard behind us a curious combination of sounds. The faint sound of the snakes as they glided across the sand, the delicate footfalls of the scorpion, the padding of Procyon and his brothers, the touf . . . touf of the toad, as it hopped and landed, hopped and landed. Then we heard the whirr of the hornet, and it alighted on Gran'papa's shoulder. It was this that made us turn.

We petted them all again and talked to them. Gran'papa said, "Don't come. We're going to a place not so good as this, but to-morrow we'll come back."

They seemed to understand, for this time only Procyon came with us. When we looked back they were grouped in a half-circle: on the outside were the two snakes; then came Procyon's brothers; and between them, in the very middle, stood the toad. They were all silent except the toad, who said good-bye in his harsh, sad voice.

CHAPTER V

Next morning we set out again for the Far Shore. We took Dobbin with us, for Gran'papa was tired after his long walk on the previous day. Dobbin was an old, dappled grey horse and we kept a young mare as well to do most of the work. Father and Mother would have sold Dobbin, but Gran'papa was very fond of him, and he often came with us on our walks. Sometimes he carried Gran'papa for part of the way, and sometimes I got a ride, but as a rule he just followed us, nosing in Gran'papa's pockets whenever he got the chance, in the hope of finding apples or carrots. It was more than a year now since he had worked on the farm, though sometimes he would draw a cartload of turf from the bog.

At first Dobbin had been nervous of Procyon, but soon he grew accustomed to him. He had always been a quiet horse, and that morning he followed us very soberly. He was carrying *our* lunch and his own, and soon I took off my jacket and added it to his burden.

"Do you think we'll meet the Dragon to-day?" I kept asking Gran'papa, but he wouldn't give a definite reply. So I stopped asking him, and ran backwards and forwards with Procyon. This made me very hot, and I was glad of the cooling breeze when we crossed the summit of the hill. It was just as bright as the day before, but hotter. There was not a cloud in the sky, and the sea looked perfectly still. Presently I gave up chasing Procyon, and walked quietly with Gran'papa and Dobbin.

At about ten o'clock we sat down by the side of a stream, to rest. It was not the stream of Neencroom, but another, which flowed into the sea at a different and more northerly bay. We intended to follow it, and then walk along the shore, till we came to the hollow among the sandhills. We had stopped where the stream was wide and shallow, and I lay down on a large, flat stone, and dipped my face in the water. Dobbin must have been hot too, for I heard his hooves clatter on the stones as he came and stood beside me. Gran'papa called to me to take off his load; so I unhitched it, and carried it to the bank.

Procyon couldn't find us for a minute or two, but when he did, he splashed into the water, and began to lap it up. Then he found a little pool, where curious water insects darted backwards and forwards. He tried to catch them in his big mouth, but of course he couldn't, and they were so small that he would never have known if he had.

"I'd like to take off all my clothes," I said, "and lie down here, in the stream."

"Take them off then," Gran'papa replied, "but it's hardly worth while; you'll be bathing very soon—as soon as we get to the shore."

So I didn't, though Gran'papa himself had taken off his shoes and stockings, and was sitting on the bank with his feet in the water.

"What happens to them all in winter time?" I asked, pointing to a very rigid-looking stick insect, which was moving slowly across the bottom of the pool. "Do they die in winter, like butterflies and bees?"

Suddenly Dobbin lifted his head from the water: he gave a nervous whinny, and his nostrils quivered.

"What's the matter with him?" I asked.

"I don't know." Gran'papa frowned. "Procyon smells something too."

Procyon had lifted his head from the water with an expectant air. "It's the Dragon," I exclaimed, and instantly I knew exactly what he was like, and I was not afraid—but Gran'papa looked worried, as if he had realized for the first time that there *might* be some danger.

"I should never have brought you," he muttered, "but I was sure it was all right. It was stupid of me, but I felt so sure."

"Is it *not* all right?" I asked, and my confidence evaporated in a flash.

"It was because of the other animals," he said, in a voice which once more was completely calm. "They're so nice that the Dragon is sure to be nice also—big animals always *are* nice."

But I felt that he was trying to reassure me, and a moment later, when he was struck by a sudden idea, I realized that he was not confident at all.

"Get on to that horse," he ordered. "Get on to Dobbin—never mind the luggage . . ."

"What about . . ." I began.

"I'll come after. Now . . ." But it was no use. Dobbin uttered a shrill and frightened neigh, and before either of us could stop him, had bolted madly for home.

We watched him for a moment without speaking. "Well," said Gran'papa, and he turned round again.

"I didn't want to go home alone," I told him, and then we heard, THUMP . . . THUMP . . . THUMP. It was faint at first, but it was getting nearer. There was nowhere to go, nowhere to hide—just the open, heather-covered hill.

Gran'papa put on his shoes and stockings. "Don't run," he said, "unless I tell you to."

We couldn't see the Dragon yet, though we knew where he was; he was between us and the sea, hidden by a mound, and by the slope of the hill.

"Perhaps he won't see us," I said hopefully, but at that moment Procyon bounded away from us over the hillock; and undoubtedly he would tell the Dragon. I jumped up the bank to stop him, but I was not quick enough. A moment later he returned—and behind him was the Dragon.

I didn't move; I just stared; because the Dragon was the most beautiful creature I had ever seen. He had a thick skin, of which the basic colour was a deep, browny green. On that, as if delicately woven, was a mottled pattern of gold. He had four legs, and four wings, and strong, four-toed feet. The wings, which were almost transparent, were pressed close against his back. When the sun shone through them, they showed faint, rainbow colourings. His tail, which was really part of his body, was thick and curved. His neck was curved too, and his head was large. His eyes were big, and rather sad. He was splendid to see.

He was looking at me, and at once my fears were forgotten. He was pleased, and I ran to him. He put down his head, and I put my arm round his neck. We stood there together, quite still, and everything that was present passed away.

I saw a strange, grey-toned world, the edge of a forest, and beyond—a vast plain. In the forest and on the plain were strange creatures, dragons, and hairy elephants with curling tusks; a grim tiger padded past, showing one long, pointed tooth.

It was winter and I saw the Dragon; he was alone in a little glade of the forest. He was restless, because, between the toes of his left fore foot, there was caught a long trailer of dead bramble. He gripped the bramble with his mouth, and pulled and pulled, but he could not dislodge it. His foot was very sore, and his mouth also was pricked with the thorns.

A boy appeared at the far end of the glade. He was strange, and wild, and nervous. He carried a spear, and he looked sharply this way, and that. When he saw the Dragon he stopped dead. But the Dragon wished that the boy would come and take away the thorny bramble.

Again the boy looked sharply to either side. Then he ran forward to the Dragon. He put down his spear, and quickly he unloosed the bramble. He picked up the spear again, and used the point to remove some of the thorns, which had broken off. He was very, very tense, while he worked.

Suddenly I saw Gran'papa again; he got up from the bed of

the stream, and came towards us. Immediately I felt the Dragon stiffen.

"Don't be silly," I said. "It's Gran'papa."

"Go away," the Dragon told Gran'papa.

Gran'papa stopped. "I'll go away," he said, "but Wolfe must come too."

"The boy will be quite safe."

I took my arm from round the Dragon's neck. "I won't stay unless you're nice to Gran'papa. He's kind to all the animals, and all the other animals like him."

"Is he *really* good?" the Dragon asked doubtfully.

"He *is*," I said, and I knew that the same answer came from Procyon, though *then* I didn't know how.

"You should just see what the animals on the Far Shore think," I said, "and all the dogs in the village, and the cats too—and the horses and the donkeys."

"For your sake I will be friends with him, though I decided long ago that never again would I be friends with a man."

Again I saw the grey plain and on it was one of the hairy elephants. He was walking along slowly, surrounded by men—small, skinny men. The elephant was friendly, and as he walked his trunk swayed slowly from side to side. But about the men there was something strange and unpleasant. They drew away a little from the elephant; some dropped behind; none was directly in front. All of a sudden the elephant lurched, and seemed to sink. The picture was wiped away, and I stared into grey, blank space.

The Dragon wished to go to the hollow among the sandhills and we all set off together.

Never have I stumbled so often as I stumbled on that walk; for I walked in a vision, and had no eyes for the present. I saw all sorts of scenes, passing in a rapid whirl, and scenes such as I had never imagined before. In all of these scenes there were men—in some only one man—but behind each scene there was Gran'papa, just as he was, walking beside us now on the heather. Sometimes he was vague in the background, and the scene went on before him, so as almost to blot him out; sometimes he was quite clear, though

accompanied and surrounded by the wild men of the plain: sometimes he was alone. Yet, whether hidden or fully revealed, he was
always the same.

Again I stumbled, but Gran'papa caught me, and I did not fall.
"What's the matter, Wolfe?" Gran'papa asked. "Are you quite well?"

"He sees my thoughts," the Dragon answered for me, "and for-
gets to watch the path. Let him ride on my back."

I scrambled up, not to his back really, but to the low curve of his
neck, before Gran'papa could prevent me. For Gran'papa, at first,
did not understand the Dragon so easily as I did.

"What does he say?" he asked.

I told him.

"How can you look at his thoughts?"

"I don't know, Gran'papa; I just see them."

"You *do* see them?"

"Yes, Gran'papa; I see elephants, and forests, and dragons, and
strange men—and you're there too."

"It's queer," Gran'papa said. "*I* see something too. But for me
it's so vague, and blurred and confused, that I can't understand it."

"*I* see everything quite clearly."

"Yes. . . . I think I understand what he says. . . . But there's
something behind it—an impression of scenes and thoughts. Presently, perhaps, I shall see as much as you."

As we went on I could feel that the Dragon was beginning to
like Gran'papa, and when we reached the shore I found thoughts
of Gran'papa's among the Dragon's. For the Dragon didn't speak
at all. It seemed as if he asked questions, and answered them, but
in doing so he made no sound. He was able to make us know his
thoughts; also he could understand ours. So when I write, as I shall
do, that the Dragon "said" something, it will just mean that he
communicated with us.

"You have lived a long time, old man; have you ever seen a
dragon like me?"

The Dragon knew the answer before Gran'papa could reply.
Gran'papa *did* reply; we always spoke at first, and nearly always
later on.

We walked along the shore, close to the breaking waves, and the
noise of the Dragon's feet was splodge, splodge, on the wet sand.

"There is no heat here," the Dragon thought, "and that is why it reminded me of the grey plain, and the forest. It was far from here, but once some of us went there. We made a long journey that time, but in the end we returned."

"Perhaps it was Russia you visited," Gran'papa said, but names had no meaning for the Dragon. So Gran'papa asked, "Did you cross the sea?"

"It was land all the way," the Dragon replied—and this puzzled Gran'papa. Yet the Dragon did not explain. He was thinking of everything as it had been, a beach with waving palms, a coral reef, and a lagoon. Even the sun was hotter, and beyond the beach was a rich, luxuriant forest.

By the time we came to the hollow in the sand dunes Gran'papa and the Dragon trusted each other completely. So Gran'papa settled down, as he had done on the previous day, and he allowed me to go on with the Dragon to see if more eggs had hatched out in the sun. I watched the snakes wriggle into Gran'papa's pockets, and the toads hop on to his chest—but Procyon was more adventurous than his brothers and came with me and the Dragon.

When we got to the shaley slope there was one more empty shell, but of course we couldn't tell what sort of creature had come out of it.

Again I listened to all the eggs, but from none came any sound. While I was doing this the Dragon scraped the shale on different parts of the slope, and presently he discovered more eggs; for the place must once have been a huge nest where all the creatures laid. As he pulled out the eggs he let them go, and they rolled down gently to where I was standing. There were a great many, but I collected all that he found, and placed them in a sunny, sheltered place, where I hoped they would hatch.

Presently the Dragon stopped digging and came to me. I went with him to a place where there was thick grass. He opened his mouth, and put down an egg which was smaller than the rest in front of me. It was a present. He had found it with the others, and chosen it because of the beautiful colouring of the shell. It was a deep, varied green, with a sort of liquid pattern running round and round it.

After he had given it to me the Dragon glanced up the valley, as if he had not thought of it before, and asked "What is *there*?"

"That is the jungle," I answered, but my thoughts told him more.

"Why do you dislike it?" he asked. "Why are you afraid?" But I couldn't explain. There was nothing strange to him in the blue-eyed plant, or the fleshy undergrowth. He had been familiar with it in his previous life, and it was not with horror, but with a special tenderness, that he pictured it to himself.

It was strange to watch him. First came my picture, filled with the remembered horror of a nightmare. Yet to the Dragon the colours were familiar, and as I watched they softened and seemed to blend. Then new things grew—new trees, new plants, new flowers. Insects I had not seen buzzed in the undergrowth. Small, brightly-coloured birds fluttered among the trees, which had imperceptibly grown bigger.

The whole picture possessed a dreamy allurement; it was beautiful, yet still I did not like it.

And then came the dragons. There were about a dozen of them, and they walked abreast through the forest. They appeared from a distance, coming through the trees and trampling the undergrowth with their feet. Presently they stopped and began to graze.

The picture vanished, and for perhaps a minute there was nothing to see but a slaty grey.

"I am going there," the Dragon decided, "but first I must leave you with your Grandfather."

I assured him that I could go myself, but he seemed to think that I had been entrusted to his care. The distance was short, but he came with me to the edge of the hollow. Then he turned abruptly and made his way up the valley.

"Will he come back?" I asked Gran'papa.

"Not for a good while, I expect," and he was right. I bathed and Gran'papa and Procyon watched me. We spent the whole afternoon on the shore, but the Dragon did not return.

On the way home I carried the green egg carefully.

CHAPTER VI

I got the egg home safely enough, but Gran'papa told me not to tell anyone either about it or our meeting with the Dragon. So I didn't.

I made a little nest for the egg, on top of the big stack of straw in the yard. I put it there early next morning, for during the night I had kept it hidden in my bed. In the evening I brought it in again; and I hoped that the heat of the sun by day, and the warmth of my bed at night, would soon make it hatch.

For nearly a week after that we did not go over the hill. Gran'-papa was tired, and he was afraid to take Dobbin in case he should bolt again at sight of the Dragon.

So every morning he brought out a chair, and sat all day long in the sun in front of the cottage. Sometimes he read; sometimes he talked to me; sometimes he watched the fishing boats; and some-times he thought without doing any of these things.

Peter and I played about on the hillside between the cottage and the village, and Procyon played with us. Gran'papa wouldn't let me go alone to the Far Shore, and Peter, of course, knew nothing of what was there.

Every time I came to talk to Gran'papa he would ask me if I had learned anything from Procyon; usually I hadn't. When I was with him I occasionally received impressions, but they were not thoughts, nor memories, nor ideas. Once I knew that Father Binyon was coming, because Procyon had seen him first, but that was all.

This was very disappointing for Gran'papa, because Gran'papa was trying to find out how animals talked to each other—for he *believed* that they could talk—that they communicated by an exchange of thoughts, as the Dragon had communicated with us. He believed that human beings must once have possessed this power, though why they should have abandoned it for the much inferior method—speech—he could not understand.

He would sit with Procyon or one of the dogs by his side, and his eyes closed. The first time I saw him like this I thought he was asleep, but suddenly he opened his eyes and looked at me. "I make my mind a blank," he said, "and then I wait to receive ideas: but none come—at least not from the animals."

He would sit for hours with old Bran, waiting for a message—and Bran liked it well enough, for all the while Gran'papa would stroke him, and scratch behind his ears.

One day when I was sitting beside him, and stroking the other end of Bran, Gran'papa said, "Our apparatus is *there* all right, but it's rusty for want of use."

"But we used it with the Dragon," I pointed out, though instead of paying proper attention I was watching the ducks. Their beaks were all muddied, and they were searching for worms in the slime at the edge of the duck-pond.

"Yes"—Gran'papa was not distracted by the ducks—"but the Dragon is much stronger than these other creatures. His thoughts are stronger, or his power of projecting them is stronger. The Dragon is like a lighthouse in a fog."

"And the ducks are like ships on the sea."

"Never mind about the ducks," he said a little impatiently. "You always let your mind wander. Concentrate. You understand the animals better than I do. So you should be able to help me."

"Why do I understand them better?" I asked.

"Indeed I don't know," he said. "It's most undeserved."

"Perhaps it's because my mind wanders. Maybe it wanders into Procyon's mind sometimes."

"I don't think so," he replied, after a moment's consideration. "If that were so you could wander into the dogs' minds too, but you don't—and it's not that dogs don't think. They do think—dream too—you must often have watched them dreaming. . . ." He looked down at Bran. "*You* think, don't you, Bran?"

Bran wagged his tail, and then, to make his thoughtfulness quite clear, stood on his hind legs and licked Gran'papa's face.

"You see," Gran'papa said and patted him, "it's an expression of emotion, an attempt to communicate. But the question is, why doesn't he do it as the Dragon does?"

"Maybe *his* apparatus is rusty too," I suggested.

"I expect it is," Gran'papa agreed. "In fact it couldn't be anything else. For thousands of years his ancestors have been in contact with humanity: they were bound to lose something." Gran'papa was always down on Humanity. You would almost have thought he was a kind of animal himself.

Just then Peter came tearing round the corner of the cottage. There were wisps of straw sticking to his clothes and hair, and he had something in his hand. He was always poking about and discovering things. "Look what *I've* found," he exclaimed. It was the green egg, which the Dragon had dug up. You couldn't keep anything from him.

"That's mine," I said quickly. "The Dragon gave it to me."

"The Dragon!" So then of course we had to tell him all about it.

"But you must keep it a secret," Gran'papa finished. "You mustn't let anybody know."

"Can't I even tell my da?" Peter asked, and he added, "I usually tell him things."

I could see that this put Gran'papa in a difficulty. He didn't like to say that Peter must keep a secret from his father. Yet in the end it was what he did say. "Ask him to come and see me," he compromised, "and I'll tell him myself."

So the next afternoon, before it was time to go fishing, Michael came to see Gran'papa, and *he* was told too. "I won't speak about it," he promised, "but what are you frightened of?"

"You know what they are"—Gran'papa glanced down towards the village—"they'd try to kill the Dragon—and Heaven knows what would happen then."

"He'd destroy them, you mean?" Michael looked grave.

"Every one," Gran'papa answered, pausing emphatically after each of the words. "They couldn't do a thing against him."

Michael was silent for a moment. He stared down at the village. There was no one in sight. A sort of afternoon lifelessness overhung the whole countryside. "Are you not afeared he'll do that anyhow?" he said presently.

"Not unless they attack him; he's very friendly."

"He's friendly to the two of *you*; but will it be the same with the rest of us?"

"I don't expect so," I chimed in. "He doesn't like people." Gran'-papa frowned and I knew I'd made a mistake.

"That's all nonsense," Gran'papa said sharply. "So far he has only met Wolfe and me, and we got on very well together."

I was expecting that after Michael had gone away Gran'papa would scold me for saying something foolish but instead he began again about that theory of his.

"You and I should be able to do it," he said. "It must be a matter of sympathy and understanding—and we understand each other fairly well, don't we?"

"Yes, Gran'papa. I think so."

"Well then, we'll sit down here and try it. You make your mind a blank. I'll think of things—simple things—and perhaps you'll be able to see them. Now shut your eyes and don't watch the ducks."

When you sat in front of the cottage it was very hard not to look at the ducks. So I did as he told me. At least I sat down and shut my eyes, but it was difficult to make my mind a blank. "Gran'papa," I began, "mightn't it help if we held hands? Your thoughts could travel that way perhaps."

I felt the grasp of his hand and waited. In my mind there formed a grey, translucent mistiness which, it seemed, could contain the whole universe. It eddied and swirled and flowed—and then suddenly I saw the Dragon—but somehow he looked different, even bigger than he really was.

"The Dragon!" I exclaimed.

"Tch," said Gran'papa.

"Weren't you thinking of that?"

"No: I was thinking of the fishing boats and the light upon the water."

I closed my eyes again and looked into blankness. Then came rocks and stones, and the slope of shale. *There* were the eggs, and one burst—and all of a sudden I felt hungry. Something came out, but it was not that I saw. I saw the inside of the egg, white and shining, and an appetizing, sticky substance which Procyon was licking with enjoyment. It looked very good.

I opened my eyes and told Gran'papa what I had seen.

He sighed. "I was looking at the 'Old Man's Nob'," he said, "and thinking of it," and he pointed to a distant hill on the far side of the lough.

I too looked at the hill. "Why do they call it that, Gran'papa?" I asked.

"I don't know," he replied. "It's always had that name so long as I can remember. Now try again."

I tried. I looked at blankness, but immediately it was replaced by the black, three-legged pot, filled with potato skins, and soft mush and scraps. It had been intended for the pigs, but Procyon somehow or other had managed to get a share. I saw this very vividly, I could almost taste it, and though it was really horrid, it seemed delicious. I wanted to get some and eat it.

I told Gran'papa and, though it wasn't my fault, he began to get cross. "The Dragon and Procyon: Procyon and the Dragon: your mind's filled with nothing else."

"I'm sorry," I said. "I can't help it. They just come—and I wanted to eat the things he was eating."

"But *why?*—they're disgusting." And all of a sudden he looked very pleased, and then he frowned. "I believe I've got it." He held up his hand as he'd a way of doing sometimes. "Don't speak to me—not a word. I must think."

I waited, and I felt quite excited, and Gran'papa frowned and frowned. At last he looked at me and smiled. "Yes. That's it," he said. "Now listen:

"In the time of the Dragon, and of Procyon's father and mother, all men could communicate with each other and with all other animals, just the way the Dragon does now." He paused, and looked at me thoughtfully. Then he went on, "I don't know why, but for some reason or other—just laziness perhaps—Man made less and less use of this faculty—and now he does not use it at all. I can't say whether the other animals have retained it or not, but at any rate most of them have no desire to speak to Man. Dogs might want to, but by now all the animals must think that Man is deaf and dumb in this respect. Perhaps they even call us 'the dumb animals'."

"You mean, Gran'papa, that the Dragon had been accustomed to men who *could* communicate."

"Yes—he just thought we were the same as everything else— and *his* faculty of sending messages and receiving them is very strong. Everything in his age must have been stronger—the air, the sun, the plants. So his strength made up for our deficiencies."

"All the same," I said, "you'd think we might have got *something*, when we were trying so hard."

"You did get something."

"Not very much—and you said it was wrong."

"I know: but it wasn't wrong. Those were Procyon's thoughts—and it was that gave me my idea."

"But, Gran'papa! How do you know they were Procyon's thoughts?"

"I don't know, of course; but we have to guess. And the guess if it isn't quite true, may at least be not very far from the truth—as Socrates used to tell his pupils. What we really do know is that we get direct messages from the Dragon, and so direct, and so clear that at first we mistook them for speech. Procyon's thoughts are different because they have Procyon's individuality. He remembers past pleasures, and they appear to him as pictures. *You* would never have seen them if your mind hadn't been blank. They weren't intended as messages—it was only that you were in a very receptive mood."

"But why didn't I get *your* messages instead?" I objected. "You were closer to me, and they were what I wanted to get."

"Because I'm not a primeval creature," he said, half smiling, half regretful. "I haven't the full vigour of that younger world. And that's all theory too, a theory built on guesses and imagination, like the stories Socrates told while he was trying to find the true story that would fit in with everything and explain everything. He called them myths and his pupil Plato wrote them down years afterwards."

"I'm sure *your* myth's right, Gran'papa."

"Well," he said, "I think it is: in which case it's not a myth."

"I'm sure it's not," I told him.

"That's very kind of you, Wolfe, because *I'm* not sure of anything," which meant of course that he was sure of this at least.

"Supper's ready," Mother called, and we both got up immediately, because she was always annoyed if we dawdled.

After supper I went down to the harbour, and met Peter there. The boats were going out, and the fishermen were standing in groups and talking. There were other boys too, and we played among the boats till the last one was launched.

When I reached home again I was scolded for being so late, and sent straight to bed. However, I climbed out through the window, and brought in the egg from the top of the stack. I held it to my ear, and thought I could detect a slight stirring from inside. I put it beside me in the bed, and soon forgetting all about it, and about Gran'papa's theory too, I fell asleep.

I was awakened by a movement at my feet. For a moment I was startled, and then I remembered. What was it, I wondered— a lizard, a snake, a scorpion? I could feel it rubbing against my toes, and I jumped out of bed and lit the candle. I rolled back the clothes, and there it was—a tiny lizard. It was bright red, with black spots like a ladybird, and though it seemed a little dazed, it had an extraordinary appearance of liveliness. I put down my hand, and it ran up my arm to my shoulder. My first impulse was to show it to Gran'papa, and I turned to the door. Then I heard footsteps and voices from the next room, and blew out my candle. The others had not yet gone to bed, and someone was coming. I lay down again hastily, pulled the clothes over me, and pretended to be asleep. I held the lizard close against my chest.

The door opened, and through half-closed eyelids I saw Father, with part of the lighted room behind him. "What are *you* up to?" he demanded, though not angrily, as he peered in. He must have heard the sound of flint and steel when I struck the light.

I closed my eyes more tightly and perhaps he noticed this. "You're pretending," he said, but he closed the door without troubling further. He was like that, and I heard him telling Mother that I was sound asleep.

For some moments I remained still, but slowly I opened my eyes. The light was shining under the door, and I could hear Mother and Gran'papa talking. I wished they would go to bed, for I wanted to show Gran'papa my lizard. I wondered if we could keep it secret any longer, or if we would have to tell Mother and Father.

It was hard to stay awake, for I was very sleepy, but at last I heard the scrape of chairs as they were pushed back. So I had to close my eyes again for Mother always came in to look at me before she went to sleep. She came now, but in a minute or two went out, closing the door softly behind her. The sounds became fewer and more disconnected. Then there was no more sound; they had gone to sleep.

Softly I got up and stole to the door. I opened it, and stood for a moment, looking into the kitchen. From the fire there was only a faint glow, because it had been banked up with wet turf for the night. Nevertheless there were weak reflections, and brass pans on the walls winked now and then at pots under the dresser.

I crossed the kitchen with the lizard in my arms. I paused a moment at the hearth, because of the pleasant warmth of the stone against the soles of my feet. Then I knocked on Gran'papa's door.

"Come in," he called in a low voice, and I pushed it open. He was sitting up in bed, and the candle was still alight on the table by his side.

"Gran'papa," I said, and stopped; for, seeing him like that, in his nightshirt, he seemed very frail and old, and I felt a great tenderness for him.

"The egg has burst," he said. "I'm as clever now as the Dragon."

"How did you know?" I exclaimed.

"I guessed when we heard the noises from your room. What is it?"

I showed him, and put the lizard on his bed, where it remained quite still upon the patchwork coverlet, blinking in a bewildered fashion.

"It's a lizard, isn't it?"

"I suppose it is," he replied, "or at least an approximation to one, for I don't think there are any red lizards nowadays. But whatever he is, I expect he'd like a drink of milk. Warm a plate at the fire and pour some milk on to it. That'll take the chill off at any rate."

I did as he suggested, and then he sent me back to bed.

"Can I keep it?" I asked.

"We can discuss that in the morning. It depends on your mother. I wish now that we had told her in the beginning."

I knew it would depend on her, and I got up specially early to show her the lizard before breakfast. "Look what came out of an egg I had," I said, being careful not to mention the Dragon.

For a moment she didn't look, for she was busy stirring the porridge. Then there was a terrible clatter, as she dropped the lid of the pot. "Sakes alive," she exclaimed, starting back, "what have you got there?"

"It's just a lizard, Mammy. . . ."

"Whatever it is," she said, "take it out of this at once . . ." but at that moment Gran'papa came in.

"Nonsense," he interrupted. "A lizard in the house is very lucky. It's unlucky to put one out."

Now Mother was a great believer in luck. "Oh . . ." she said slowly, "is it?" So she allowed me to put the lizard down on the table while I got it a saucer of milk—and she was quite interested in it.

But the lizard didn't seem to care about the milk. He just stayed quite still on the table and blinked his eyes; and presently a fly lit on the table and began to walk towards him. Suddenly there was no fly. It was magic; none of us had seen anything, but we knew it was the lizard.

Then he got off the table and began to scuttle round the room. Whenever he came near a fly the fly disappeared. "Mercy me!" Mother exclaimed, "did you ever see the like!"

We never had. There were a lot of flies in the room that morning, but by the time we had finished breakfast there was not one left. Mother was delighted; she hated flies. "It *is* lucky," she said, and very soon she was calling it *her* lizard.

CHAPTER VII

Soon after breakfast I set off for the village to show the lizard to Peter and his father. Mother didn't want me to take it away, and she came to the door specially to remind me to bring it back. I carried it in my pocket, and Procyon came with me.

I had only gone a little way down the lane, and Procyon was somewhere near though out of sight, when I met Father Binyon.

"Good morning, Father," I said.

Though it was still early, Father Binyon looked hot. He always looked hot when he was coming uphill. Now, before replying, he took off his hat and wiped his forehead with a not very clean handkerchief.

"Good morning, my son," he answered at last. Then suddenly an expression of astonishment came over his face. He stared fixedly at something behind my back. "In Heaven's name," he demanded, "tell me, am I seeing things, or what's that in the ditch?"

I turned quickly and saw Procyon watching us over a grassy bank. Only his head and forepaws were showing, and perhaps he did look rather strange. "Oh, that's our dog," I said lightly, "our new dog. Didn't you hear about him? He's called Procyon."

"A queer name," Father Binyon remarked, "but the dog's queerer. It's him I suppose they're all talking about—and I thought it was just some new kind of mongrel you'd got. That's not a dog at all."

"Is he not?" I asked, for I had got so accustomed to Procyon that I had really begun to think he was an ordinary dog. Now I remembered that he wasn't, and I began to be afraid that Father Binyon would ask all sorts of awkward questions and perhaps even begin to suspect about the Dragon—and at that moment I felt a wriggle in my pocket and I put my hand into it quickly. Father Binyon was staring at me. I felt myself going crimson.

"Of course he's not a dog," the priest snapped, "and you know that as well as I do. Call him. I want to see him."

"Procyon!" I tried to whistle as well as call, but could only produce a feeble, watery hiss.

However Procyon came. He bounded over the bank and rushed to me in the most playful way, wagging his tail. Then he jumped up on me and I had to turn quickly for fear he should bruise the lizard. "What on earth have you there?" Father Binyon demanded, "in that pocket?"

"Oh"—I very nearly said "nothing"—"Oh, just—just I like keeping my hand in it."

The priest snorted, and I knew he didn't believe me, but after all Gran'papa's instructions what could I do? I half expected he would make me show him the lizard, but instead he pointed to Procyon. "Where did you get him?" he asked.

"Oh—him?" I answered—for I was still thinking of the lizard. "Oh, he came to me up there." I took my hand away from my pocket to point. "I found him in the valley—you know, the Valley of Neencroom."

I glanced down, and there, poking out of the corner of my pocket, was a little speckled head. I pushed it back in, and glanced quickly at the priest. Fortunately he was looking up towards Neen-croom.

Presently he turned to me again. I could feel the lizard wriggling, but I held it tightly. "And will you be going over the hill to-day?"

"I expect we will. We haven't been since last week."

"Last week! That's not long. You don't meet Michael's Sea Serpent on these excursions of yours?" It was a curious question. Did he suspect something, or had he just asked it by chance? Well, we hadn't met him yet, though we hoped to.

"No," I answered, and I wished he'd go on—or that I was allowed to talk openly.

However, this seemed to please him. "No," he repeated emphatically, "and nor did anyone else. Nobody's seen him, but Michael himself."

Of course *I* had seen him, though only in the distance. Yet instead of telling Father Binyon so, I said, "But we all saw the Dragon, when he came to the cottage that night."

"So it was a dragon, was it?" Father Binyon asked slowly. "You seem to know a good deal about it." He looked at me in a peculiar way, and I couldn't say anything. Eventually, abruptly, he broke the tension himself. "Is your Grandfather in?" he asked.

"He's up at the house."

"I'll go then and see him." He continued on his way and so did I—and now I was just as hot as he had been. I passed his house and the church and hurried along the road to the harbour.

This was really the village—the harbour, the boat-house, and this one row of cottages. Here lived all the fishermen, who were fishermen only. The others, who were farmers as well, lived in different places in the surrounding countryside. The Rymples lived in the third cottage from the boathouse, and I found them at breakfast. Their cottage was divided into two rooms only, and their kitchen was very like ours, except that it wasn't so big. Indeed the kitchens in all the cottages were very much the same.

Michael and Peter were sitting at a white scrubbed table, eating porridge from bowls. Michael had a chair, but Peter was on a tall, three-legged stool. He had a touzled half-awake kind of look and he hadn't got his jersey on. When I came in he glanced up. His spoon was in his mouth, and he said, "Hullo", without taking it away. Then he went on with his porridge.

Michael was properly dressed and he said it was a nice morning. Then he went on with his porridge too.

They didn't pay any attention to me; so presently I said, "What do you think's in my pocket?"

"Air," Peter answered, and he looked up this time and took the spoon away from his mouth.

"No; don't be silly." He thought he'd been clever, because that had been a joke once. "I really *have* something—and something exciting too."

"Another egg?"

From under the half-open door came a sniffing noise, and I went over and let in Procyon. Immediately there was a low growl, and I realized that Finn, the Rymples' dog, disapproved. I hadn't noticed him before, but now he came out from below the table, where he had been lying. I was afraid there would be a fight, but as soon as Finn discovered that Procyon wasn't a real dog—and it only took him two sniffs to find out—he didn't mind so much, and they settled down quite peacefully on opposite sides of the table.

"Well, *is* it an egg?" Peter asked again.

I shook my head. "Guess."

Suddenly I felt myself reeling backwards. Michael had caught me in a sort of huge handful, that was partly me and partly my jersey and underclothing. "We'll see for ourselves," he declared.

"Oh be careful," I screamed, and at that instant the lizard escaped from my pocket and ran up my arm to my shoulder.

Michael got a start and let go, so that I nearly fell. "What is it?" he asked. "Would it sting you?"

"No, it's quite harmless—except to flies. It eats flies and drinks milk. Do you remember the egg we showed you the other day—it came out of that; but don't forget about it being a secret."

"Sure *everything's* a secret with you," Peter said, but Michael came in on my side.

"He's right to do what his grandfather tells him. If others were a little more obedient it would be no harm." Peter was abashed and Michael turned to me. "Of course we won't say anything," he promised. "Now let's see it eating the flies."

So I put the lizard on the table, just as I had done at home, and Michael put down a little honey. I expect he thought of that because he was a fisherman and knew that fish needed bait. Very soon a fly came buzzing down to the table and alit near the honey, but it never tasted it. Other flies came too, and Michael wished the lizard would catch them more slowly so that he could see it happening. Presently we couldn't see any more flies in the room, for Michael and Peter had caught some in their hands and brought them to the lizard—and it had taken them out of their hands—just as soon as their hands had opened, before the fly had a chance to escape.

Then they both wanted me to take it into the next-door house, but as I'd agreed not to tell anyone else, I couldn't very well. Besides it was time to go back. So I put the lizard in my pocket and set off for home.

At exactly the same place in the lane I once more met the priest. I would have hurried on but he stopped me.

"There's plenty of time," he told me. "Your mother's just packing the basket."

"Then we *are* going?" I said.

"Apparently so. Are you glad to get your own way?" This was a surprise, for though I had known vaguely that he suspected something and disapproved of our going over the hill, he had never actually said anything against it, and I had no guilty conscience about it. Yet by just assuming that I should have had he made me feel most uncomfortable.

"I'm glad we're *going*."

"I know you are. Your grandfather knew that you wanted to go—that's why he's taking you. I don't suppose he would have gone on his own account."

"Wouldn't he?" I hesitated. "I thought . . ."

"And your mother would certainly rather you stayed. You can be a help to her you know, when you like—and now she has the additional work of packing the basket for you."

"I could pack the basket," I said in a shamefaced way, because I knew that I didn't want to—and wouldn't.

"You could," he answered drily. He paused to let the words sink in. "But you prefer to go down to the village to show *something* to the Rymples—something which, judging by your behaviour, you're ashamed of."

This time I was really confused, because I had been very careful to conceal the lizard from him. Nevertheless I didn't show it to him even now.

He was looking at me intently and presently he went on: "Remember: what is pleasant is not always what is right. You know that yourself: your conscience tells you—and when you have done something which you know to be wrong, you try to hide it."

"But, Father," I protested, "I didn't think that it was wrong to have the lizard."

"I didn't say that you did. All that I'm trying to point out is that the Devil is much cleverer than either you or I. We must always be on guard for he comes in strange disguises. We must try to know him and to avoid him." His voice now was quiet and persuasive.

"Yes Father," I murmured.

"But that isn't enough. He's so cunning that we can't always know him. He can make himself very attractive; he can show us something very pleasant to do. We may not recognize him; nevertheless God always gives us some warning—some little prick of the conscience perhaps. The conscience is a very sensitive thing and we must pay attention to its slightest indications. If we are doubtful or suspicious we must avoid the doubtful act, the doubtful person: it is the only safe way. We must think of the people around us—what is best for them and what will make them happiest. It is they, those nearest to us, but especially our own parents, to whom, after God, we owe our duty most—your mother for instance is nearer to you than your grandfather."

He stopped and I was rather puzzled. He looked at me for a moment. "Run along home now," he said, "and think about what I've told you."

When I got there I found Mother in the kitchen. She was packing the basket, sure enough, and she looked very cross. So I really wondered if I ought to find Gran'papa and tell him I didn't want to go. However, she soon put that out of my head. "What's your grandfather want?" she snapped at me. "Why can't he eat in his own house like a Christian, without taking his food to the sea shore?"

"Christ ate on the sea shore," I reminded her rather priggishly,

"—fish." Gran'papa was my ally, and whatever the calls of conscience, an attack on *him* was bound to make me hostile.

"That was different," she declared, "—and mind now, don't you
start preaching at *me*—anyhow you're just as bad as your grandfather. I sometimes wonder if there's any of me in you at all."

"*You* gave him his good looks," said Gran'papa, who had come
in by the back door.

She laughed. "I see what you're after. You want the basket. If
you go and get Dobbin I'll send Wolfe out with it. It's nearly ready."

He went away and she turned to me. "Where are you going
to-day?" she asked.

"I expect Gran'papa will take me to the Far Shore."

She must have known, or at least guessed that we were going
there, but instantly her mood altered once more. "And will you see
that horrible creature, whatever he is?"

"He's not horrible."

"Wolfe," she said in an appealing voice. "Don't go—to please
me. I know no good will come of it."

I expect I should have given in, but Gran'papa reappeared at the
doorway.

"What's all this nonsense?" he demanded. "Wolfe's coming of
course."

"A lot *you* care about him," Mother said. "You like him with
you—and you risk his life for your own amusement."

"It's foolish to talk that way," Gran'papa answered calmly. "You
might as well say he shouldn't go near Dobbin in case Dobbin bites
his head off."

"Dobbin's not a devil."

"Nor is the Dragon—but what's the good of telling you so. Is
the food ready?"

She indicated the basket with a jerk of her head, and he picked
it up. "Come on, Wolfe."

I went, without looking at Mother. I felt sorry, but I wanted to
go very much. "Does Mother know about the Dragon?" I whispered to Gran'papa.

"Oh, everyone knows," he answered, "or will know very shortly.
I wasn't going to tell lies about him. This place is priest-ridden. It
was none of Father Binyon's business, but he wants to meddle."

"You told him then?"

"Yes—and your mother and your father. They don't know what to think—Father Binyon doesn't know either. I told him all about it, and he said it *seemed* all right, but it would be better to leave the animals alone."

"Why?"

"Oh, he doesn't know, or couldn't say, but in things like this it's always safer to disapprove: then other people will do the same. He *knows*—at least I think he does—that the Dragon isn't a devil; but that won't prevent him from denouncing him as such."

"Even if it's not true?"

"The truth doesn't matter to him, nor to the Church. It's the attitude they think about, and I know what that'll be."

"They won't approve?"

"Of course they won't—it's a wonder he didn't speak to you as well."

"He did."

"He did! Why didn't you tell me?"

"It was just now," I explained, "and it was so muddling—and it was about you too—part of it."

"About me!" Gran'papa exclaimed. "What did he say about me?"

"Oh, I don't know. Do you not *like* going to the Far Shore, Gran'papa? Do you just go to please me?"

Gran'papa looked at me in astonishment. "What ideas have you got into your head?" he asked. "Did Father Binyon tell you that?"

"Not exactly. I don't know exactly what he told me."

"He seems to have been talking nonsense," Gran'papa said angrily. "I think you'd better put it right out of your head—forget all about it."

"All right, Gran'papa," I answered; but, as you see, I must have remembered it or I couldn't have written it down in this book. Even now, though my memory is not so good as it used to be, I very rarely forget things, even if I try.

CHAPTER VIII

We had been strolling towards the stable, and, while the last few sentences were being spoken, had been standing outside its door. Gran'papa had already saddled Dobbin and now I went in and led him out. Gran'papa mounted him, and with Procyon we set off up the hillside in silence.

Gran'papa's head was bent forward and he looked troubled. I knew he didn't want to talk and I walked along gravely, trying to guess what he was thinking. I imagined he was thinking about his conversation with the priest, but he looked so displeased that I didn't like to ask him—and guessing is no fun unless you can hear the answer afterwards. So I began to run after Procyon and when I came back to Gran'papa I had forgotten that he didn't want to talk.

"Do you think the Sea Serpent will be nice?" I asked, for it had suddenly occurred to me how dangerous it would be if he wasn't.

"I think he's bound to be," Gran'papa answered, and his voice showed that he was in a very serious mood, "—according to our standards at least. In his age, I expect, the standards were higher."

"Why Gran'papa?" I said, "how do you mean?"

He didn't reply immediately for we were crossing a boggy place and had to pick our steps carefully. We chose different paths and it was some little time before we came together again. As soon as we were close enough Gran'papa answered: "Because everyone was nice then—much nicer than now."

This somehow annoyed me slightly. I felt that the present was *my* time, and I wanted to champion it. "The *men* weren't nice," I said. "Look at what they did to the poor elephant."

"Yes," he agreed, "Man was the worst of the animals then, but isn't he still?"

I was close beside him now and I walked on thinking, with one hand holding his stirrup and the other clutching the pocket where I still had the lizard. At last I remembered a sermon of Father Binyon's. "Father Binyon says that man is lord over the animals."

"That's true, I dare say, but lords aren't everything. Just think what animals do for Man, and how Man repays them."

I thought about it for a while. "Dogs," I said presently.

"Dogs don't count. They're overlords too, and practically men."

So I couldn't say anything at all, because I knew too well how animals were treated. I thought of cows who provided milk for us, year after year; and as a reward we took away their sons and killed them, and ate them. And as soon as they themselves could no longer provide milk, we killed *them*, and ate them also. And when a horse who had served us for years grew old, we killed him too, rather than continue to feed him. And when we had killed him, we didn't even leave him his skin to lie in, but took that because we could use it.

"And rabbits," said Gran'papa, who must have been watching me. "Man is the same in everything—there is practically no creature whom he does not kill."

"But Gran'papa, animals kill each other."

"Some of them do: it's probably Man's influence and example. In the Dragon's age it appears that Man alone was the killer."

Gran'papa was always like this. He preferred animals to human beings and he rode along frowning, till I asked, "Would you rather have lived then than now?"

"Much rather," he answered emphatically. "Every new period seems worse than the last." He said this gloomily, but presently he continued in a slow, reflective murmur, that resembled a little the purring of a cat: "In the Dark Ages they looked back and regretted the culture of the Greeks and Latins; but that was as far as they *could* look. The Greeks too looked back, because the Golden Age, which had existed long before, was better than their own. Even in the Golden Age, I expect, they looked back further to an age more golden still—and the Dragon's age must have been before even that—before Rome, before Greece, before Babylon, in the time when the Sphinx was real—not just a memory in sandworn stone."

He stopped speaking and stared straight ahead. I would have asked him to go on, but again he seemed immersed in his own thoughts and I did not like to break in on them. Only occasionally, and when he was alone with me did he speak in this way. He spoke in a quiet voice, which rose and fell a little, in regular cadences.

It may seem strange when I say that this way of speaking pleased me very much, but it did, and if I hadn't been able to understand him I would have listened just the same to the mere sound of the words, and I hoped now that he would go on again—he looked as if he might.

Dobbin's reins were lying loosely in his hands: he allowed Dobbin to pick his own path, and I picked mine, till presently we reached the top of the hill and saw the Far Shore below us. No other living creature was visible, but I stared—and the impression has never faded—at the smooth, deep water and the white line round the rocks: from the hill it always seemed calmer than it really was.

It had been very hot coming up, but now a cool breeze blew in our faces and we walked more comfortably. There was no track here, and nearly every time we chose a fresh way through the heather.

Gran'papa looked down at me. "Do you like my sermons?" he asked.

"It wasn't a sermon," I replied. "It wasn't long enough, and I did like it—and I don't like sermons very much."

"If it wasn't a sermon," he asked, "what was it? It wasn't conversation."

"I don't know," I said. "If it *was* a sermon it was far better than Father Binyon's. If you'd been a priest, Gran'papa, I'm sure they'd have made you Pope."

"Do you think so, Wolfe? I very much doubt it."

"Why?" I asked.

"Well, for one thing I don't agree with all their doctrines."

"Then you could give them new doctrines."

"No: I don't like new doctrines. If I gave them anything it would be something older— Now, I wonder where the Dragon is."

"Perhaps he's in his cave," I suggested.

He nodded. "Perhaps—or else in the jungle, or on the shore—but Procyon should find him for us."

"Where *is* Procyon?" I wondered. I looked round, and then whistled and called. At last I saw him in front and far below us—but he came leaping through the heather, as easily and quickly as if uphill had been down.

Gran'papa looked at him doubtfully. "How will we let him know what we want? Can we?"

"We'll just tell him," I said, and I stroked Procyon, who had arrived, panting, at the place where we stood.

Gran'papa didn't believe that "just telling" would be any good, but as he hadn't any other suggestions we tried it.

Procyon ought to have been exhausted after his rapid ascent of the hill, but he was only impatient to know what we wanted. So, in deliberate tones, I commanded, "Take us to the Dragon."

I had grown so accustomed to wonderful things that I really expected him to obey as promptly as a genie. Instead he just stared at me a little, puzzled and surprised: then he wagged his tail to show that it was all right.

"That's not the way to speak to him," Gran'papa said. "You have to speak to him the way you speak to a dog." He turned to Procyon. "Fetch him out—the Dragon—find him—good dog—good Procyon;" but he was no more successful than I had been. Procyon just began to scratch up the grass, and we knew of course that the Dragon wasn't there.

For some moments neither of us spoke; we looked at Procyon and pondered.

"Think of the Dragon," Gran'papa suggested at last. "Concentrate on him, and try to make a picture of him for Procyon to see. I'll do the same, though I don't know if my thoughts can affect him at all."

I thought of the Dragon. I thought of him at the moment when he had given me the egg on the shaly slope. I concentrated on that picture as much as I could. The Dragon was face to face with me, and he put his head down and opened his mouth. Gradually, however, another picture began to obtrude on the first. It was a side view of the Dragon, seen from very low down: he seemed immensely big, bigger even than he was.

"Do you think Procyon sees him yet?" Gran'papa asked.

"Yes," I answered abstractedly, and I still gazed at the picture. "What colour are his feet?" I said, "—the soles of his feet, the Dragon's feet."

"Bless my soul!" Gran'papa exclaimed. "I never examined them. Weren't they always on the ground?"

"I never saw them either, but one of them's pink—a rather worn-out pink, like some dogs' paws."

"How do you know if you never saw them?"

"I can see a picture of the Dragon now. A moment ago he lifted one paw. If that wasn't your picture it must have been Procyon's: it wasn't mine." As I spoke we looked down at Procyon, and the picture of the Dragon faded into the background of my mind, though it didn't disappear altogether.

"He still looks puzzled," Gran'papa remarked. "He may see a picture of the Dragon—and still not know that we want him."

That was just what had happened, but presently I had another idea. "Should we look round as if we were hunting for him?" I suggested.

Gran'papa thought this a good plan. "Try," he said, "and keep the Dragon in your mind at the same time."

So we began to do this and suddenly Procyon tugged at my trouser leg. I looked down at him. Vaguely I saw a cave in a hollow of the hillside, and looking out from the darkness was the face of the Dragon.

"He knows, he understands," I exclaimed. "He's found him."

"Where?" Gran'papa asked.

"I don't know. In a cave somewhere, but he'll take us to him."

"Well, we'd better leave Dobbin here," Gran'papa said. "He'll stay all right, and we can get him later."

So we followed Procyon. He led us towards the headland, and suddenly I recognized where he was taking us. It was not very far away, and though there had been no cave before, the Dragon could easily have made one.

Soon we came to the place. It was a sort of sheltered terrace on the hillside, and not far away was a stream. Looking out of his cave was the Dragon, just as I had seen him in Procyon's mind. The cave was new, and all around on the hillside was the earth which had come out of it.

"I was wishing you would return," the Dragon said. "Ever since I met you I have wished it, and I wondered why you stayed away."

"I wanted to come and see you," I told him, "but I wasn't allowed to come alone."

"That's all very well," Gran'papa replied, "but wait till you get to my age. . . ."

However, the Dragon was pleased. "There's no danger," he assured Gran'papa. "*I* should look after him; he could easily come alone."

"The egg hatched," I said, "and look what was in it."

All this time I had been holding the lizard in my pocket, but now I let him out. "Isn't he nice? He might be a young dragon. Do dragons start very small?"

"Not as small as that. That is a little creature which flies in the forest."

I had put the lizard down on a flat rock in the sunshine so that the Dragon could see it. Now it unfolded two delicate, transparent wings. In a moment it was gone: it flew towards the jungle.

"It's better that it should do that," Gran'papa said, but *I* was sorry to lose it and knew Mother would be cross.

Yet when the Dragon asked, "Would you like to meet the Sea Serpent?" I was quite happy again at once and forgot all about the lizard. How the Dragon asked questions I can't quite explain, but they came, just as clearly and as definitely as all his pictures and thoughts and ideas.

"Yes," I answered. "I'd like to."

"Then we must fetch Dobbin," Gran'papa said. "I don't want to walk much."

"That creature!" The Dragon despised Dobbin. "What's he so frightened and nervous about?"

"Horses are all nervous," Gran'papa answered, "but they are faithful and hard-working as well." However, it was no good arguing with the Dragon. He had made up his mind and was quite obstinate about it.

"Shall I go and get him?" I asked.

"I think we'll both go," Gran'papa decided, "and it would be better if the Dragon stayed here; otherwise we'd never catch Dobbin to-day."

So we went back for Dobbin. We found him nosing about for grass, though there wasn't very much, quite close to where we had left him. He let us catch him and we walked back along the path, one of us on either side, holding his bridle. At first he came quietly enough, but soon he must have smelt something or suspected something, for gradually we could feel him getting more and more restless; every few paces he would stop, and at last we had to pull him along by force. Then he saw the Dragon and went quite wild with fear. He reared and plunged and Gran'papa shouted "Whoa! Whoa!" I had never seen him wild before: indeed I thought he was too old a horse to behave like that.

At last he tired himself out and became quite still, but we went on holding his bridle lest he should make a sudden attempt to bolt. However, he gave no more trouble.

I thought what a peculiar contrast the two animals made. The Dragon was calm, a little melancholy, and a little haughty. Poor Dobbin was trembling and hot, his sides heaved, and though his mild face was subdued and resigned now, I saw his eyes rolling with fear. Yet presently he got over that too—or most of it—and Gran'papa mounted him and we set off to visit the Sea Serpent.

As we went the Dragon watched Dobbin curiously. "That creature does what you want," he said presently, "because you have gained control of his spirit; yet he is bigger and stronger than both of you put together."

"In return for what he does we feed him and take care of him," Gran'papa replied.

"Can he not feed himself, and take care of himself?"

"Not very well: our care is better than his."

"It's not because of *that*, that he works for you."—The Dragon was exploring the dim, misty regions of Dobbin's mind—"He obeys you because he's compelled to obey you—I don't know why. Your compulsion is against his will: now, at this moment, he is frightened, and he wants to go home. He longs for a green meadow close to your cottage—and in spite of all this he has a great affection for you—a sort of devotion."

"Were there no horses when you lived before?" I asked.

"No." There was a pause; then the Dragon went on slowly, with a sort of melancholy pride: "When I lived before, Man was not the greatest of the beasts. We were the greatest; but we did not oppress the other animals, nor molest them in any way. It surprises me that Man has been allowed to do what he has done."

"It must have been done gradually," Gran'papa told him, "and it was all done so long ago that now it is never questioned. The animals Man has tamed could not be happy without him. . . ."

"Are they happy with him? Your horse is not happy. He is patient, and sad, and enduring, but not happy: he never was happy."

"I don't know whether they're happy or not," Gran'papa said, "but if they were free they would be even less happy than they are now. In the daytime, when the sun was out, they might enjoy themselves for a little; in the evening they would return to Man."

"The horse *was* happy—once; and he remembers one particular day, in a big field with his mother. There were other foals in the field, and they galloped up and down in the sunshine."

Talking in this way, comparing the present with the past, we came to the shore.

We left Dobbin on a grassy patch behind the sandhills, because we knew he would be frightened again if he saw the Sea Serpent. "Even if he doesn't stay," Gran'papa said, "he'll only go home—and that doesn't matter much." So we took off his saddle and bridle while the Dragon watched us.

"Are these the only animals left," he asked, "these animals who live with you and serve you?"

"Oh no," Gran'papa answered. "There are the wild animals too."

"There are rabbits and foxes, and stoats and weasels," I began, "and lions and tigers and wild elephants. . . ."

"The lions and the tigers and the elephants are not in this country," Gran'papa said. "They live in India, in Africa—in hot jungles such as *you* remember."

We were walking along the beach now, close to the edge of the water. When we had gone some distance I looked back at the line of our footprints on the wet sand. In the centre were the Dragon's, big and distinct. One on each side and not so deep were Gran'papa's and mine, and fainter still were Procyon's, crossing backwards and forwards in long spirals over the other three.

"How can I get to these jungles?" the Dragon asked.

"It isn't possible."

"Are there other dragons there?"

"No; there are no dragons anywhere; you are the only one."

He sighed: "And the Sea Serpent is the only Sea Serpent—if

there were another I don't suppose he would meet me so often on the shore."

"When will he come?" I asked.

"I don't know. You'll see him presently."

Half-way along the strand we stopped and sat down where we thought the Sea Serpent would be most likely to notice us, but very soon I got tired of sitting. "Can I bathe now?" I asked Gran'papa, "while we're waiting for him."

"No, not yet," Gran'papa replied. "Go and visit the snakes and the lizards and the toads. You can bathe in the afternoon"—yet he must have thought more than this, for the Dragon said:

"There's no need to be afraid of the Sea Serpent. He won't harm him."

The water was blue and sparkling. As I looked at the waves I felt a longing to be in them that was intense as a passion.

"Oh let me bathe now," I begged. "Please let me, Gran'papa."

He shook his head, and I turned again towards the sea.

"Oh look," I shouted. "Just look—look! Look!"

They looked. "It is *he*," the Dragon said.

"It's the Sea Serpent. Oh, isn't he lovely! Oh, Gran'papa, *do* look at him."

"My dear child, I *am* looking at him."

"Isn't he beautiful, Gran'papa? Isn't he . . . oh look at the foam."

"He's certainly magnificent."

He was. He had come round the point and was moving very fast. His head was held high above the water, and his sinuous neck parted the waves. His long body behind him came in green, undulating curves.

Very soon he reached the shore. He lay in the shallow water, half on the sand, half in the sea. The Dragon went towards him, and we followed. Procyon was already there, sniffing inquisitively; but the Sea Serpent paid no attention to Procyon.

"These are they," the Dragon told the Sea Serpent, "an old man and a little one."

The Sea Serpent stared at us. "They are not like men."

"They *are* men," the Dragon answered. "All men are different now, and these men are better than the others."

"I'd like to be a Sea Serpent," I said. "I'm very fond of bathing.

I'd like to bathe all the time—the way you do—but I get cold when I stay in too long."

"It *is* cold now," the Sea Serpent agreed.

"It is cold, cold," the Dragon thought.

"I don't think it's cold," I said. "I mean the weather's very hot. I can stay in longer this summer than I've ever been able to before."

"In the old time it was always hot. . . ." I was sure they told each other this every time they met.

"Gran'papa," I said, "can I bathe now?" And this time he had no objection.

So I undressed quickly, and ran into the water. When it reached my knees I threw myself forward into a wave, and began to swim. The long, tapering body of the Sea Serpent was floating in the water. I swam along beside it: I dived underneath it, and I tried to clamber over it. Presently I succeeded. It was very slippery, and I slid over with a splash, and went under water at the other side. I tried again, and at last I managed to get astride of the Sea Serpent and sit there. The warm sun beat down upon my back.

The Sea Serpent began to be interested. "Would you like a ride?" he asked, "—a ride on my back? I'll take you for a ride across the bay."

"No, no," Gran'papa cried. "Wolfe's been in long enough. Wolfe, you'd better come out."

So I had to come. I wasn't cold really, and as soon as I'd dressed I felt as if I'd hardly bathed at all. All the same I was very hungry. "Shall we start our lunch now?" I asked Gran'papa.

Gran'papa frowned a little. "What about the others?" he said, seeming to forget they could understand. "It looks very greedy to sit down and eat, all by ourselves. Yet we can't share with them."

"*I* have been feeding all morning," the Sea Serpent told us, "but I get tired of the shore. I will go back to the deep water for a little, and return before the evening."

"Like you I feel hungry." The Dragon yawned, and straightened his tail. "I shall go with Procyon and we'll find food in the forest."

In a few minutes we were alone, which shows, as Gran'papa pointed out, that there was tact, even in the earliest times. We sat down on the shore and ate our meal. Then we went to the stream and drank. After that Gran'papa found a shady place behind a rock, and settled down to go to sleep.

Everything was silent except the waves which broke continuously on the shore.

CHAPTER IX

Gran'papa slept very quietly, breathed very quietly. Occasionally he sighed, and it seemed as if he were about to wake up; but he went on sleeping.

I wasn't sleepy, and presently I got up. I found a small piece of drift-wood, and I began to cut it with my knife into the shape of a boat. From another piece of wood I made a short mast, but I had no sail. I put my boat in a shallow pool and began to push it about. "It's a galley," I said. "It has no sails: it is rowed by fifty men, and it is bringing a cargo of silk from China to Arabia." And I loaded it with green seaweed and began my voyage across the pool.

It was a shallow pool, which was not always there, but had been left by some vagary of the waves and the tide. The water was very warm because of the sunlight, and it was pleasant to paddle in. All the same I would rather have sailed one of my proper boats in deeper, colder water. I had very good toy boats at home: my boats were better than those of any other boy in the village. They could sail faster, and they were nicer to look at. It was because I was friends with Larry Donovan, the carpenter, and he allowed me to work in his shop. I was always careful with his tools and he helped me a great deal himself.

My best boat was hollowed out of white wood. The hull was very thin—so thin, that when I was making it I could see the light through it, if I held it up. It was fairly broad and rather flat, and the keel was a separate piece, screwed on through the bottom, and weighted with lead. For the deck I planed another piece of wood till it was very thin too. I nailed it on with the smallest nails I could get, and puttied it all round. Then I painted my boat white, and when the paint was dry I fitted a bowsprit. It had a very tall mast and Mother made me two sails—a mainsail and a jib. There was no rudder.

"What are you doing?" Gran'papa asked, for I was standing in the middle of the pool, quite still.

"I was thinking of the *Seagull*," I answered, for that was what my boat was called.

"Well, I've been thinking of *you*," he said. "How long is it since you did any lessons?"

"I don't know." I pondered. "It doesn't seem very long."

But Gran'papa thought it was quite long enough. "You'll have to work sometimes," he said. "You don't want to grow up a dunce."

"We haven't any books," I objected, but I wondered if he had brought some without my knowledge.

He hadn't. "We don't need any," he said. "This is going to be a nice lesson—Geography. We'll make a map of the World."

"On the sand?" I asked.

"On the sand," he repeated.

Immediately I saw how the lesson might be changed, so that I could go on sailing boats while *he* drew the map. "This pool could be the sea," I suggested craftily.

"Which sea?" he said, almost as if he were a schoolmaster again. "There are a great many seas, and you ought to know them."

This sounded like a really serious lesson, and maybe the pool wasn't the same shape as any of the proper, geographical seas, but I did want to work it in. "It's a bit like the Mediterranean," I answered doubtfully, and after some hesitation. "Isn't it?—long and narrow."

Gran'papa looked at it critically. "It's not a very obvious likeness," he said, "but it'll do—and perhaps we can improve it a little. Now I'll draw the rest of the world with my stick, and you can fill it in."

"Fill it in?" I murmured reluctantly: I'd hoped he would do that himself.

"Yes," he returned a little crossly. "Sure you can sail boats any time. I want you to mark the towns, and countries, and seas."

But it wasn't really that I just wanted to sail boats: I wanted to dream, and you can't do that any time—only when you are in the mood for it.

He began to draw, and still standing in the pool I watched him. It was really interesting, so certainly did he form the headlands, and inlets, and bays, till at last he achieved a shape that I recognized. "That's Africa," I said, and I lifted one foot from the water to point.

"Yes—but that's not enough. Mark Egypt and Ethiopia, the great desert and the land of the Moors."

I set to work. He had drawn me maps of Africa before, and I wanted to show him that I remembered them, and wasn't growing up a dunce after all.

I became so engrossed that I didn't see the return of the animals. It was Procyon whom I noticed first: I was puzzling over the course of the Nile, and Gran'papa was making pyramids with wet sand, when we heard a splashing in the water behind us, and saw Procyon paddling in the Mediterranean.

We looked up. The Dragon and the Sea Serpent were watching us solemnly, but Procyon wasn't interested: he waded slowly through the Adriatic, and then set off across Europe, settling down eventually in the very centre of Russia. The other two were more careful and kept outside our world.

"What is it?" they wondered, and gradually they both drew closer, peering at the outlines which seemed to them so mysterious.

"A map," I told them.

"What's a map?" And when I compared it to a picture, a diagram, a model, they still didn't understand, because they had never seen pictures or diagrams or models.

"It shows where things are," I said vaguely. "Over there, in those countries, are all the lions and tigers"—and I drew a lion and a tiger to show them. "We are up here on this island—that's all the size it is compared with the rest of the world."

I pointed, and they leaned forward with the greatest interest, but I could see they didn't understand a thing about it. The same question came from each of them: "Where?" they asked.

I showed them again, but still they were puzzled. "If that's where we are now"—the Dragon stared intensely, and his thoughts came slowly—"where was I—before?" Once more I saw the grey forests; they dimmed and disappeared, and in their place came the palm trees and the summer shore.

"You were here all the time," Gran'papa answered, in a matter-of-fact tone, "buried in the earth." I don't think Gran'papa saw the palm trees, the forest, or the summer beach; or if he did they were not very clear.

"It wasn't here," the Dragon said stubbornly, and I knew that he was right, though Gran'papa was right too.

"It's gone," the Sea Serpent mourned. "It's gone: where is it now?"

"It's nowhere," Gran'papa said. "Nowhere, but in your minds. To find it we would need a time-map, and even then, there is no means of travel."

"We can only travel on," the Dragon thought, "—no slower, no faster; it was always the same."

The conversation was not a very cheerful one, but presently the Sea Serpent brightened up a little. "What's a map for?" he asked, with sudden curiosity.

"It is to guide sailors from one place to another."

"I understand now. *You* find your way by the shape of the land. *I* find mine by the depth of the sea."

"Where is the deepest place?" I asked.

"I don't know. It is deep out there, but where it is very deep indeed, I do not go."

"Gran'papa," I said positively, "I'm going to bathe again."

He was always cautious, and he shook his head. "It's too soon after your meal: you might get cramp: it's always better to wait two hours." But seeing that I looked disappointed he added, "Now just sit down quietly and perhaps the Dragon will tell us what happened on the last day he remembers of the old time."

It was a strange story, if you could call it a story. It was a dream, a nightmare. This is what we saw:

—It was morning. The brightly coloured dragons opened their eyes and stretched themselves sleepily. They were in a grassy hollow near the sea shore. The sea was not visible, because the dragons looked towards the forest. The forest was close to them. There were a few trees in the hollow; to the right and to the left there were more trees. Most of the trees were green, though the leaves of some had a coppery tinge. There were many other shades, from a green dark as pines, to a light green like young grass. There were flowers too—vivid splashes of colour—on the trees and among them. They were brilliant red, and yellow, and purple—immense, exotic. . . . Now everything was fresh with the freshness of morning, and the sun was shining.

—Yet something was wrong: there was something strange in the air; it spread to the dragons. They looked at each other in a puzzled way: they sniffed with their big nostrils and pawed the ground uneasily.

—It was just the sort of day they liked—the right time of year, the right place. What was wrong?

—They didn't know. The forest and the sky remained the same, yet the dragons were filled with fear. Gradually their dread increased, though in the picture nothing changed. The trees continued to sway gently.

—The air had grown heavier, and the sky was a deeper, darker blue. All the dragons looked at the sky together.

—Suddenly the ground shook.

—Everything was still again. The sun continued to shine, but the green branches no longer swayed. The whole forest was motionless. The dragons remained close together, panic-stricken.

—There followed a rumbling, a confusion of noise, remembered noise. Again the ground shook, and trembled, and continued to tremble.

—There was a mountain. It swelled up beyond the forest like a bubble, a brown and green bubble. Round the bottom of it there were trees.

—The top of the mountain rose more quickly than the rest: it had exploded. The mountain disappeared; the light disappeared. It was quite dark. There was a memory of sudden pain, pain in the Dragon's head and ears.

—After that all was chaos. Cracking branches, noise, noise, noise. The earth swaying like a rowing boat in a heavy sea. The sound of falling trees; smoke, thick and choking. Hot earth and stones and cinders dropping everywhere. Instead of the darkness a red light, gradually increasing. A horrible sun. Thick clouds of blinding sand. A torrent of water pouring from nowhere into a deep hole. An extraordinary, tossing sea; *it* had risen up too, a huge, black-blue wall. Again trees, a tottering, tumbling cliff. Dead birds, a dead dragon. Darkness, a strange odour, things falling. . . .

"That is all you remember?" Gran'papa asked presently.

"There *was* nothing more," said the Dragon.

CHAPTER X

For a long time no one spoke. Only Procyon slept. The Dragon and the Sea Serpent, with melancholy eyes, were staring back into the past. I was infected with their sadness as I watched their ancient world. For that world appealed to me: I would have liked to be a dragon, or a sea serpent, or even the wild looking boy whom the Dragon had shown me in the forest.

Gran'papa was looking at the sea. "The same sea?" he said, "or isn't it?"

"*Could* it be any other?" I asked.

"Not any other—no; but it's not the same. It has different coasts, a different shape—and shape, after all, endures longer than anything. This year's grass and leaves and flowers are different from last year's. Touch that rock—touch it with your finger."

I did so.

"If you come back next year, and touch it again, in exactly the same place, you will touch something else. The rock will have worn away a little. You changed it slightly even by touching it, and you changed your finger also. Your finger renews itself; the sea renews itself—but not the rock: the rock wears out."

"That's queer, Gran'papa."

"Everything's queer if you think about it. How would you like to go to sleep, and wake up again after thousands, perhaps millions of years, all alone in a strange and different world."

"I would like it," I said.

"Not if you really cared for anyone here," he answered, and for a moment he seemed a little hurt. Then he smiled. "Think of it—if you found the whole world ruled by a race of cats, very superior cats, far more self-important than cats are now."

"Are cats self-important?"

"Of course they are—self-important, cold, disdainful."

"But look at how they rub against your legs, Gran'papa."

"Yes, they like that, but that's a weakness. These new cats would have no such weaknesses. They wouldn't see how you could be of any possible use to them, and by that time usefulness to *them* would be the only thing that mattered in the world. So you, an isolated, disconnected figure, with strange notions from another time, would probably be in their way—and they would try to get rid of you. How would you like to fight a hundred cats, cats who had long ago got rid of their fur, and with it all desire to be stroked and scratched; cats who wore clothes and didn't purr, and had never heard 'puss, puss' in their lives?"

"I haven't seen a puss yet," said the Dragon, who had been paying great attention. "What are they like?"

"They are the strangest and most unaccountable of all creatures," Gran'papa answered—"at least of all *our* creatures."

"Meaiow," I mewed.

"What's that?" asked the Sea Serpent, waking up with a start. He had been asleep for nearly ten minutes.

"That's a cat," I said, "—the noise they make."

"One of them," Gran'papa added.

"Who?"

"Cats." We had to tell him all over again, and when we had finished he invited me to come and bathe.

I undressed quickly and ran down to the sea. Gran'papa and the Dragon were standing with Procyon, watching the Sea Serpent as he entered the water. His beautiful, green body glistened in the sunlight as the waves broke over it. I rushed in beside him. "Would you like a ride now?" he asked.

I answered without opening my mouth, and scrambled onto his back.

"You have found out that there is no need to make those strange noises?" he thought.

"Yes. Start to swim," I wished, and immediately, with his very first wriggle, I fell off again into the sea.

"What are you doing?" Gran'papa shouted, as soon as my head appeared above the water. "You're not to go for a ride."

"But Gran'papa," I protested, "even if I do fall off, I can swim—I could swim right across the bay."

He said nothing further, except that we were to keep close to the shore. "Then, if anything happens, you'll be safe."

I scrambled up again, but it was no use; as soon as the Sea Serpent began to move I fell off into the water. A third time I clambered up, but this time I fell flat. I was red and smarting from my chest downwards.

"All the same, I'm going to," I muttered, rubbing my stomach.

Then I had an idea. "Please wait," I whispered to the Sea Serpent. I came out of the water and ran along the shore towards the sandhills. They all stared after me, and I think Gran'papa called to know where I was going, but I pretended not to hear. I went through the sandhills, avoiding the sharp tufts of spiky grass which would have pricked my bare feet. I came to the field where we had left Dobbin. He *had* gone, but the saddle and bridle were still there. I gathered them in my arms and went back more slowly to the others.

When the Dragon saw the harness he recognized it. "They'll make you like one of their own animals," he told the Sea Serpent. "You'd better be careful."

The Sea Serpent didn't mind. "I will be his animal if he likes," he said.

Gran'papa was watching, not certain whether to be amused or to stop me. "You've given yourself a lot of trouble for nothing," he said. "The girths are too short."

So they would have been if I had put the saddle on the Sea Serpent's back. His neck was thinner, and I put it there instead. I didn't put the bit in his mouth, but looped the reins round just under his chin, so that I had something to hold on to. This time I didn't fall off, and before Gran'papa could say a word we were at the other end of the bay.

At first the water came only to my knees, but it mounted gradually as our speed increased, till it was swirling round my waist. I had to cling tightly to the saddle to prevent myself being swept away. It was the loveliest, the most exciting feeling I had ever experienced. I was sitting in the middle of a rushing, sunlit sea. It swirled past me and around me; on either side were two walls of white-flecked, light-green water; behind was the long sinuous body of the Sea Serpent, and further back still, a trail of swirling foam.

I looked in front, over the Sea Serpent's head, which was low down on the surface of the water. Not far away were the rocks of the headland.

Faintly across the water I heard Gran'papa's voice. "Come back," he called, "come back." Then his voice was drowned by the rushing water and the breaking waves.

I didn't want to go back, but I shouted to the Sea Serpent that we must. I don't know if he knew that I was speaking to him. At any rate he went on: he seemed quite impersonal now—just something mighty rushing through the water. I clung more tightly to the saddle. I looked at the stretch of shore, the dark hill, the grass on the hillside—how quietly they watched this extraordinary scene—the most extraordinary for a thousand, perhaps a million years.

We were nearer the cliffs now, sombre, shadowy cliffs, with dark water beating at their foot. We were close to that restless, hungry sound, that monstrous sucking, that ponderous rise and fall. It seemed for a moment as if the Sea Serpent would hurl himself on those hard, black rocks; I held my breath. Then, just at the last second, with a quick and dizzying swerve he shot away again towards the open sea.

After this he darted backwards and forwards in the bay, and I felt again the exhilaration of this huge, powerful movement, which seemed faster than a galloping horse.

At last he turned, and swam more slowly towards the shore. I could hardly stand when I reached it. I thanked him and lay down exhausted, to rest and dry in the sunlight. The girths of the saddle were saturated with water and it was with difficulty that Gran'papa undid them. Then he unlooped the reins, and put them with the saddle down on the sand.

"It's time to go home," he said.

CHAPTER XI

W hen we had hidden the saddle and the reins in a cave, we set off. The Sea Serpent swam away, but the Dragon came with us to the top of the hill. Then he returned to his cave, and we went on with Procyon: we reached home just in time for supper.

Both Father and Mother had been anxious, because Dobbin had arrived all alone some time before. Father had actually gone to the village to try to collect a search-party. "I would have gone by myself," he said. "Then I was afraid the devils had got you, and I didn't like."

We were sitting at the table and Gran'papa looked at Father very hard. "And could you not get a party?" he asked.

Father seemed uncomfortable. He tilted up his plate by pressing on the edge of it with one finger. It was a habit of his. "I could not," he answered. "There wasn't one would come with me."

"So what did you do then?" Something in Gran'papa's voice made me uneasy, but I could see that it was worse for Father, though he pretended not to notice it.

"I came home, and I met his Reverence. 'What's the matter?' he says, and I told him. 'Sure they're all right,' he says. 'Didn't I see them with my own eyes not an hour ago and the horse coming home by himself.'"

"Father Binyon," said Gran'papa, "—I wonder where *he'd* been. It's not often he goes out of his way without a reason, and he never goes in that direction. What was he doing?"

"Sure how would I know," Father said. "He maybe *had* reason."

"Perhaps he had," Gran'papa reflected, and that was all.

On Thursday, and Friday, and Saturday, we again visited the Far Shore. The weather remained fine and each day was hotter than the last. I had many more rides on the back of the Sea Serpent, and Gran'papa and the Dragon had long talks together.

We told the animals that we wouldn't be there on Sunday because both Dobbin and Gran'papa needed the rest.

So when Sunday arrived I felt rather disappointed. After four interesting days, here was a dull one, and because of that, though I awoke at the usual time, I just lay on in bed and thought.

It was no good getting up, because on Sunday I wore different clothes, which Mother would bring in presently. To dress now would have meant dressing twice, and that seemed a waste of time. I didn't like my Sunday clothes; for one thing I had to wear shoes and stockings, which cramped my feet and made me hot and uncomfortable. I looked with affection at my everyday clothes— my corduroy trousers, and my navy-blue jersey.

To-morrow I would wear them, and we would go again to the

Far Bay. To-day I would bathe with the village boys in the harbour. How dull that would seem after my rides on the Sea Serpent, and it would be difficult, too, not to tell about them.

What would the Sea Serpent do to-day? Would he meet the Dragon as usual, and would Procyon be there? I thought so; Procyon would go when we were at church—he often disappeared anyhow. It would have been queer if they had all been devils the way the village people thought. Then they *would* have had to go away every now and again.

It was a pity we couldn't go over the hill to-day, but it really was too far for Gran'papa to walk—and Dobbin's Sunday rest was never broken. "It's only fair," Gran'papa had said, "and besides, he's as much a Christian as anyone else."

"That's all very well," Mother answered—she wanted a trap like the Flanagans' so that we could drive to church on Sunday mornings—"but doesn't he rest all the time?"

"*I* don't work very much," Gran'papa replied, "nor does Wolfe. Of course Dobbin and I are getting old."

He *was* very old, I thought, and then I must have fallen asleep again, for all of a sudden I found that Mother was in the room, with my clean clothes.

I got up, and washed and dressed, pulling on my shoes and stockings reluctantly, last of all. After that we had breakfast, and as soon as the dishes were washed we set off in a hurry for church.

None of us knew the exact time. We had a clock in the kitchen, and Gran'papa had a watch, which didn't go: but we could tell the time by the sun, and by something else too, more difficult to explain. We all knew, through some vague, communal feeling, that it was Sunday morning, and about time for church; but whether we were late or early was more difficult to say.

Mother thought we were late. But she always thought we were late, and hurried us along uncomfortably.

"Sure the bell hasn't started yet," Father remarked suddenly, and we slowed down with sighs of relief, for it was a sunken lane, and very hot.

"We must be early indeed," Gran'papa said.

"Perhaps it has *stopped*," Mother suggested, "and they're all inside."

"Climb up on the bank, Wolfe," Father told me, "and see if you can see anyone."

I scrambled up the bank and looked down on the grey church. It had no steeple, but a big bell in front of the door, with a thatched roof over it.

"There's a crowd," I said. "They're all in the churchyard and at the door, but no one's going in."

"What are they doing?" Father asked, and he got up beside me to have a look.

"Come on," Mother cried. "We'll hurry, and find out what's happened."

Soon we were in full view of the church, and when we got nearer, people began to look at us and to point. There was nobody else outside the churchyard. As we went through the gate and got closer we grew increasingly uncomfortable. They had drawn together now into two tightly-packed crowds. There was a little avenue between the crowds and it led to the church door.

Father stopped, and for a moment even Gran'papa seemed uncertain, but Mother did not hesitate; she went straight up the middle of the avenue, between the dark hedges of people. I went after her, and Gran'papa took my hand. Father followed us. There wasn't a sound: we were walking on grass, and nobody spoke.

In the porch we met Father Binyon. He shook hands with Mother, and nodded to Father.

"What's the matter?" Gran'papa asked.

Father Binyon turned his back, without answering. He didn't speak to me either, which was unusual. His face was very red; his eyebrows were drawn together in a black and furious line. I had never seen him so angry. The two crowds had joined: the avenue had vanished.

"Mercy me!" I heard Mother exclaim in a low voice, and I took a step forward and peered into the shadowy darkness of the porch. For the first time I saw what had happened.

The church had only one aisle, which ran straight up the centre to the chancel steps. Now only the very beginning of the aisle was visible: the rest was occupied by something large and green: I recognized the Dragon.

Mother was peering in curiously. "What is it?" she asked, and she

put out her hand towards the Dragon's tail. Then the tail moved—
nothing, only a slow, transverse movement, but in this confined
space a strong gust of wind was forced past us and through the
door. It fluttered our clothes and ceased. Mother whirled round
sharply; she caught my arm and pulled me outside.

Gran'papa had wandered away by himself among the tomb-
stones, and I would have liked to go with him. But Mother held
me tightly and kept me with her near the door of the church. Presently the priest came and stood on the steps beside us. Pointing to
Father and Mother, he spoke to the people. "These two are not to
blame," he said. "They know no more of this visitation than the
rest of you. It is the old man who is the cause of it. I saw him yesterday on the Far Beach: he was with this creature and another; *it*
disappeared into the sea. Now stay here, and I shall see what can
be done. Remember that these two have not harmed anyone. Do
not avoid them, but speak to them as usual."

There was a pause after he had finished: then Michael Rymple
came up and greeted us. After that they all came and began to talk.
Mother let go my arm, and I slipped away to join Gran'papa.

He was peering at an ancient gravestone, which was no longer
upright, but had not quite fallen down. "What's it all about?" he
asked, and he may have been speaking of the half-obliterated
legend on the tomb.

"It's the Dragon," I answered, and for a moment I wanted to
laugh. "He's inside the church. I think he's asleep."

"Indeed: how long has he been there?"

"I don't know, Gran'papa—he's right up the middle—you can't
get in. What are you going to do?"

"Do? What should *I* do?"

"But Gran'papa, Father Binyon's very angry."

"Perhaps he is; but I didn't put the Dragon there."

"He says it's your fault—he told them that. Look—here they
are."

The crowd was moving towards us, but Gran'papa paid no
attention. He peered again at the stone, and touched the words
with his stick. "'In fide Jesu Christi . . .' You know what that means
anyhow—but we must have a lesson here some day and see how
you get on."

But I couldn't listen. "Here they are, Gran'papa," I repeated. "They're all coming—oh no . . ." For Father Binyon held up his hand, and they stopped abruptly. He came on again, and now only Father and Mother were with him. Then they too stopped, and the priest made the last few paces alone.

"Good morning, Mr. Emmet." He spoke in a brisk and business-like manner, but his tone was not cordial.

"Good morning," Gran'papa replied in a dry, cold voice. It wasn't so long since they had been friendly and it was curious to hear them behaving in this way towards each other.

I could see that it upset the priest, in spite of the fact that he had ignored Gran'papa and turned his back on him in the porch. For a moment he looked sad, as if he were regretting his own behaviour. Then he asked quite softly, "Why have you done this?"

"Done *what?*" said Gran'papa bluntly.

"Put that creature in the church," the priest answered quickly, his irritation returning at once. "Do you tell me you didn't know there was anything there?"

"Wolfe has just mentioned that the Dragon is in the church," Gran'papa replied quietly, "and that you have announced that I am responsible. Until then, actually, I did not know for certain what had happened."

"Could you not ask?"

"I did ask. I asked you. You heard me, but you turned your back immediately without replying. As I don't care for that sort of thing I didn't ask anyone else."

I saw Father Binyon bite his lip. I had never seen him discon-certed before. "Well . . ." he hesitated. "Could you not take it away now?" It was a request, but his voice was truculent.

"I don't see why I should," Gran'papa answered, twitching his eyebrows a little, and speaking very coldly. "I didn't bring him here any more than you did. Why don't *you* take him away?"

Father Binyon shrugged his shoulders. "Do you see all the people behind me?" he asked.

"I couldn't help but see them," Gran'papa replied shortly for they were not very far away and were gradually edging nearer in an endeavour to hear what was going on.

"Very well," Father Binyon said slowly. "At present they all believe that that creature is a demon and that it was you who put it in the church."

"And do you share this innocent belief?" Gran'papa asked sarcastically. "Besides, what do you mean? Is this supposed to be a threat?"

"Possibly it is," the priest replied, "though I don't believe that you put it there, or even that you brought it here originally, but what it is I cannot tell."

"You think it *may* be a demon then?" Gran'papa seemed more interested now than angry.

But the priest did not answer directly. He indicated the people behind him, who were watching in silence with expectant faces. "*They* do," he said, "and also that you are a sorcerer—and unless I tell them you are *not* they will treat you as a sorcerer."

"And before you enlighten them, I suppose, I must get the Dragon out of the church?"

"That's what I want you to do."

"Well, I *won't*," said Gran'papa. "I'd like to see you get him out for yourself."

"Maybe you'll see more than you expect."

"And maybe less than *you* expect," Gran'papa retorted. "Remember: the Dragon is old; the old are often obstinate."

The priest looked at him earnestly. "I give you this one chance," he said.

"And I still prefer not to take it," Gran'papa answered, "and anyhow, if I did call the Dragon away, it would only *prove* to them that I was a sorcerer."

Father Binyon looked at Gran'papa again: it was a very hard look. "Then give up the boy," he said. "*He's* not to blame. He acted innocently enough, though he had some warning. It's not fair to his mother to expose him to danger. Mr. Emmet, you are one against many, against all. Even your son and daughter are against you."

I held Gran'papa's hand tightly, but he seemed quite undisturbed. I wondered what would happen. Would all the people in the village turn upon Gran'papa and me?

"I am not alone," Gran'papa said. "Wolfe is still my friend, and so is the Dragon. We have other allies too—strange allies and strange friends. Wolfe, whistle."

In those days I had a very shrill and penetrating whistle and I screwed up my lips now and whistled with all my might. As I whistled I kept my eyes on the hill, and a green streak came from behind our cottage. It crossed a grey wall and became invisible in a field the same colour as itself. Still I whistled, and Father Binyon, seeing me looking up, looked up also. The people saw the direction of our looks. They pointed to the sky, and nudged each other, and drew close together. But in the sky there was nothing to see except a few drifting clouds. The hill looked quiet too. I could see our cottage in the distance, and dotted here and there over the countryside there were many others, gleaming white in the sunshine.

"What is it?" Father Binyon asked uneasily. "Do you want something more?"

"Wait a little," Gran'papa answered. I was pleased, and I went on whistling.

I heard a faint thud of feet: it grew louder, then ceased. Again I heard them. There was a scrabbling on the churchyard wall. A green head appeared and two paws. Certainly they looked strange, and immediately they vanished.

I thought that some of them would recognize Procyon, but no one did. Even Father Binyon was startled, and a sort of gasp came from the crowd.

"Oh!" I murmured. "He's fallen."

"*He'll* be all right," Gran'papa whispered, but I had started to go and see, when Procyon appeared again, at a place where the wall was broken down. He scrambled over and came bounding towards us.

"Sure it's only the dog!" Mother exclaimed: "What are you all so scared about?"

The people began to reassure each other, but Gran'papa made them fearful again. "He's not a real dog," he said, in deliberate tones, which everyone could hear. "We pretended he was a dog, but those who said he wasn't a dog were right. He's one of our allies. He's not very strong himself, but in a few minutes he could summon others—and no one could stop him. They would come through the air and along the ground. If you harmed us now, it is unlikely that any would escape. But if they did escape, that would not be the end. We have a powerful ally who lives in the sea, and he could wreck every boat that left the harbour."

"All this is empty talk," Father Binyon said coldly, but everyone else was impressed.

"Wolfe," Mother whispered, "come with me."

"Please, can't I stay with Gran'papa?"

"Go with your mother," Gran'papa told me. "We'll have a walk together in the afternoon."

"You will not," Mother said, and she looked so angry that I was frightened. "You'll never see him again, nor speak to him—sorcerer."

"In that case you'd better stay," Gran'papa said to me. He spoke quite gently, and I still held his hand.

Mother would have tried to snatch me from him, but the priest talked to her in a low voice. "You'll have him in the end," I heard, and the three of them went off together.

Father Binyon said something to the people, but as he had his back to us we didn't hear what it was. At any rate they moved further away, and he went through the gate that led to his own house. We remained where we were, and Gran'papa continued to scrutinize the tombstone. I looked at the crowd and saw that every eye was fixed on us.

"Why do they think *you* brought the Dragon here?" I asked Gran'papa.

"Because they're stupid," he answered. "Anything they don't understand they think is wrong—and there's very little they *do* understand. They don't understand me: they don't understand the Dragon. 'Evil breeds evil,' they say—so I must have brought the Dragon."

"But they've known you so long, Gran'papa: they didn't always think you were evil."

"They always thought me a little strange—and of course it's much easier to think bad of someone than good."

"And do they think the Dragon is a devil?"

"It seems so; and if he is a devil then I must be a sorcerer. Your mother was just expressing the popular feeling." His voice was rather bitter, but I didn't see why he should mind being called a sorcerer.

"I wish you could really raise up dragons," I said, "—whole armies of them—then nobody would dare to say anything, would they, Gran'papa?"

"It would be very convenient," he answered dryly. "Unfortunately I can't."

"But if Father Binyon *thinks* you can, he must be frightened of you."

"I don't know what Father Binyon thinks. He thinks whatever it is wise to think—wise, and suitable."

"Here he is," I said, "and look at the big book he's got. What is it?"

"I don't know. I have an idea he's going to read an exorcism—in which case it would be the *Rituale Romanum*, I expect."

"What's an exorcism?" I asked.

"Oh, it's a sort of religious incantation. It's intended for casting out devils."

"Where does it cast them to?" I wondered.

"Back to Hell, I should imagine; but we'll see presently."

"Will he try to send the Dragon to Hell, Gran'papa?"

Gran'papa smiled and patted my shoulder. "Don't be afraid: the Dragon is not a demon, nor is he evil. The prayer will not affect him."

I felt reassured. "What do *they* think's going to happen?" I asked, and I pointed to the crowd.

"They don't know—nobody knows: but they hope something spectacular—the opening of the earth, or the sudden appearance of an angel—though that would frighten them as much as anything else. Perhaps they just think that the Dragon will leave the church and fly away."

"But nothing like that *will* happen, will it, Gran'papa?"

"You never know what will happen. At any rate, as I say, we shall see."

"I hope nothing does happen," I whispered.

"I shouldn't worry," he said. "Nothing will."

"Look," I whispered. "Father Binyon's going to start."

We moved nearer, but the priest paid no attention to us. He turned to the people and said:

"If anyone here has come out of idle curiosity, let him go home.

This is a solemn and fearful occasion. Doubtless God had good purpose in allowing this monster to be sent among us. It has come as a warning, showing that some of us are nearer to perdition than to grace.

"Perhaps this warning will be judged enough: perhaps it is only a precursor of some dreadful punishment God has prepared for those of us who do not forsake our sins.

"There are certain ceremonies which the councils of the Church have ordained shall be performed on occasions such as this. It is necessary that witnesses should be present—not those who come out of vulgar inquisitiveness, expecting some extraordinary spectacle, but rather those who come humbly and hopefully, praying God to remove the affliction which has been laid upon them.

"I shall now read the exorcism. We must not be too hopeful of immediate success. Often, as history shows us, it has only been after prayer, and fasting, and repeated adjurations, that the Evil One has yielded, and given up his hold. We must remember that there was an evil spirit which even the blessed apostles themselves could not cast out."

I listened in breathless silence and so did everyone else. There was no sound but the sounds of nature, from the fields, and the stream, and the sea. Then Father Binyon advanced to the door of the church, and after crossing himself, began with these words which I have copied out of the very book he used:

"Exorciso te, immundissime spiritus, omnis incursio adversarii, omne phantasma, omnis legio, in nomine Domini nostri Jesu Christi; eradicare et effugare ab hoc plasmate Dei. Ipse tibi imperat. . . ."

After "Jesu Christi", and after "Dei", he crossed himself. I could have translated the first sentence fairly well, though I didn't know what "immundissime" meant. But it wasn't all as easy as that; there were more and more words which I didn't understand, though Father Binyon spoke very slowly and solemnly, and Gran'papa, with a strange expression on his face, made a rough translation for me, as he went along.

Sometimes I listened to him, sometimes to the priest. Some parts I heard in Latin, some parts in English. Some I missed altogether, and some I heard in both languages.

"Ipse tibi imperat," I heard again, "qui mari, ventis et tempesta-
tibus imperavit. Audi ergo et time satana. . . ."

And then Gran'papa's faintly ironic voice: "Hear then and fear
O Satan, enemy to the Faith, enemy of the human race, stealer of
corpses, plunderer of life. . . ."

From inside the church came the sound of a faint movement, as
if the Dragon were changing his position. "I hope he isn't going to
come out," Gran'papa said. "That would spoil everything."

The people heard also and leaned forward expectantly. Father
Binyon faltered, as if wondering whether, after all, he were too
near for safety. But the noise ceased, and he went on more firmly,
Gran'papa translating as before.

". . . root of evil, form of corruption, seducer of men, betrayer
of peoples. . . ."

I wondered if the Dragon heard or understood, and how he
liked to be called such names.

". . . causa discordiae, excitator dolorum. Quid stas et resistas . . ."

"Will it go on for long?" I asked Gran'papa.

He shook his head and frowned at me to be silent. I looked
round, and again I listened.

"Recedo ergo in nomine Patris et Filii et Spiritus Sancti, da
locum Spiritui Sancto, per hoc signum Crucis Jesu Christi Domini
nostri. Qui cum Patre et eodem Spiritu sancto vivit et regnat Deus
per omnia saecula saeculorum."

Again and again as Father Binyon read he made the sign of the
cross.

"Adiuro te serpens antique. . . ."

"I adjure you, ancient serpent. . . ."

". . . per Judicem vivorum et mortuorum, per factorem tuum,
per eum qui habet potestatem mittendi te in gehennam. . . ."

I liked the fearful rolling of the words, and wondered that the
Dragon dared to remain after such an exhortation, for after all he
was a kind of ancient serpent. Yet, but for that first slight movement, all had been still within the church, though sometimes, in
the dead silence that occurred between the words of the priest, I
fancied I could hear the regular sound of the Dragon's breathing.

"He's still asleep," I whispered, and again I heard Gran'papa's
translation.

"Go thus; go not for me, but by the ministry of Christ. For that power urges you, which by his Cross subdued you. That arm—O tremble—which thrust you with groans into Hell. . . ."

At this point Father Binyon dropped his voice and became indistinct. "He sees it's no good," I exclaimed triumphantly.

"Hush," Gran'papa said.

A faint breeze blew across the hillside and stirred the long grass among the tombs. In the fields the young corn bent before it, and for an instant its green was tinged with grey.

Then the priest raised his voice again and I looked at *him*. "Imperat tibi Deus, Imperat tibi Maiestas Christi, Imperat tibi Deus Pater, Imperat tibi. . . . Imperat tibi. . . ."

How many times those words were repeated I did not know. The priest crossed himself almost incessantly; but the Dragon slept on. He was commanded by the Father and by the Son; by the Holy Spirit and by the Sanctity of the Cross: by the Faith of the Apostles; by Peter and by Paul; by the blood of the Martyrs and by the pious intercession of the Saints.

"Adiuro ergo te, draco nequissime, in nomine Agni immaculati, qui ambulavit super aspidem et basiliscum, qui conculcavit leonem et draconem, ut disceda ab hac Ecclesia, discedas ab Ecclesia Dei, contremisce et effuge."

For a long time the priest remained, standing silent before the door of the church; the people, equally silent, watched him.

At last he turned and faced them. "Go away now," he said slowly. "Perhaps this creature can only be cast out by prayer and fasting: perhaps other means will avail. To-morrow, if he is still here, we must all fast. In the meantime go to your homes."

The people went, and Gran'papa and I would have followed them, but Father Binyon beckoned to us. "Wait," he called, "I want to speak to you." While we waited, he went and stood a little further away, watching the people. When the last of them had passed through the churchyard gate, he turned and came towards us. He no longer looked angry: his face was calm and stern.

"Well," he said, "you have seen and you have heard."

"What do you really believe?" Gran'papa asked, and it seemed to me that there was more genuine curiosity than unfriendliness in the question.

"I believe that all things work together for the good of those who love God and serve him, but the ways of God are mysterious." He paused and seemed to reflect. Then he went on slowly, "I have tried, and for the moment at least I have failed, in my attempt to get this creature away from the church. Are you satisfied? Will you help me now, or must we wait till it leaves of its own accord?"

"We will help you," Gran'papa answered, "—or at least we will try." Before he had actually spoken I was conscious that Gran'papa's feeling had changed. In the beginning he had been hostile to the priest. Now a half sympathy was taking the place of hostility. "I too love God," he said, "and I endeavour to serve Him."

"Why, then, do you disobey His Church?"

Gran'papa pondered. "Who knows," he asked, "which is His church, and who serves best?"

"There is only one Church," the priest replied.

Gran'papa closed his mouth suddenly. "All right," he said, "we'll do our best."

But Father Binyon lingered: the hostility had gone out of his voice too. "Do you think it will take you long?" he asked.

"I don't know; I don't expect so."

"In what direction will the creature go when it leaves the church?"

"He will go up the mountain."

"Then I will stand over there," the priest said, and he made his way to a low mound, near the seaward wall of the graveyard. At the same time Gran'papa and I went towards the church.

"What shall we do?" I asked. "How will he know that it's us?"

"We'll go to the far end," Gran'papa answered, "and you must climb in at the window."

When we got to the eastern end of the church, Gran'papa bent down, and I scrambled onto his back and looked through the window. There was the Dragon, just as I had expected, with his eyes closed, and his sleepy old head on the chancel steps. How anybody could think him wicked I couldn't imagine.

I dropped down into the church a little fearfully, and I was very careful not to stand upon the altar, which was just below the window. Inside the church it was very hot, for the Dragon's breath came in long, steamy blasts. A warm, dragony smell filled the whole place.

"Dragon!" I called, and he opened one green, lazy eye.

"What's the matter?"

"Exorciso te," I couldn't help beginning. "You're in the church. You shouldn't be here. You must go outside."

He opened the other eye, and looked at me benevolently. "When you said that you couldn't visit me to-day, I thought that I would come to you instead. I came early; no one was out, and it was cold. This was the only place where it wasn't cold. I came in, and I warmed it with the heat of my body: then it was pleasant, and I fell asleep."

"But you must go now," I said. "It was wrong to come—or at least Father Binyon thinks so. You see nobody else could get in to say their prayers. Didn't you hear him?"

"I heard nothing—only the sounds of memory and of sleep, the sounds of long ago, the sounds of my dreams."

"There's no wind now," I said. "The sun's out, and it's very hot. Gran'papa's waiting for you."

"Does *he* want me to leave this place?"

"Yes, he does—but go carefully; don't break anything."

"I'm not clumsy," he answered. "It was you who spilled the milk," but at that very moment he broke one of the rails of the chancel. There was no more damage, however; he backed down the church very carefully, and we all met outside.

"How did you come to be there?" Gran'papa asked, and the Dragon told him.

I was stroking Procyon, when I happened to glance up. "Oh look," I exclaimed, "look at all the people." Father Binyon was still on his mound, and besides ourselves there was no one else in the churchyard; but all along the wall there were people, and their heads looked like knobs on battlements.

The Dragon saw them. "Those are men," he thought. "They were always like that. Where shall we go now?"

"I want you to go back to your cave, or back to the Far Shore," Gran'papa said.

"And you will not come with me?"

"No, not to-day. We shall visit you again in the morning."

"Why won't you come with me?" the Dragon asked.

"Because I am tired to-day, and so is Dobbin."

"Why then may I not stay here? It is because of the other men: because they would not like it—and you are afraid of them."

"Yes," Gran'papa admitted. "I am afraid of them."

"But there is no need to be afraid," the Dragon told him. "What are men to me?"

"I don't want anyone to be harmed," Gran'papa said.

The Dragon looked at him. "I understand. Each cleaves to his own kind. You like men, even if they are your enemies, better than you like me."

"No, I don't," Gran'papa said. "I like you very much, and there are many men whom I don't like at all—nevertheless I do not wish to harm them. So go back now to your cave, and we will come to you to-morrow."

The Dragon said no more, and we went out of the churchyard by the gate, and up the lane which led to our house and to the mountain. When we had gone a little way I looked round: all the people were following us. At first they were silent, but gradually they began to talk. Then their voices grew louder and threatening.

"Take him away," someone shouted. "Take him out of this." After that they all shouted it.

We went on up the lane without speaking, and I wondered how long the people would follow us, and how far we should go with the Dragon. Suddenly a stick whizzed through the air. "Drive th'ould donkey home," Peadar Flaherty bawled. I didn't like Peadar: he was a dirty, clumsy youth.

The crowd, however, was amused. "An ould donkey," they repeated, "—that's all it is," and they picked up stones, and lumps of earth, and sticks, and began to throw them at the Dragon. They didn't throw them at us, and they didn't hit us. This was quite easy for them, because the Dragon was so big. I don't know whether they were angry with Gran'papa and me, or not. I know that they couldn't have understood, or even imagined, that the Dragon was our friend. They thought, perhaps, that Gran'papa had called up the Dragon for some strange purpose, and had been unable to send him away. They were ignorant and superstitious enough to have believed anything.

Actually the Dragon hardly felt the stones, and they didn't

bother him at all. For a time he plodded steadily up the hill as if nothing were happening; then he felt our anger, how we despised our own people, and hated them. He turned round. The people stopped abruptly, and for fully a minute no one moved.

Peadar Flaherty was in the front row of the crowd, and it was he who broke the silence. "What are you frightened of?" he shouted, "—yon ould cucumber on legs?" He threw another stone. It hit Procyon, who uttered a sharp yelp of pain.

I was raging. "Go at him, at him," I shouted to the Dragon. "Kill him, kill him."

Whether or not I really wanted Peadar to be killed, I can't say now. I only know that those were the words I used.

Procyon paused for a moment to lick himself, then he darted forward with his teeth bared. The Dragon growled, a deep, loud, rumbling growl. It warned the crowd. They turned and ran: they scrambled over the ditches and up the banks. In a moment the lane was cleared. The Dragon charged. He needed a few yards to gather speed. I ran after him shouting, but it was impossible to keep up with him. He went straight on down the lane, past the church, and through the village. I stopped and looked round for Procyon, but I couldn't see him anywhere. So I went back to Gran'papa. He was exactly where I had left him.

"Come," he said, and began walking towards home.

"But Gran'papa, don't you want to watch the Dragon?"

"No—we'll hear of the harm that he is doing soon enough."

"But doesn't it serve them right, Gran'papa?"

"Yes, but I wish it hadn't happened."

"Let's see where he is now," I said, forgetting for the moment that it was I who had urged him to charge. "Perhaps we can stop him."

He turned, and we looked down at the village. The only human being in sight was Father Binyon—and in a field nearer the harbour was the Dragon. He was trampling over the young corn; beside him was Procyon.

By degrees they were coming towards us, and we went to meet them. "You are doing a lot of harm," Gran'papa said. "This is the people's food you are destroying. How will they like *me*, when my friends take away their livelihood?"

"If I kill them," the Dragon answered simply, "then they will like nobody and hate nobody."

"Come into the lane," Gran'papa told him, "and don't do any more damage."

So the Dragon came into the lane, and this time nobody followed us.

CHAPTER XII

Thus it was, and through no fault of ours—or perhaps even of Father Binyon's really—that all the trouble began.

We reached a sheltered hollow among the heather, and here we stopped to rest. The Dragon sank down gradually till his long neck and chin were resting on the ground; Gran'papa found a gentle slope to support his back: Procyon and I flung ourselves down on our stomachs and looked at the way we had come.

Still Father Binyon stood alone upon his mound, but as we watched, we began to see stealthy movements along the ditches and through the hedges. One by one the people were returning to their homes, though no one came up the lane that led to our cottage.

"Now you must go on," Gran'papa said presently. "Go back to your own side of the hill, and we will visit you in the morning."

"Why should I not stay here?" the Dragon asked. "Whom will I harm?—and you can come again in the afternoon. Wolfe is hungry now and wishes for his dinner."

"And what will *you* eat?"

"I can do without for the present. I will wait till I get back to the jungle."

But Gran'papa was doubtful. "Don't eat the corn," he said, "nor the young grass in the pastures."

"It is safer too that I should remain," the Dragon continued. "These men, instead of being grateful that you have saved them, may be angry because I spoiled their corn. So it is better for *you* that I should stay."

Procyon got up and stretched himself. He yawned; we got up too, and leaving the Dragon, went down the hillside to the cottage.

There was nobody there, but our Sunday dinner had been prepared the night before. We found bread and cold meat in the cupboard. We put them on the table and sat down in our usual places—except Procyon; Procyon's usual place was the floor, but to-day, knowing that things were different, he got onto Mother's chair and helped himself from the table. It was quite wrong, but neither of us stopped him. Indeed I liked it, and Gran'papa seemed abstracted and didn't notice.

"Your father and mother are against us," he said at last. "That's why they haven't come back."

"*Won't* they come back?" I asked, and my only feeling was curiosity.

"I think they will," he answered, "but when, and with what intentions?"

He paused, "With what intentions?" I repeated, for I guessed that there was more to come.

"It may be all right," he said, "only I don't know. I don't want to lose you," he added suddenly. "That's what I'm afraid of—they might easily try."

"But I won't go," I told him, "and if they make me, I'll run away from them."

"It's better that they shouldn't get the chance," he said. "To-night you can sleep in *my* room, and you must stay close to me all the time."

So after we had finished dinner and washed the plates, we moved my bed into his room, and planned to barricade the door. Then we went back to the Dragon.

When we got near to him we saw that his eyes were closed, and we thought he had fallen asleep in the sunshine, but he hadn't. As we came up he opened his eyes, with a sort of lazy alertness, and looked at us.

"Could you not find grass, or leaves that you liked?" I asked, for when he had been feeding he had always a green stain round his mouth, and pieces of leaf on his chin.

"I will get food in the evening," he answered.

So we all lay down in the hollow, and Gran'papa and Procyon and the Dragon went to sleep. I alone remained awake. I went to the edge of the hollow, and lay down and watched the village.

Usually on summer Sundays the men sat on the quay-side, and watched the boats, and talked, and spat into the water; and others would walk along the shore towards the point. To-day they had all gathered in one group between the harbour and the church: the women were there too, and the children. They moved about a little, but none went far away. I watched them as one watches the water in a stream, though from this distance I could recognize nobody.

Presently Gran'papa and the Dragon woke up. The Dragon asked about the exorcism, and Gran'papa talked of magic, and devils, and sorcery. Procyon woke up too and came over to me to be petted. So I petted him, and at the same time I listened to Gran'papa talking.

I think it was about five o'clock when I saw Father and Mother coming up the lane. I told Gran'papa, and we all watched them. They were quite alone, and they went into the cottage without seeing us. We spent the rest of the afternoon watching the cottage, and wondering what they were doing, but as they didn't come out again we could only guess.

When supper-time came Gran'papa said we had better go back home and see what was happening. The Dragon said that he would stay for a little and watch. If all was well he would go back to his cave, but if not, we were to call; and if anything went wrong during the night we were to send Procyon, and he would come. So again we went down the hill and entered the cottage by the back door.

Father was on a chair at the fire, and the kettle, which hung from the crane, was boiling. Mother was setting the table, and when she saw us she laid two more places.

Then began the strangest and most unpleasant meal I have ever eaten, for nobody spoke. Nobody spoke when we came into the cottage, nobody spoke at supper. And after supper nobody spoke, though we sat round the fire together all evening. My bedtime came at last, and without being told I got up to go. I took a step or two towards my own room, and stopped. At the same moment both Mother and Gran'papa spoke.

"Your bed's in your own room," Mother said, "and that's where you'll sleep."

"Aren't you going to say good-night?" Gran'papa asked.

I didn't answer, but stood still, without knowing what to do. There was a long silence until Gran'papa spoke again.

"Go to your own room then, but say good-night first."

So I said good-night to them all, and when I got to bed I was so tired that I fell asleep immediately.

CHAPTER XIII

I don't know how long I had been asleep when I was awakened by Mother's voice, which, rising from a murmur that at first had only intruded upon my dreams, gradually became shriller and shriller.

I sat up with a start. Father spoke hurriedly and nervously. I could tell that he was trying to calm her. I jumped out of bed, and tip-toed to the door to listen. There was a crack in it, and I could see Mother and Father and Gran'papa, all seated round the fire.

"He's *my* child," Mother sobbed, "and I can do what I like with him."

"I know he's your child," Gran'papa answered with a sort of exasperated weariness, "and if you'll agree and be sensible he will go on being yours—if not. . . . Well, you'll see very little of him."

"I *will* see him," Mother declared, "and if I'd a husband who was a man, not a . . . a . . ."

She stopped, unable to find a suitable description for Father, and Gran'papa spoke in an even, deliberate voice: "There's no need to make a fuss. I only want a guarantee that things will go on as usual—that you won't try to keep him away from me."

Nearly always, when other people got angry, Gran'papa got quieter and colder. Usually it made the other people angrier, and it made Mother angrier now. She turned to Father: "David!" she exclaimed, and her voice was so loud and sharp that instinctively I drew back a little from the door.

Father I think was startled also—I expect he was a little frightened of both of them—and besides he didn't like being appealed to. "Sure what can *I* do?" he asked. "Why shouldn't they go on?"

"And have Wolfe mixing up with the devils—after all Father Binyon said too? I declare you're nearly as bad yourself."

"All right," Gran'papa said, "don't give in; there's no need to, but he'll sleep in my room, and stay with me all the time—and you'll not be able to speak to him either, not a word, mind you."

He finished up in quite a different tone of voice and there was an astonished little silence for a moment. "There," Father said, "what's the good of talking?" I couldn't see Father now, but I knew he looked across at Mother, and I knew the exact expression on his face.

"Do you agree then?" Gran'papa asked, "—both of you?"

"Yes," Father answered at once, but Mother said nothing.

"Both of you," Gran'papa repeated, and there was a long pause.

Then Mother's voice came sullenly and almost inaudibly. "Yes," she said.

"That means," Gran'papa explained slowly and deliberately, "that you won't have anything to do with any scheme for having Wolfe taken away from here. Or if Father Binyon has such a scheme, you'll tell me about it—and at once. Also you mustn't ask Wolfe to promise that he won't go to the Far Bay, or prevent him doing anything else that I'm likely to want. Do you promise that?"

"We promise."

This came from Father, but Mother said, "I don't think a promise to you matters. I don't think it's a promise at all."

"Well I can't say I place much faith in it myself," Gran'papa replied, "but if you break *this* promise you won't see any more of Wolfe for some time—that's all."

I held my breath. From behind me had come a slight noise. I turned towards the window and waited. It came again—a thin scratching against the glass. Perhaps, I thought, it was Father Binyon. He might be waiting outside the window, and when I opened it he would snatch hold of me and pull me out and take me goodness knows where.

So I stood still and wondered what I should do.

The noise was repeated—just the same—and this time I recognized it. "Procyon," I murmured, and stealing across the room I unfastened the window.

Procyon it was, sure enough, and he sprang inside, landing on the floor with a soft thud. Then he jumped up on me to lick my hands. After that he licked my feet—and his tongue was as cold as ice. I got into bed quickly and took him with me so that he wouldn't make a noise.

But he did make a noise, for he wouldn't stay still, and his back feet kept digging into me and tickling me. I had to bury my head in the pillow for fear Mother would hear me laughing. At first he had been on top of me, but I pushed him to one side, and that seemed all right till suddenly he began again, wriggling and kicking to get his head out. I pushed back the clothes—but of course he hadn't the sense to keep quiet. He gave a shrill, excited yelp, and immediately the door burst open, and there was Mother with the light streaming in all round her. "Wolfe," she said, "what have you got there?"

She sounded ready to pour out the full force of her temper upon me, and I knew I was going to get the smacking she would have liked to give Gran'papa. I didn't dare to say anything, and she strode across the room and snatched the clothes from my bed. Behind her were Father and Gran'papa.

I lay there, looking up at them, clasping Procyon, and blinking uncomfortably in the sudden stream of light. Without the bed-clothes I felt very small and unprotected.

"Just look at those sheets!" Mother exclaimed, and she aimed an indignant slap at Procyon: but she missed him—for he gave a sudden jump and darted round her, and out through the door before she could catch him.

I was left cowering miserably in front of her, and I wasn't so lucky as Procyon had been. "How often have I told you"—yet even now she was less angry than she had been—"that that creature is *not* to go on your bed." Nevertheless she turned me over as she spoke. With every word came a smack, and her hands were hard. But I didn't even feel like crying, because I knew she wasn't really angry. Instead I thought about my nose. It was pressed firmly against the pillow, and I wondered if it would be turned up in the morning.

Then Mother stopped. Her maternal rights were re-established, and I felt a warm tingling sensation that was rather pleasant. Mother pulled up the clothes again and tucked them in. "Now," she said, and it sounded almost as if she were laughing, "be a good boy and go to sleep—but no more nonsense."

I was left in the darkness once more, and this time I slept till morning.

CHAPTER XIV

On Monday, as Gran'papa had promised, we went again to the Dragon's cave. We spent the whole day on that side of the hill and did not return home till supper-time. After supper we were both tired and sat together on the wooden bench in front of the cottage, asking each other riddles.

I asked Gran'papa, "What was Eve's straw bonnet made of?" and Gran'papa guessed this right. "Straw."

Then he asked me, "If Moses was the son of Pharaoh's daughter, who was the daughter of Pharaoh's son?"

I couldn't guess, and Gran'papa said it was Moses, but I didn't see how it could have been Moses, because Moses is a boy's name.

I was trying to think of another riddle, when Gran'papa pointed down towards the village. "Who are those?" he said, "coming up past the church?"

I looked. "Finnegan," I told him, "and Cauley and old Flaherty, Peadar's father."

"And who are the others?"

"I think one's Carney," I answered, "and Brogan. I don't know who the other is. It might be Flanagan and it might be Brennan."

"It'll be Brennan," Gran'papa said, "but what are they doing? Do they look as if they were coming here?"

"They do. They wouldn't be going anywhere else, unless they were going over the mountain."

We watched them for a little, till suddenly a young calf full of energy and life bounded into view at the corner of the lane. "Look out, Wolfe," Gran'papa said. "Shut that gate or he'll be into the corn."

I jumped up and crossed the lane. I hadn't time to shut the gate, but I waved my hands and he went past with a kick of his heels, and his tail in the air. Then I closed the gate and ran after him towards the byre, where I caught him and tied him to a ring on the wall.

Then I went back to Gran'papa. I looked down to the bottom of the lane. "They *are* coming here," I said.

A moment later Father appeared from the same direction as the calf. He was driving the four full-grown cows and another calf. The cows were brown, and black, and cream, and black and cream, and their tails swung evenly. They came slowly and leisurely, munching all the time, and snatching an occasional mouthful from the banks under the hedges. Behind them, and a little in front of Father, walked Bran and Rory.

"Now Wolfe," Father said, "you'll have to help," and I returned with him to the byre. Gran'papa remained upon the bench.

Father milked the black cow, who was older than the others, and I milked the brown one. Mother milked the remaining two, and took in the milk when she had finished. After that Father and I fed the calves out of small wooden pails. When they had licked the pails dry the calves turned them upside down and rattled them on the ground. Then we closed them in a shed and went towards the house, with the pails in our hands.

"Maybe you'd better not go in," Father said uncertainly, but I pretended not to hear and he didn't stop me.

Mother was pouring the milk into crocks to be skimmed in the morning, while the six men whom we had seen were sitting on chairs round the fire. Gran'papa was in his own chair, in his own corner, and the others were talking to him. Father stayed outside. I sat down on a stool and began to listen. Gran'papa made a sign to me. I knew he wanted me to sit beside him, but for some reason, I don't quite know what, I didn't go, and he didn't call me.

"Just this, Mr. Emmet," Cauley was saying when I came in, "we want rid of him." It was the Dragon I supposed, but it might have been Procyon—and I wondered where Procyon was. I hadn't seen him since supper.

"Oh! Why is that?" Gran'papa didn't really seem interested, and his eyes wandered away from Cauley, and rested again upon me.

This lack of attention must have been irritating. "Never mind why," Cauley replied quickly and truculently. "We want rid of him. He trampled over Finnegan's corn, which didn't help it much, and how's any of us to feel safe with the likes of him around—tell us that now." Cauley was a little dark man, with a red and vehement face.

Mother had stopped work to listen to him, and now she straightened up and looked across the room. I knew that she was not on our side. Very softly I shifted my stool so that I was hidden from her behind the dresser, for I didn't think she had seen me come in.

"He's really quite harmless," Gran'papa replied gently. "He won't do any more harm—he wouldn't have done any at all if you hadn't stoned him."

"He's done harm enough as it is," Finnegan growled. "More harm . . . if I catch him. . . ."

"What would you do?" Gran'papa asked.

Finnegan didn't seem to have thought of that. He mumbled something which nobody could hear, and Cauley went on instead. "That's it," he said, speaking less rudely than before. "We want you to catch him for us, Mr. Emmet. You know Walsh's big barn?"

"You're a lot of fools," Mother interrupted. I was sure she had been longing to join in all the time. "Do you not know? He keeps a pet dragon of his own in the house. You'd better kill that first."

Of course I got a fright then—for there had been no need to worry about the real Dragon: *he* could look after himself—but Procyon! I was so raging with Mother that I jumped to my feet and she saw me at once. "Get out of this," she ordered. "Who let you in?" She picked me up and bundled me through the door, but I managed to kick her shins on the way. She dropped me outside and I went to look for Procyon.

Then I saw Father; he was dreamily watching the ducks swimming in the duck-pond. "Where's Procyon?" I said.

"He's in the pig house, and you're not to let him out."

I didn't say anything, but I went round the back of the cottage so that Father couldn't see me. I found Procyon in the pig house, and he was very glad to escape. I decided to go with him to the Dragon's cave, and we set off up the hillside.

It was one of those warm evenings in early summer, when, just because you can't see it so well, life seems to be going on far more intensely than in the daytime. Not that it was dark really, but everything was enveloped in the soft, grey dusk.

As usual at this time there was a faint luminosity crowning the top of the hill, which showed me, that though the sun must have set there also, it was lighter on the far side than here.

In the very air now, hot and still, I began to feel an excitement. Something, I was sure, was going to happen, and I began to run so as to reach the Dragon more quickly.

I was right: suddenly I heard voices. The men had come out of the cottage to kill Procyon—and what had happened to Gran'papa? I threw myself down on the heather, and putting my hand over Procyon's mouth, I watched.

I could hear Mother's voice, and Father's, and Cauley's. Then Father came round the corner of the cottage, with Cauley and Finnegan and Brennan. I guessed that the others must still be inside keeping Gran'papa a prisoner.

The four of them went into the byre and when they came out Cauley and Brennan had pitchforks. They went towards the pig house. Now they'd get a surprise—but we mustn't be caught, if they came to look for us. So as soon as they had gone inside I got up and ran as hard as I could.

To run up hill is very tiring; nevertheless I didn't stop once, or look round once to see what was happening. I had got a good start and I didn't think they would be able to see me when I had gone a little farther.

Procyon loped along beside me, and it was so easy for him that I very nearly sent him on ahead to bring the Dragon, in case Gran'papa was held a prisoner. He could have got there much quicker than we were going now, and he would have given some sort of message to the Dragon, but it might possibly have had the wrong effect. The Dragon might have rushed down to destroy the village, with ideas of vengeance or rescue, and really have done Gran'papa no good whatever.

So I thought it better to go on myself, and once I reached the top it was easier. Of course I knew that I was more visible while I was crossing the sky-line, but it was not for very long, and I felt fairly confident that now I wouldn't be caught.

I did imagine, however, just as I started to go down the opposite side, that I heard a faint shout. I believe really that it was only my imagination, but it made me hurry the more, though the sweat was already running down into my eyes.

I came at last to the cave, and the Dragon was sound asleep. We woke him up, and though I was too breathless to speak, he very soon understood what had happened. "We must go at once," he said, and I saw he was afraid that the men might kill Gran'papa. I hadn't thought of them doing that, but I did now, and I wished that I had sent Procyon after all.

"Get onto my back," the Dragon ordered. "Hold on tight: you mustn't fall off." I didn't, but how I stayed on I don't know, for we made that journey in what seemed little more than a moment. The air whistled past my ears . . . and there we were at the back of the cottage. Then I did fall off. "Now," the Dragon told me, before I could get to my feet, "run in at once, and say to those men if they're still there, that the Dragon is here, and waiting for them; and come out again immediately and tell me about your grandfather."

I went in through the back door, and by this time it was so dark that for a moment I could see nothing but the flickering firelight. Then Father spoke. "Where have you been?" he asked. He was sitting by the hearth.

"I was up the hill," I answered. "Where's Gran'papa?"

"Never you mind. Did *you* take away that creature?"

"Procyon? Yes."

He got up and caught me by the arm. "Didn't I tell you not to?"

I paid no attention. "Where's Gran'papa?" I repeated.

"Never mind about him."

"Let go my arm," I said. "The Dragon's outside, and if I'm not back in two minutes he's going to trample the house down, and kill you."

"I don't believe it."

"Just go and look out of the back window," I told him, "and see if you don't believe me."

He kept hold of my arm while he walked to the window and looked out. There, glowing faintly, he saw the Dragon, and he dropped my arm very suddenly. He nodded towards Gran'papa's door. "In there," he said.

I went to the door quickly and knocked. "Hurry up," Father shouted after me, "you've no time to lose."

"Come in," Gran'papa called, after I had knocked a second time.

He was lying on the bed: his face was pale and his eyes were only slightly open. "Gran'papa," I said, "are you all right?"

"Yes," he answered, "just a little shaken."

"What happened, Gran'papa?"

"Nothing." His voice sounded weary. "They wanted to kill Procyon."

"I took him away," I said.

"Yes, but I didn't know that till afterwards." He closed his eyes; then he opened them slowly and smiled. "You're a good boy: you saved Procyon's life."

"They didn't do anything to you?" I asked. "The Dragon's outside and he wants to know."

"No, they didn't do anything: they only held me—and your Father let them do that." The last words were muttered in a very low tone, and I waited some minutes before he spoke again. "Go and tell the Dragon I am not harmed and thank him for coming."

I went out, closing the door softly. "You'd better hurry," Father said anxiously as I crossed the kitchen. "He's peering in the window at me—and I don't like it at all."

Just outside the back door was the head of the Dragon. "You were a long time," he complained. "You shouldn't have dawdled. So they did attack your grandfather, did they?"

"They only held him."

"Yes, but he's not well. They made him ill. I wish I'd caught them."

"So do I," I said, and I wondered what Finnegan would have done then.

"Go back to your grandfather," the Dragon told me, "and ask him if he'll come and live with me. There he will be perfectly safe, and I'll make a new cave for you both, as big as you wish."

I went in again and saw Mother standing at the front door, with three or four pieces of turf in her hand. "Where are you going?" she demanded.

"Don't stop him, don't stop him," Father cried, jumping to his feet. "He's got the Dragon there, waiting on him."

So Mother didn't keep me—though I'm sure she wanted to scold—and I went to tell Gran'papa of the Dragon's invitation. Gran'papa considered for a long time, then he said: "To-night I am tired and not well; I couldn't go to-night."

It seemed such a lovely invitation that I couldn't understand why Gran'papa didn't accept at once—but grown-ups are never in a hurry to do anything, and I asked, "Could we go in the morning?" for I knew I would enjoy living in a cave.

Gran'papa didn't seem to realize that he would enjoy it too. "What would we eat?" he said.

Of course I hadn't thought of that, but I felt sure we'd get something—and then I looked at Gran'papa, and suddenly I noticed that he was looking very ill indeed. "Oh Gran'papa," I exclaimed—for he really *was* very old, "you're not going to *die*, are you?"

He smiled and that made him look a lot better. "Not just at the moment," he answered.

"Oh, don't die at all, Gran'papa," I begged him, and he said he wouldn't die so long as I wanted him, but I knew that that would be always, and that people can't live for ever, especially when they are as old as Gran'papa. I felt reassured all the same.

"Now run along," he told me presently. "You've kept the Dragon waiting far too long—and I expect I'll still be here when you come back."

"But what shall I tell him?" I asked.

"Tell him I'll have to think it over, but that I can't go to-night—and thank him very much."

"We could catch fish," I suggested. "That would be something to eat—and it would be great fun."

"Oh there are lots of things," he answered vaguely, and lay back against the pillows. I took his message to the Dragon.

CHAPTER XV

Usually Gran'papa was up before me, but when I went to his room next morning he was still in bed. "I'm going to have a rest to-day," he told me, "but I want you to go and see the Dragon just as usual. Tell him I'll be over tomorrow."

Without Gran'papa I didn't enjoy the Far Shore so much, but it was fun all the same and I stayed till nearly supper-time.

When I returned Mother was at the back door waiting for me. At first she didn't see me, because she was looking straight into the sun. I thought I must be late and slowed down a little, expecting a scolding. Then I saw that she was not cross at all: she was only frowning because the sun was in her eyes.

Indeed she looked particularly kind and motherly, and as soon as I realized this I hurried on. She was bathed in golden sunlight and all the harshness had gone from her face. For those few moments she was part of a sublimated landscape, part of the ideal.

Suddenly she saw me and called. Her voice was not quite right; it was out of tone with the picture—but it was nearly right, and I hid away the criticism lest it should break the spell. I ran to her and she kissed me, and *that* was quite right—though it was most unusual.

I expect that she had been affected by the mood of the evening—though not so much as I had been, for presently she recollected herself. She remembered that the boats would soon be coming in and that she had wanted to send me down to the village to get some mackerel. "Hurry back," she told me, "and don't dawdle."

Father had come up as she spoke, and he heard the last words. "Where's he going to?" he asked.

The spell was completely broken now. Father had broken it, and that perhaps was why Mother answered so crossly.

"He's going to the village," she said, "and why not? I'd like to know."

Father looked at her uncertainly. "Is it all right?" he asked in a mysterious manner.

"Of course it is."

Father hesitated. "I was . . . I was just afraid. . . ."

"Fiddlesticks!" Mother replied. "Would I send him if it wasn't? It's not *him* they mind."

I ran down the lane, wondering what they had meant, but very soon I forgot all about it. I was anxious to get to the harbour before the boats.

I saw no one in the village—I didn't really expect to—for all the wives and children would be waiting on the quay. I found them there, sure enough, as well as Father Binyon and two old fishermen who no longer worked. I heard a hum of conversation, which would stop suddenly every now and then when somebody hailed the boats and everyone waited for a reply.

"I'm only just in time," I thought—and then I paused. I had

meant to push through the crowd so as to get served quickly, but all at once the backs of the people looked hostile. I remembered how unfriendly they had been on Sunday and I was frightened. Then I looked at Father Binyon. I knew that while he was there no harm would come to me, and I began to edge through the people as I had intended at first.

They were too busy watching the boats to hinder me, and gradually I wriggled my way to the very front. Below me was the water, smooth, and not very deep. The sand at the bottom appeared to be a pale, yellowish green and on it there was a dead dog-fish. A little further out floated some loose sea-weed which resembled a bunch of brown bubbles. Beyond the end of the quay the tide was flowing in, in a series of small, lapping waves, but here the water rose without a ripple and almost imperceptibly.

The boats now were gliding into the smooth water: some of the fishermen were standing up; others were taking in their oars, or turning them round to fend off the wall of the quay. On came the boats, making no sound, but the voices of the people grew louder. The talk of the fishermen merged with the conversation of those on shore. Children who stood too near the edge were pulled back sharply and scolded. Still smaller children were held up and told to wave to their fathers.

There were some jokes and some laughter, but the men were discontented because the catch had been bad.

"It's been very bad all summer," a woman grumbled. "There's something wrong, you'd think."

"Nonsense," Father Binyon told her, "it'll improve one of these days—you see if it doesn't."

The leading boat was just below us as he spoke, and Brennan was slipping a rope through an iron ring set in the stone of the quay. "It won't get better," he growled, "not while there's a wizard among us."

I felt uneasy and began to slip back a little, though Brennan was looking down and hadn't noticed me. Then suddenly I felt the stare of another fisherman. "*There's* the wizard's brat," he exclaimed. "How could we bring in fish with *him* standing there. He's the worst of the lot."

I tried to shrink further into the crowd, but the women round about, who hadn't noticed me till then, drew away quickly, pulling their children with them. I was left standing by myself.

I would have made a dive through them and run for home if I hadn't still remembered about the mackerel.

They were all looking at me now and suddenly, from the second boat, which had come up on the outside of the first, Brogan addressed me. "Aye," he said, "there you are. There's always one of you watching. That's why you took the house on the hill. You can see us from there. When we go out you tell the fish—and they all clear off right and quick—and when we're ashore, in they come again. Sure haven't I seen them myself, leppin' all round on a Sunday?" He spat disgustedly into the water.

"That's true enough," agreed one or two voices, in very grave tones, and then Cauley chimed in.

"Didn't he say he was a wizard?" he asked.

"As good as said it," Brennan replied. "He said that green beast of theirs wasn't a real dog—and it wasn't neither, for we couldn't kill it. Look at the way it escaped, an' it locked up tight in the pig house. It was magic, I tell you."

"What are you here for, boy?" asked another fisherman less unkindly.

"Mother sent me for some mackerel," I answered timidly, but that only annoyed them more.

"No fish will you get from us," they growled.

I would have run away then, but in front were the fishermen, the boats, and the water; behind was a ring of people, with the children peering through inquisitively.

"I'll give you some fish," Michael said suddenly, but immediately a grim voice contradicted him:

"Not from this boat, Michael Rymple."

An angry argument began and I was feeling very frightened, when a hand grasped my arm. I started away, but it was Father Binyon. "Come along," he said quietly, "this is no place for you."

Immediately my anxiety vanished. I was under his protection. I was safe.

He held me close to him and frowned down at the angry men. "Stop that at once," he ordered. "It's disgraceful"—and there was a dead silence.

Then he turned round and faced the others. "Now," he said, "no more of this. Get along home the lot of you."

They went, and he turned again to the fishermen. "You're very foolish," he told them. "Whatever the old man may have done, how could this child know magic?"

They all looked ashamed of themselves, but I think some of them were still angry as well.

There was now no one on the quay and we walked along it and through the village together. I saw faces at some of the doors, but nobody dared to come out. I myself felt rather frightened of Father Binyon, though just then he was on my side. All the same, I felt he was good and kind, as well as stern.

But he walked quite silently, which made me rather uncomfortable. So as soon as we were outside the village I said, "Mother told me to hurry back. I think I'd better go on."

"All right," he answered, "but I want to speak to you. However, it'll do another time. Tell your Mother she'd better keep you out of the village for a while."

I hesitated, because I didn't know whether he'd finished or not, and then I thanked him for helping me. He smiled and told me to run along. I did so, and I was quite glad he hadn't spoken to me. When grown-ups wished to speak to me like that it usually meant trouble of one kind or another.

CHAPTER XVI

My next meeting with Father Binyon was on Friday evening. I found him waiting for me on the bank at one side of the lane, when I crossed the hill-top on my way back from the Far Shore. Immediately I remembered the talk he had in store for me and I thought of hiding, but he noticed me at once and waved with his stick.

Though I really quite liked him, and was grateful to him for rescuing me at the harbour, I went towards him slowly, uncertain whether to regard him as a friend or an enemy. At any rate, I was afraid his talk would become a talking-to, and I wished that Gran'papa was there to prevent it. It was always more fun with

Gran'papa, and he and the priest got on very well together—or at least they *had* till the Dragon came. But Gran'papa wasn't quite better yet—not that he was ill exactly; he was tired and a little upset. He had spent two days in bed; after that he sat outside in front of the cottage. However, I knew there was nothing to worry about: Gran'papa was just being careful. Next week, he had promised, he would go again to the Far Shore.

Father Binyon hailed me cheerfully. "Well," he said, "and what have *you* been up to?"

I told him where I'd been and he went on: "How's your grand-father to-day? And why didn't you tell me he was ill?"

I didn't know what to say. My only chance had been on Tuesday at the harbour, and it wasn't very surprising that I hadn't thought of it then. I was still wondering, too, if Father Binyon was friends with us or not. He hadn't seemed to be on Sunday, but then he'd been so nice at the quay. It was all very muddling.

"Did you hear what made Gran'papa ill?" I asked suddenly.

"Yes," he said—but he didn't tell me what he thought about it. Indeed he said nothing more for some time, and *I* couldn't think of anything either. I felt most uncomfortable. I didn't quite trust him yet, though he was walking along slowly with one hand on my shoulder.

"He's wondering how to begin," I decided suddenly; and imme-diately I became most anxious to know what he had to say. The very idea that he had difficulty made me long for him to start, but when he did it was only to say, "You don't play much with the other boys—and you prefer the Far Shore to our own."

"I often play with Peter," I answered quickly, "and on Sundays I bathe with the other boys in the harbour."

Of course I knew it was only a beginning, yet it seemed to be changing into a sort of game. It was his turn again and he said rather slowly, "But you would rather be with your grandfather, I think."

"Yes," I said, feeling a little disappointed. Perhaps this wasn't the talk after all; perhaps he'd forgotten about it or given it up.

I stopped, for we had reached the place where the lane branched off for home. "Would you like to *see* Gran'papa?" I asked.

"Not now," he replied, "another time. I'll have to go home

now; my supper's waiting. Will *you* come and have supper with me?"

I had never been in Father Binyon's house and the invitation surprised me. I hesitated. "Mother won't know where I am."

"Yes, she will. I told her I'd look out for you. She's not expecting you now."

"But shouldn't I go home first?"

He smiled and shook his head. "No. We're late already, and Bridie'll be angry with us."

I went with him, feeling rather shy, but pleased too—and I half hoped we'd meet Peter or some of the other boys. We neither of us spoke much till we reached his house and he told Bridie that I had come to supper. She grumbled a little because we were late, but she appeared to be expecting me. Very soon she had supper ready. It was fried fish.

We sat at one end of a big table and I told Father Binyon about my boats. He too had been fond of sailing boats, when he was a boy, and he had had one boat which was very fast—but he didn't think it was so fast as my *Seagull*.

From where I sat I could see into the garden. It was filled with currant bushes and apple-trees, and long grass and weeds. There were wild roses and honeysuckle, and the currant bushes were choked with convolvulus. It was a lovely garden. Presently I saw the grass tremble and above it showed the tip of a tail. It was Polyphemus, Father Binyon's cat. He was a big tabby cat and he would sit for hours on the top of Father Binyon's wall, with one eye closed and the other open. That was why he was called Polyphemus, because it really looked as if he had only one eye, the other was so hidden in fur.

"Here's Polyphemus," I said, and Polyphemus jumped to the window-sill.

"Yes indeed," said Father Binyon, "he likes Fridays and fish."

"Is that why it's called Friday—because you fry fish?" I asked; but Father Binyon didn't think so.

Polyphemus landed with a solid plump on the floor; he strolled over, and began to rub himself against chair-legs, and Father Binyon's legs, and the legs of the sofa, and my legs. At the same time he began to purr. Father Binyon gave him a piece of fish, and the purring became curiously broken. He took a long time to eat it, and he ate it with the side of his mouth, the way cats always do. When he had finished, I gave him a piece too. After the fish there were buns and jam, and after that there was cake.

"Now," Father Binyon said, when I had eaten as much as I could: "it's too warm in here; let's sit in the garden."

So we took out two chairs and sat down. Polyphemus came with us, and sat on Father Binyon's knee. I said, "Puss, puss," and stroked him, but he wouldn't come to me. "Why won't he come?" I asked the priest.

"Because he's wise," Father Binyon answered, "old and wise."

"But he's not wise," I contradicted. "He's silly. I'd be nice to him if he came."

"He knows me best," Father Binyon said. "He knows I am safe and reliable, and being wise, he is content with what he knows."

Polyphemus opened both his eyes and looked wisely round at us. Then he stood up and stretched and drove his claws into the knees of Father Binyon's trousers, so that the priest winced a little and tried to pull them out. Polyphemus had been looking at me, and now he sheathed his claws of his own accord, gave a small miaow, and dropped heavily to the ground. From there he jumped to my lap, and after turning round once or twice he settled down and closed his eyes.

Neither of us spoke while he was doing this, but presently I couldn't help glancing stealthily at Father Binyon.

He noticed and smiled. "It just means he's not so wise as I thought," he said. "If he had been really wise he would have stayed where he was."

"Don't you think he was wise enough to know I was all right?"

"No one is wise enough to know that anyone is all right," Father Binyon answered. I looked down and stroked Polyphemus, and wondered if this were true.

"Are cats asleep when they purr, or only pretending?" I asked.

"I don't think it's a case of pretending," Father Binyon said, "though I don't think he's asleep. If you stop stroking him, he'll soon stop purring."

Of course I didn't want him to stop and I went on stroking steadily. All the same, the purr gradually grew weaker; it became more and more broken, till eventually it ceased. He must have fallen asleep after all.

"He's a silly old thing," said Father Binyon. "He doesn't know what'll happen to him now—besides, he's hurt my feelings."

I looked at him to make sure he meant it, because it was partly my fault. I had wanted Polyphemus and tried to make him come to me. "I'm sorry," I said.

Father Binyon smiled again. "It doesn't matter," he told me; "to avoid hurting people's feelings is one of the most difficult things in life. But also one of the most important," he presently added. "We can't always help hurting them; sometimes it is necessary; but at other times we do it unnecessarily in the pursuit of our own pleasures—and then it becomes a sin. Do you ever think about that when there is something you want to do?"

He looked at me and I felt rather embarrassed. "No," I had to admit uncomfortably.

"What makes you do things?" he asked. "Why do you bathe? Why do you go to the Far Shore?"

"Because I like bathing," I told him, though I couldn't understand the reason for his questions, "and I like going to the Far Shore."

"And why do you like going there?—It's because you like the animals, isn't it?"

"Yes," I agreed, "it's mostly because of them, but I like the Far Shore anyhow."

"And *why* do you like them," he insisted, "—the Far Shore and the animals?"

I looked at him uncomprehendingly, and began to fidget. He was asking almost exactly the same question time after time, and I couldn't answer any more, but perhaps he didn't expect any answer, for he went on himself: "It is because you find them beautiful."

"Don't *you* think they're beautiful?" I asked, but he didn't answer me directly.

"It depends on what you mean by beauty," he said. "To me there is only one kind of real beauty and that is the beauty which is the expression of goodness."

"But how is beauty the expression of goodness?" I wondered, for they seemed to me to be quite different sorts of things.

"This is how it is," he told me. "In the beginning when God

made the world everything in it was good and beautiful. Then the Devil came and he put bad things into the world, but bad things are ugly. So it was easy for people to distinguish between what was good and what was bad—and to avoid what was bad. The Devil saw this, and being very clever, he made many of his bad things look good and beautiful. But they weren't really good or beautiful, though many people are still deceived by them—and those who are deceived are led into sin."

"But how can you tell?" I asked, for if you couldn't tell it didn't seem quite fair.

"That is what is so difficult," Father Binyon answered. "It is very hard to distinguish. We have to be very careful. Even good people may be dazzled by the false beauty—but only for a time. If they really wish to be good, God will show them their mistake, so that they can repent and turn to the right way." He looked at me suddenly, with a piercing glance. "You know the right way?"

"Yes, Father," I murmured. "I think so."

"The right way"—he used the same deep tone as he had used to the Dragon in the exorcism—"the right way is the way of the Church. If you follow the commands of the Church you can't be led astray. It was to guide mankind that Christ left the Church behind him on earth. He knew that Man in himself was too imperfect, however willing he might be, to distinguish between right and wrong. But there are some things—the safe things—which you know are right and good. Cling to those things. There are others which may be right or may be wrong—you are not sure. It is better to leave those things alone."

"You mean the Dragon," I said.

"Yes—the Dragon, and the Sea Serpent, and Procyon. They may be good; they may be evil. They seem beautiful; they seem pleasant: but their beauty may be a false beauty, and the pleasure of their companionship a false pleasure."

"But Father," I interrupted, "the Dragon is really good. It wasn't *his* fault that he trampled down Finnegan's corn: it was because the people stoned him."

"I know it was," he answered. "They were foolish—but perhaps, Wolfe, you too are foolish. By visiting the Dragon you are bringing the anger of the people on your grandfather and yourself."

"But we aren't doing them any harm," I protested.

"They don't know. They think you are consorting with demons, and that that is bound to bring evil."

"But they're not demons, Father—and if it hadn't been for Gran'papa the Dragon would have killed everyone in the village."

The priest's voice became stern. "Surely you cannot think the Dragon good if he was ready to kill all the people in the village."

"He *is* good," I answered. "It was just that the people made him angry."

"Yes," he agreed, "they made him angry, but why? Was it not because he came over to this side of the hill?—and it was because of you that he came."

"We didn't want him to come."

"You may not have wanted him, but it was only because you had visited him in the first place that he came at all. If you had never visited him there would have been no evil, or if there had been you would have been innocent of it. But you were led away— you saw beauty, or what you imagined to be beauty, the beauty of the Dragon and the Sea Serpent, and you were attracted to it. You have gone a little way on the wrong path; it is not too late to turn back. Go no more to the Dragon. By not going to him you cannot sin; by going to him you may sin greatly, and cause others to sin."

My head was in a whirl and for some moments I did not answer. I wanted to go to the Dragon: I liked him, I liked them all. "What would Gran'papa say?" It was the only argument I could think of.

"Your father and mother would be glad," Father Binyon answered after a pause, "and it is our parents that scripture tells us we must obey. Besides, your grandfather has already disobeyed the commands of the Church. I have known him many years and he has always been a good man, but I told you that even the good can be led away by what is false. It is possible that if *you* turned back, he would turn also, for I suspect it is largely for your pleasure that he visits the Far Shore."

"I think he likes going himself," I said stubbornly.

Bridie had appeared at the corner of the house. Father Binyon looked up and saw her. "Well," he asked, "what is it?"

"Mr. Emmet, sir, is here for Wolfe."

"His father?"

"No, sir, the old man."

For a moment Father Binyon looked annoyed. "All right," he said, "Wolfe will be ready in a minute."

She went out and he turned again to me. "Remember, Wolfe, the Church is always ready to help those who are in doubt or trouble. Now go to your grandfather and don't forget what I have said."

CHAPTER XVII

Polyphemus, realizing suddenly that I was leaving, opened his eyes just wide enough to give me a leer of sleepy malevolence. Then, hanging limp, heavy, and apparently inanimate, he allowed me to return him to Father Binyon's knee. I left them and went alone round the corner of the house to meet Gran'papa.

Gran'papa didn't look at me directly as I approached. He was watching me, but he seemed to be looking away. "Well," he said, in a very quiet voice, "we'd better go home."

The sun was just setting behind the hill, though it was still shining with a thin and golden light on the tops of the trees and the opposite shore of the lough. It was evening, though not yet dusk, and the fishermen were gathering at the harbour. The sea was very still and the currents showed like long, smooth ribbons. Faintly I could hear the voices of the fishermen, but everything was so quiet and untroubled that the few sounds there were did not break the silence.

Suddenly I noticed that Gran'papa had not spoken a word since we left Father Binyon's house. He was looking a little queer too. "What's the matter, Gran'papa?" I asked.

"Nothing," he replied in a flat voice. "There's nothing the matter," but I thought there was.

"Are you not feeling very well?" I persisted, but he did not answer.

Instead he turned sharply and looked down the lane. "Who's that?" he asked.

How he had known there was anyone I can't imagine, but I looked round also. "It's Michael Rymple," I told him, "and he's going into Father Binyon's." Gran'papa watched for a few seconds; then we walked on.

I wondered that Michael should go to the priest's house just now, when all the other fishermen were down at the boats: but actually he had plenty of time, for the men used to gather at the boats to smoke and talk an hour or more before it was time to go out.

Then my thoughts returned to Gran'papa. I looked at him again. "Are you really quite well, Gran'papa?" I asked. "You shouldn't have bothered coming for me. It was all right—I mean Father Binyon was—he was very nice."

"I'm sure he was charming."

I didn't say anything more, because I didn't quite know what Gran'papa meant. Father Binyon *had* been nice.

I thought for a long time. "Gran'papa," I said, when we were very nearly home, "did you not want me to go to supper with Father Binyon—I mean, would you rather I hadn't gone?"

"Well," Gran'papa answered, "he hasn't been very friendly to us—to me—has he?—just recently."

"No."

"On Sunday, what was he going to do?—he was going to drive me out, wasn't he?"

Then I was very sorry. "I didn't think of that, Gran'papa. I forgot. I wouldn't have gone. I wish I hadn't gone, Gran'papa. He was very nice to me, and I didn't think. I'm sorry, Gran'papa."

Gran'papa took my hand and smiled. "That's all right," he said; "if you didn't think, it's quite different. You wouldn't do anything I didn't like if you remembered, would you?"

"No, Gran'papa."

We sat down together on the bench in front of the cottage, and waited for the fishing-boats to go out.

Presently Michael Rymple came from Father Binyon's house and went down to the harbour, and some time later the boats did go out, but one was missing.

"It must be nearly your bedtime," Gran'papa said after a while, but we sat on for a little longer.

When at last we did get up to go in, I happened to glance down the lane. "Look," I said, "here's Father Binyon."

"Father Binyon!" Gran'papa exclaimed. "What on earth is it now?"—but he went inside without waiting to see. After a moment's hesitation I followed.

"It's bedtime," Mother called, as soon as she caught sight of me. "So off you go."

I dawdled a little, looking into the fire as I passed, and stroking Bran and Rory. I had just reached my room when Father Binyon, hot and a little breathless, pushed open the half-door. "I want to speak to you," he said to Gran'papa.

"Very well," Gran'papa replied coldly. "What about?"

"Listen"—Father Binyon gasped slightly between the words— "you're in great danger. Michael Rymple's just been to see me, and he says that the fishermen are all talking about something which they won't let him hear—but he's heard this and so have I." He pulled out a large red silk handkerchief and began to mop his forehead. "You know they've had practically no fish for the last three nights—ever since they came up to kill that green crea-ture of yours. They say it's because you're a wizard—that you've bewitched them in revenge—and that they won't catch any fish till they get rid of you. Now if that was all their talk they'd let Michael hear it, and I'd hear it too—but last night and to-day there's been something more—it's Cauley and Finnegan and that lot, Michael says; and he thinks they want to murder you."

"Murder me!" Gran'papa repeated—and in those quiet peaceful surroundings the word seemed strange and a little unreal.

The priest held up his hand. "Let me finish," he said; "this is urgent. Did you see the boats? Did you count them?—only five went out; instead of six. No one's ill. It was because of that I hurried."

"You mean they'll try to-night," Gran'papa said.

"Any moment." Father Binyon went to the window and looked out. "No sign yet, but they mayn't come up the lane. Where's your son?"

"Out in the byre," Mother said.

"Then you'll do," the priest told her. "Go up behind on the hill a little way, and if you see a living soul come in and tell us."

"I wouldn't care if they did kill him—all the trouble and dis-grace he's brought on us." Mother folded her arms, and stood looking at them both.

"Woman," Father Binyon frowned terribly, and his voice made me tremble, "go and do what I tell you. If you don't, or if you fail to bring us warning, you'll never get absolution from me, though you be on your death-bed."

She went like a lamb.

As soon as the door had closed behind her the priest turned again to Gran'papa. "You'll have to go," he said. "You're not safe here. I can't do anything for you now. You'll have to go away, and I'd advise you to go to your Dragon. I didn't want you to go to him, but you'll have to now—at once."

Gran'papa looked at him oddly. "Thank you," he said, "and I'm sorry. . . ."

"Come outside," the priest interrupted, "we must watch—I wouldn't trust. . . ."

They went through the door, and I still heard the murmur of their voices.

Presently Gran'papa returned. Father was with him. They stood together talking till Mother came in by the back door. "You can do your own watching," she said.

Gran'papa didn't answer: he looked at *me*. "Wolfe, I'll have to go."

His voice and face were sad, but *I* was pleased at the prospect of such an adventure, for I was sure he would take me with him. "I'll go too," I announced.

"You'll stay *here*," Mother said, and Father added, "Of course he'll stay here."

I felt rebellious. "Why can't I go?" I exclaimed. "I'd be a great help. I'd light the fire, and I'd get stuff to burn, and I'd come home and fetch things that were wanted."

"I know you would," Gran'papa answered, "and I'd like you to come; but it's not that."

Father was still standing near the door. "There are men coming up from the village," he said to Gran'papa. "You'd better go on."

Mother turned to me. "And *you'd* better go to your bed," she ordered. "Come on now—this minute."

Gran'papa came over and kissed me. "Good-bye," he whispered, "and be a good boy."

"Good-bye," I answered in a sort of daze, and Mother pushed me into my own room and shut the door behind her.

"Get undressed," she told me.

I did so and she watched. I did it slowly and fumblingly, but she helped me. I got into bed and she blew out the candle. "Good night," she said, and left me alone.

A few minutes later the back door opened and closed, and I heard Gran'papa's footsteps on the path behind the house. Then, for the first time I think, I realized that he was going away, and I began to cry. I imagined him going over the hillside, in danger, unhappy, and alone. I imagined the men who might be waiting to spring out on him and murder him.

Suddenly I stopped crying. "I *will* go," I muttered. I jumped out of bed and dressed quickly, but quietly. Then I crossed the room on tip-toe, and softly opened the window. I clambered out, and stood for a moment listening: no one seemed to have heard me. I looked up the hill, and there, not so very far away, was a figure, vague in the dusk, but I knew it was Gran'papa.

It was not dark, but all the shapes were indistinct, all the outlines vague. Somewhere in the obscurity there were murderers lurking—and Gran'papa was further off than I had thought. I hurried after him, and though he seemed to be walking slowly he was almost at the top of the hill before I caught him up. When I was still a yard or two behind, he heard me, and turned sharply round. "It's only me, Gran'papa," I whispered, panting. "Oh Gran'papa, I'm frightened."

"Good gracious, child," he exclaimed, "you gave me quite a start."

"I'm sorry, Gran'papa, but I was afraid they would hear us."

"Who?"

"The men."

"Have they come?" he asked.

I shook my head. "No, not yet."

Gran'papa frowned. "Then why did you come after me?"

"Gran'papa," I told him timidly, "I want to be with you. I'd much rather live with *you* than with the others—and you *are* going to live with the Dragon, aren't you?"

He half smiled, then frowned again and looked puzzled. "Wolfe," he said slowly, "you must go home. It won't be safe living with the Dragon. You *must* go home."

"But why," I pleaded, "why won't it be safe? They're all afraid of the Dragon: they won't dare. . . ."

"Wolfe," Gran'papa's voice had become rather stern, "if you don't go by yourself, I'll have to take you back."

"But Gran'papa, that wouldn't be safe either."

"Then go alone," he answered.

I took a few steps and stopped. "Please, Gran'papa," I begged.

His mouth was very tightly shut, but suddenly his expression relaxed. "You *can't* go back," he said. "They're coming."

I glanced hurriedly down the hill. There were five men between us and the cottage, but I only saw them for a moment. Then we turned and went on quickly.

We were really in danger now. The men were not very far away. We were standing against the sky-line and they must have seen us quite clearly. Perhaps they would try to catch us before we reached the Dragon's cave. Yet because I was with Gran'papa I was no longer really frightened. It wasn't that I *thought* we were safe; it was just that I had complete confidence in him.

We didn't run—I don't know if Gran'papa could have run very well—but we walked fast. As soon as we had crossed the hill-top we went straight towards the cave. As usual it was lighter on this side of the hill and we had no difficulty in seeing our way, nor, once they had crossed the summit, would our enemies have any difficulty in seeing us. But they never appeared. I expect they were too afraid of the Dragon. At any rate we came to his cave safely and found him at home.

"So you've come," the Dragon thought, and he was pleased. "They've driven you out, have they? Just like them."

"They've driven *me* out," Gran'papa replied. "I'd have been better to come when you first asked me. Here we are anyhow—Wolfe for to-night only—but *I've* come for an indefinite period."

I didn't say anything, but the Dragon knew quite well that I hoped *I* had come for an indefinite period also. "The time doesn't matter," he told Gran'papa, "and I'm glad you've come."

He looked glad too, and helped us to gather heather, with which we made beds in the back of the cave. Then we were quite safe, for to reach us it would be necessary to pass the Dragon. He promised that in the morning he would dig a new cave for us, opening off his own. I noticed that, though the new cave would be for both of us, Gran'papa did not oppose the plan. I felt sure he was going to allow me to stay.

In spite of all the excitement, and the unaccustomed nature of our beds, we both fell asleep quickly and slept soundly.

CHAPTER XVIII

When I awoke the sun was shining brightly outside. Gran'papa was standing at the mouth of the cave, and the Dragon was nowhere to be seen. I lay for a little without speaking, till presently Gran'papa turned round and saw that I was awake.

"You're a lazy boy," he said. Yet in spite of the tone of his voice, he seemed to be troubled about something.

"Is it very late?" I asked, and I got up and went over to him.

"It is," he answered, "but it doesn't matter—there's nothing to hurry for."

"No breakfast," I murmured, and I felt rather shocked. Immediately I began to be hungry.

"Nor dinner, nor tea, nor any other meal," he replied half ironically, "but you can wash in the stream: that's something to do while we think about it."

"Where's the Dragon?" I asked, for though I looked up the hill and down, I could see no sign of him.

"Oh," Gran'papa said, rather enviously, "he was up at dawn, and now he's in the jungle or somewhere, having a good meal."

"I wish *we* could eat leaves," I sighed; and went to the stream to wash.

Procyon came with me. He had been munching grass while I was talking to Gran'papa, but the interruption of his breakfast did not matter; for him there was food everywhere.

I splashed for a little in the cool water, and after that I felt hungrier than ever. We went back to Gran'papa, and I lay down on my front, because I didn't feel so empty in that position.

Gran'papa didn't say much: he wanted the Dragon to come back, and he was considering sending me home. I didn't want to go home, but I did want something to eat. I thought of the fish I'd had last night, and of stews and steaks and chops. And Procyon sat beside me and nibbled the grass contentedly.

"Why can't *you* do something?" I said. "I mean Procyon," I explained to Gran'papa, who was looking at me in surprise. "He should be able to get us something."

"Yes, indeed," Gran'papa agreed. "By this time all the dinners in the village are nearly cooked. No one would notice Procyon. He could dart into somebody's house, snatch the pot from the fire, and bring it back to us in his mouth. After all, *they* had their breakfasts."

"It would have stew in it," I said, and we became silent.

"Why can't we fish?" I exclaimed suddenly.

"No lines, no hooks," Gran'papa answered. "I thought of it long ago."

Again we were silent.

It was past mid-day now: I must have been awake for over two hours, two tedious hours. I wondered how long Gran'papa had been awake. I asked him.

"I don't know," he said. "But when you get to my age time passes quickly."

It was queer that—the sun moving across the sky, and clocks ticking. For Gran'papa it moved faster; and the clocks ticked faster—yet for both of us it was still between twelve and one o'clock.

"Where's Procyon?" I wondered.

Gran'papa glanced round, but didn't answer.

"He was here a moment ago," I went on. "I suppose he's feeding somewhere."

"Wolfe," Gran'papa said determinedly, "you'll *have* to go. It's no good your staying here. *I* would go if I could. You'll just have to go straight home—now."

"But Gran'papa. . . ."

He ignored the interruption. "You'll probably meet your father on the hill. If not, I don't expect you'll see anyone. If you do, try to avoid them. Get home as quickly as you can. Then your mother will look after you, and no one need know you were ever away."

"Could I not wait till evening?" I pleaded. "It's hot now, and I don't *feel* like going."

"You won't feel any better then," he said. "You'll have missed more meals by that time."

Of course I would have been much more comfortable at home, but being hungry had made me cross and obstinate. Besides I intended to stay with Gran'papa and I wasn't going back if I could help it. "I'm not so likely to be seen if I wait," I answered.

"No," he agreed doubtfully, and began to consider, while I sat beside him trying to think of fresh arguments in case he made another attempt to send me home. But for a long time he didn't speak at all—and then Procyon returned.

"Here's Procyon," I said, and I was glad to change the subject. "Look—up there beyond the cave."

Gran'papa looked. "So it is," he said, "but what *has* he got in his mouth?"

We both watched, and I was the first to answer the question. "It's a pot," I exclaimed, "and I'm *sure* it's got stew in it."

I was right; it had. Procyon came trotting down the hill, holding up his head steadily and proudly. Not a drop seemed to have been spilled. Gran'papa looked very pleased and patted him. "You're a marvel," he said. Procyon put the pot down between us and we pulled out the pieces with our fingers; we hadn't anything else to use.

"Now whose can this be?" Gran'papa wondered presently. He had nearly finished, and he paused with a piece of meat half-way to his mouth so that the gravy dripped onto his trousers.

"It's ours," I replied, pulling a handful of grass to wipe away the gravy. "That's our pot. Mother and Father will have no dinner to-day." I began to laugh, for I could picture Mother's astonishment when she found the pot gone. Next she'd get cross, and there'd be nobody to blame, which would make it worse.

We shared the remainder of the gravy between us, drinking out of the pot in turn. Then we stretched ourselves, and lay back, and looked up at the sky. For the first time that day we both felt quite happy and comfortable.

"Two Elijahs and a four-legged raven," Gran'papa remarked presently, and I wondered what the ravens did bring to Elijah— nothing so nice as what we'd got I felt sure, but then the ravens wouldn't have been so clever as Procyon. Besides, Elijah wouldn't have known how to talk to them.

It was because I was still thinking of Elijah and the way he had been fed that I presently remarked, "*We* just have to wish, and we get what we want."

"Do you think so?" Gran'papa looked interested. It was the sort of thing he liked to discuss. "I fancy we got the first thing that came handy."

"But I *wished* for stew."

"And not anything else?"

"I thought of some things," I admitted, "but we can try again this evening. We'll wish for something and see if he brings it."

Gran'papa looked doubtful. "I don't quite like it. It's dangerous for Procyon. If only the Dragon . . ."

But at that moment I saw the Dragon. "Look!" I exclaimed. "There he is—coming up from the shore."

Gran'papa didn't finish what he had been saying and we both watched the Dragon in silence. As he came closer I had a feeling as if someone were speaking to me and I couldn't quite catch what was being said. Suddenly I realized it was the Dragon and at the same moment I understood him.

"He wants us to go to the shore," I told Gran'papa. "The Sea Serpent's there, and they've been waiting for us all morning."

"We've been waiting for *him*," Gran'papa grumbled. "A nice way you have of treating visitors," he went on, as soon as the Dragon was close. The Dragon looked at him in perplexity, unable to understand this mixing of moods. "What were we to eat?—nothing, I suppose."

The Dragon understood that we had been hungry, but he could not understand that it was in any way his fault. "Are you angry with me?" he asked.

"Of course not," Gran'papa told him, but I think he must have been nearly angry or the Dragon wouldn't have thought of it.

"What do you want me to do?" was the Dragon's next question. He already knew how Procyon had brought us our dinner and that Gran'papa thought it dangerous.

"We want you to come with us," Gran'papa answered quickly, "while we go home again and arrange about our food supplies. We want you first of all as a protector, but at the same time you will appear as a sort of threat to remind the villagers what may happen if they don't do as we wish."

While he spoke I was conscious of the Dragon's thoughts. The Dragon listened carefully to Gran'papa, and sometimes his perception was ahead of Gran'papa's words, and sometimes it lagged behind. "Then you won't come to the shore," was his first thought; nevertheless he took in what Gran'papa was saying.

"We must go down to the cottage and find my son," Gran'papa concluded. "I will tell him that food must be brought to us every day, or else you will harm the village."

"What shall I do to them?" the Dragon said curiously. I saw that in his mind was a vague picture of himself trampling down the cottages and chasing the people, and that the picture rather pleased him.

I don't think Gran'papa saw this. "You won't do anything," he replied. "It won't be necessary: they'll be so frightened they'll agree to whatever I want."

"Shall we go now?" the Dragon asked.

"Yes, now," Gran'papa said, but he got up rather slowly.

We walked languidly, Gran'papa and I, for it was sultry weather. The Dragon on the contrary felt more than usually energetic. So did Procyon: he scampered up and down, and peered into every rabbit hole. I believe that watching him and imagining how uncomfortable he *ought* to have been increased our own tiredness. We went more and more slowly. There was no shade from the burning sun and the way seemed steeper than ever before.

Suddenly, without a word, Gran'papa sat down. He gave one glance at me and then lay back and closed his eyes.

"Gran'papa! Are you all right, Gran'papa?" I asked, peering down at him, and feeling a little frightened.

"I will be soon," he replied. "I can't go on just yet."

I was rather worried, but I didn't know what to do, till presently, without opening his eyes, he told me. "Get the Dragon to stand between me and the sun," he said, "so as to give me a little shade."

I explained to the Dragon and showed him just where to stand. He thought it strange that we shouldn't like so much sun, but he was very obliging and stood quite still and patient. I lay down in this shade too and presently Procyon came and licked both our faces. I found it cool and pleasant. Then I heard him lying down somewhere near, but though I was slightly curious to know whether he was in the shade or the sunshine I didn't trouble to open my eyes and look.

"Don't you wish," I said to Gran'papa, "that the sun would go behind a cloud and it would rain—big, cool drops?"

He didn't answer and I didn't mind in the slightest.

After a while I spoke again. "It's nice, isn't it?" I remarked, and this time he gave a sort of lazy grunt of agreement. It *was* pleasant, now that we were rested and out of the sun, only I couldn't forget that we had to go on. Then, just as suddenly as he had sat down, Gran'papa sat up, propping himself on his hands, and so did I. "Come on, we'll have to go," he said—but we didn't just at once. We looked down at the expanse of sea and sky. From here part of the sky seemed below us. It was the part which was over the sea, and blended with the sea, in the hazy line of the horizon. It was the most satisfying beauty that ever could be. It was so complete that I felt neither sadness nor longing. It was calm because of the immensity of the slightly moving water, the open arch of the sky. . . . There was a blending of colours and tones— the water, dark over rocks, translucent over sand—and the miracle in this summer picture was the constant, imperceptible, and subtle change. It seemed static, yet even now, unnoticed, shadows were creeping out from rocks and stones, and down there on the shore the tide was flowing in.

We went on at last, and when eventually we reached the cairn at the top of the hill, there was a faint breeze. Here we stopped to consider our plans. "Where shall we find your son?" the Dragon asked.

"He will be either on the hill or about the farm," Gran'papa said, looking downwards.

"There he is," I cried. "He's working in the potato field."

"Perhaps I'd better go alone," Gran'papa told the Dragon. "If you came too he might be frightened, he might run away."

"Do as you think best," the Dragon answered, "but remember, men are treacherous. Keep in the open and if by any chance you should be threatened, say that I am watching you."

"I will remember," Gran'papa said. "Wolfe, you stay here with the Dragon. Procyon, come with me."

Father had his back to us. He was weeding the potatoes with a hoe. I sat down, and we both watched Gran'papa, who was following the path towards home. Procyon, knowing that the errand was serious, did not wander in his usual way, but trotted soberly beside Gran'papa.

Father stopped working. He leaned forward, resting both his hands on top of the hoe, and gazed down at the lough. Returning to the harbour was the Rymples' boat. Michael was in it himself, with another fisherman—I couldn't see whom—but Peter was not there. Far out, near the northern horizon, was a ship under full sail. It was going, perhaps, to the Americas.

Gran'papa had reached the edge of the field. He began to climb over the low place in the dyke which divided the field from the open heather. His foot knocked against a loose stone: it dropped onto other stones, which had fallen similarly on previous occasions. We heard the clatter distinctly.

Father looked round. He stared for a moment at Gran'papa. He may even have seen me and the Dragon. At any rate he dropped his hoe and ran.

"David," Gran'papa called, looking a little precarious on top of the wall. "David, there's no need to be afraid. I won't—I can't do anything. Stop!"

But Father ran on till he reached the back door of the cottage, and then he hurried inside. A moment later I saw him, with Mother, going down the lane towards the village.

For some little time Gran'papa remained upon the wall. Then he climbed down and began to cross the field. The lane was hidden from him, and I shouted after him to tell him that Mother and Father had left the cottage, but he was too far away to hear what I said. He turned and waved, and went on down the slope.

The Dragon had a sudden fear. "There's an ambush for him in the cottage. He's going into it—and I told him to stay in the open."

"How do you know?" I asked.

"I know men. Get onto my back."

I scrambled up, and again we sped down the hillside like lightning. Gran'papa was very near the cottage door. "Stop," I shouted, "stop!" and the Dragon bellowed. Gran'papa heard us. He turned, and waited in surprise.

"There are men hiding there," I gasped, as soon as we reached him. "They're in ambush to kill you."

"How do you know?"

"The Dragon knows."

He looked at the Dragon. "Are you sure?"

The Dragon now did not seem so very sure. "If they *are* there," he told us at last, "I can find them out—but you promised me that you would stay in the open."

"I know I did," Gran'papa admitted. "I'm sorry. I forgot all about it."

The Dragon clambered down, and pressed his nose against the back door of the cottage. His hind legs remained part way up the bank, and he gave a mighty sniff. He waited a moment, then he pouffed a great breath that made the windows rattle and one of the doors slam. After that he stood quite still, his mind alert for any wandering thoughts or emotions that might betray the presence of a lurking enemy within: but the cottage was empty.

Gran'papa and Procyon and I entered. The Dragon couldn't, but he stayed at the door.

"What shall we do now?" we pondered—all of us except Procyon. *He* had found something delicious heating over the fire and I heard him gobbling up the scraps which had been intended for the pigs.

"Well," Gran'papa said presently, "if they won't allow us to talk to them we'll have to write. Wolfe, see what food you can find, and pack enough in a basket to do us till tomorrow."

I obeyed, and he got up and went to his own room. I saw him open the desk, sit down at it, and take a piece of paper. He dipped a quill in the ink, and after a momentary pause he began to write.

He wrote for a considerable time and we waited for him, expecting every moment that he would finish. At last he did. He scattered sand on the letter, folded it and sealed it. Then he returned to the kitchen and put it in the middle of the table. It was addressed "To David and Rebecca Emmet", but I never learned what exactly he had written. All he told us was that he had ordered them to leave provisions for us at the cairn every day at noon.

"There's somebody coming," the Dragon warned us, and we hastened out of the cottage and a little way up the hillside. Then we looked back. A party of men had left the village and was approaching the cottage. They were armed with pitchforks.

"At any rate," Gran'papa said, after regarding them for a moment, "I've time to get Dobbin, and I'm going to. I won't tramp any more."

"I'll saddle him for you," I offered.

"No," he answered, "you'd better go on with Procyon, so as to get a good start. The Dragon can wait for me. I won't be long."

"Why not fight them now, when they have come to fight," the Dragon urged. "You would not need to do anything. I could kill them all in a moment, and after that there would be peace."

He spoke quite indifferently. He neither wanted to kill them nor cared if he did. He was merely suggesting what seemed to him the best solution of the problem.

"No," Gran'papa answered frowning. He turned to me. "Go on now," he said. "There's no time to lose." He himself went towards the stable.

I climbed the hill with Procyon, turning from time to time to watch the men. They were approaching very slowly, and suddenly they saw the Dragon, and stopped altogether. They pointed and talked, and meanwhile Gran'papa came out of the stable, leading Dobbin.

When he reached the Dragon, they both looked at the party from the village. Then Gran'papa mounted Dobbin, and very soon they caught me up. We looked down again, and the men had advanced a little, but when *we* stopped, they stopped also.

We paused again when we reached the cairn, but this time we could see nobody. "They've all gone into the cottage," Gran'papa said. We set out for the cave, and when we reached it it was evening.

We unpacked the basket and ate our supper, and for a while we sat together in the sunlight.

"I haven't made you a cave after all," the Dragon said. "I'll start now."

"No, don't," Gran'papa told him. "It will do to-morrow, or some other time. . . . I believe," he went on presently, "that we're going to be very happy here—long days on the shore, evenings at the cave, sunsets over the sea. . . ."

It was nearly sunset now, and his words seemed true.

I felt that this golden evening was not so much the end of another day as the beginning of a long new era of happiness. We sat silent and reflective, watching the deepening shadows and thinking quiet, peaceful thoughts.

At that time I had never been unhappy: all my life had been pleasant and interesting, but it seemed as if the future would be better still, preserving all that had been best in my old life and adding something more. I imagined a sort of community, a fellowship which any animal might join, but of which Gran'papa and I would be the only human members.

I imagined us living there on the hillside in harmony with the plants and the trees, the hill, the sea, the rocks, and the sky. . . . I imagined this going on for ever with no winter and no storms and no discomfort.

Then I told myself a story. In the story I went down to the village alone, and I met a donkey and I spoke to him and he told me where he had been and I told the people and they were very surprised. I met a dog and the dog told me what his master had done and I told, and everyone thought me very clever because I could understand the language of the animals.

But it's all true I reflected—that might easily happen—any day. It was so nice here—and I was almost an animal myself.

The sun sank behind the sea, and the night came slowly. At last the Dragon shivered, and we went into the cave. Only Dobbin remained outside, and before going to bed I went to see that he was all right. I had tethered him by a long rope, in case he should try to return to his stable as he had done before. He was asleep and I stood for a moment by the mouth of the cave and took a last look round.

It was dark now, but I could still see the faint glimmer of the sea and the shadowy outlines of the hills. Eventually I turned and went in. I was happy.

CHAPTER XIX

We were up earlier next morning, and the Dragon did not go away to feed in the jungle. Instead he began to make a new cave, opening off his own. It seemed that he could do without food for indefinite periods, and make up by eating more at other times.

He worked very quickly and soon he had hollowed out a fair-sized room. Then we ourselves started to smooth the floor, and make bunks in the walls, while the Dragon began a stable for Dobbin.

The morning passed very quickly, and soon it was time to go to the cairn to see if provisions had been brought for us. We all went together, but though there was no cloud over the sun, and no breeze, the climb seemed easier than on the day before. It was a little after mid-day when we arrived at the top, and our food was there sure enough—quite a large supply—bread, lettuces, a roast chicken, even a bottle of brandy; everything was wrapped up in cool cabbage leaves.

We looked round. Some distance away were five armed men, watching us. Two of them had guns, one a pike, while the other two had pitchforks. One of them was Father; he had Gran'papa's old arquebus; it didn't work, but Father didn't know that, because he had never tried it.

We took the provisions and came away. Then we had our dinner, and all afternoon and evening we worked at the cave, till by bedtime it had begun to look quite comfortable.

The next day, at the same time, we returned to the cairn, and there again were the parcels in cabbage leaves, and the men watching us. The day after there were fewer men, and gradually the precautions were relaxed, till eventually children began to come with our supplies. When that happened, Gran'papa allowed me to go to the cairn alone, though he made me promise to stay at some distance till the messenger had departed.

Thus we led a very easy, pleasant life. We had made our cave as comfortable as could be, and if there was anything we wanted, we had only to leave a note at the cairn and it would be brought to us the next day. Gran'papa had got his books; I had my boats and fishing lines. We had even a table and some chairs. Now, however, we collected our supplies in the evening, for during the day we were usually on the shore.

I know we made a great difference to the animals. They liked us and we saw most of them every day. I thought sometimes that to them we were like a priest and his curate, for we visited them, just as Father Binyon visited everyone in the village. But it was to the

Dragon we made the greatest difference. He had been terribly lonely, though he had played sometimes, in rather a romping fashion, with the Sea Serpent. Yet they didn't really suit each other, and besides, the Serpent liked to be in the Sea most of the time. So the Dragon was happier now. He liked talking to Gran'papa, and to me too, and his fits of melancholy became quite infrequent.

I suppose we had been living with the Dragon for about a fortnight, when one day I met Peter Rymple on top of the hill. It is hard to judge the periods between those happenings. There was nothing to distinguish one day from another. They passed pleasantly, gliding into each other almost imperceptibly. We didn't even hear the church bell when it rang on Sundays. We were cut off from the world, and we didn't miss it, because *our* world was so much better.

Very often I wasn't at the cairn when the provisions arrived, but on the day Peter brought them I was there first and saw him coming. He didn't see me, and I lay down to wait for him. He trudged along slowly. His face was red and damp and hot, and when he was a little distance off he put down the basket to rest. "Peter," I called.

He looked all round, but I kept my head among the heather and he didn't see me. "Where are you?" he asked, a little nervously. "Are you invisible?"

"Yes," I said, but he caught sight of me and came over.

"Why didn't you come and help with the basket?" he demanded. "It's very heavy."

"I didn't think."

"Well, you can carry it now." He handed it to me; then looked at me rather curiously. "Are you having fun?" he asked.

"Oh yes," I said, and then, "What do they say about us down there?" and I nodded my head towards the village.

"They're all very angry with you," he replied, "but everyone's frightened."

"I'm sure they are," I said with satisfaction.

"We've got a new game we play," he went on. "It's called 'Dragons'. It's great fun being the Dragon. You shout and bellow and pretend to trample down the village and eat everyone up—but you get killed in the end by the others."

"The Dragon won't get killed," I told him confidently.

"Oh, but in the game they all band together and take him at night when he's asleep—and when you're dying, if you're the Dragon I mean, you give a terrible, long yell, fading away like this, as you get weaker and weaker."

He yelled.

"Don't," I said hurriedly. "They'll think I've been captured, and come to rescue me."

"The Dragon?" he exclaimed, looking rather scared.

"Of course, but he wouldn't do anything to you if you were friends with *me*. Would you like to see him?"

"I don't think so." He hesitated. "I'd like to see him if I wasn't too near."

"He won't touch you," I assured him, "if you're with me and Gran'papa. He likes boys, and besides, he's promised Gran'papa not to hurt anyone."

Still he hesitated and I urged him. "Why don't you come?—you could see the Sea Serpent too, this afternoon. Where's your father?"

"He's out after the lobsters."

"Why don't you come then?"—I repeated, "—the way you used to. You can have dinner with us—and it'll be far nicer than going home."

"You get very good things," he agreed a little wistfully.

"Well, there's always plenty," I told him. "Come on," and he came.

When we got back, we found Gran'papa sitting in the shady mouth of the cavern, reading a book. He was glad to see Peter, though at first he was afraid that Michael would be anxious when Peter did not return.

"Sure he won't be back till late," Peter answered. "He'll be going over to Dunachil with the lobsters."

So we unpacked the things and had our dinner, while Peter told us the news of the village.

"Who's providing the food?" Gran'papa asked.

"It was Finnegans' to-day. Sometimes it's one; sometimes another."

"How's that arranged?"

"Oh, Father Binyon decides. It's between the farmers—and the fishermen have to give a fish now and then. Sometimes it's from your own house it comes."

"I didn't see how it could be always from home," Gran'papa said, "but I didn't think anyone else would send it."

"Father Binyon ordered them to, and they were afraid that everything would be destroyed if they didn't. Mrs. Emmet made a terrible fuss. She said she couldn't provide all the food, and she wasn't going to, because it was as much for the good of the rest as for her."

We finished dinner and set off for the shore. The Dragon had been away all morning, and we expected to find him there.

We did. He was not far from the stream, but there was no sign of the Sea Serpent. Peter was only nervous of the Dragon for the first few minutes, and the Dragon liked him.

The tide was out, and we walked along the shore to the far end. Then Peter and I took off our clothes and scrambled over the barnacled rocks. We slid into warm, shallow pools, and lay there luxuriously. Gradually we worked our way towards the point, and Procyon followed us. His progress was uncertain. There was no firm grip for his paws, and he slithered along, changed all at once from the fastest of the party to the slowest.

Everything was relaxed—the many sea-weeds, green and brown and pink, and even white, all wet and shining in the sunlight—the sea-snails and limpets, which had loosened their hold and were cautiously changing their positions. In the pools were sea-anemones and crabs, and hermit-crabs, and codling and shrimps. We chased them all, except the anemones of course, and caught some of them, but because we didn't want them, we put them back. There were catfish too, but we didn't chase them, for we believed that they could sting.

When we got near to the point we bathed—Procyon accidentally, because he fell in and then found that he could swim. We could see Gran'papa, where he was sitting with the Dragon on the shore, but there was still no sign of the Sea Serpent. Peter was a very good swimmer. He could swim under water. When Procyon swam towards him he dived underneath and came up on the other side. Procyon couldn't understand where he had gone to, and was quite confused. Presently we came out and lay in the sun. Peter wasn't quite so brown as I was. While we were lying on the rocks we watched the water. Just below us it was dark, transparent green, looking a little thick because of its great depth. We could see one or two fish nosing round the rocks not very far below the surface. There were several jelly-fish as well. Languidly they sucked in the water and expelled it again—yet, though their method of propulsion seemed so indefinite, they were moving steadily towards the open sea.

Peter said that *they* would sting also, but I said I didn't care and was going in again. So he said he would go in too, though it was dangerous. Just as we were about to dive there swam by, with anxious haste, a whole regiment of tiny eels, all dark greeny-black. Then came another, and another, and another. There must have been five hundred or a thousand in each regiment, and yet perhaps, if he had happened to have his mouth open, the Sea Serpent might have gobbled up the whole army without knowing anything about it. We waited for them to pass, but there were always more and more and more. So at last we dived right on top of them, but when we looked round we couldn't see one. Then we heard Gran'papa calling to us to come back and get our clothes on. Procyon, though he had seemed to enjoy the previous bathe, had not come in a second time. We climbed out, and returned to Gran'papa, and dressed.

We had brought food with us, and we had our supper on the shore. Just as we were finishing we saw a line of white surf approaching from the northern point. It was the Sea Serpent, and in a moment he was with us. "Who's this?" he asked, looking curiously at Peter, who looked just as curiously, if rather timidly, back. We told him, and asked him where he had been all day.

"Northward from here," he answered, "where there is a small island. It is not far from a tall cliff on the mainland."

"Tory," I guessed.

"Rathlin," suggested Gran'papa.

"Instrahull," said Peter.

"I don't know," the Sea Serpent replied. "On one side of it there is a long, sandy bay—and I saw no men. I was lying on the shore, when a seal came to me and I learned many interesting things."

"What?" we asked.

"This seal once met another seal, whose home was in an ocean, in the far south-west. It is a pleasant ocean, where there are many fruitful islands, and he told me that *there* are sea serpents."

"It's the Pacific," Gran'papa said, "but I doubt if you could get there. You would have to go round either of two great capes. At one there are many bitter winds and constant snow. It is filled with moving blocks of ice, and is very dangerous. The other is cold too, and often stormy. Besides, they are both a long way off."

"This seal had swum through the colder strait, amid the blocks of ice," the Sea Serpent answered. "He saw there a wrecked ship, and another, which he knew was doomed, though the men worked desperately."

"But seals are accustomed to ice," Gran'papa told him. "You're not; you'd be frozen to death."

"Maybe I should," he replied, "but to meet others of my kind would be worth the risk." He moved away a little along the shore.

"Foolishness," Gran'papa declared. "Why can't he be happy here?"

"It may be foolish," the Dragon answered, "but if I had such a chance, however small, I should do the same."

I got up and followed the Sea Serpent. Presently he stopped and I found him looking rather mistily at the sea.

I didn't say what I had intended to say, but he knew nevertheless. "You don't want me to go?" he asked.

"No," I said. "I like you."

He liked me also. "I won't go now," he promised, "but later, when the sun moves south. . . ."

"Don't go then either," I pleaded. "Stay all the time."

"I couldn't. I couldn't live. I might endure the cold for a day or two at the cape, but a whole winter—it would kill me."

"How do you know about winter?"

"The seal told me."

"What about the others?" I said. "What about the Dragon? What will happen to him?"

"Oh, the Dragon . . ." and without completing his thought he plunged suddenly into the sea and swam away.

I supposed I had seen the last of him for the evening, and I went back to the others, but in about half an hour he returned, and joined us as if he had never been away.

"Let's bathe again now," I suggested, "and Peter can have a ride on the Sea Serpent."

Gran'papa wouldn't allow it. "You've bathed enough today, and besides, it's getting late." He looked at the Dragon. "Did *you* bathe when you were young?" he asked. The Dragon had never bathed, but the question made him reflect.

"Am I old now?" he wondered. "I suppose I am." He thought of his past world. "I was young then, but we live to a great age. Now I feel old, not because of the long time I was buried, but because the world has changed so. It was a better world then—not so pale and tired. . . ."

"What you call pale," Gran'papa answered, "is the softness of atmosphere, and light, and tone. It is that that makes beauty. The hills are rounded, not harsh. The colours . . ."

"I would rather they were harsh," the Dragon thought. "*Then* the sun had more light and the trees were alive. It was like the jungle up there. It too has come . . . but it is sickly and languid. Soon it will die—yet, till that very moment, it will remain more alive than your heather, or plants, or grass."

"I don't like it," Gran'papa said. "I would rather have the heather and the grass."

"This is your time," the Dragon answered. "That was mine. The sun will grow weaker, and there will be fainter creatures and paler trees. The land will become ever older and greyer. Colours will become duller, and the hue of the sea will be softer still. The sky will be less bright, and life less vigorous. . . . If you saw that now, you would wish for this. Yet to the creatures who will live then this would seem too real, too harsh, too vivid. . . . Is the jungle not real to you, more real than this?"

As he spoke we saw a vision of jungle, but I think now that it must have been some early, primeval forest that he remembered, not from that morning, but from long ago—because of the extraordinary brilliance of the sun and the brightness of the colours.

"It is real, certainly," Gran'papa replied, in an impressed voice.

Then all of a sudden he remembered other things. "It's very

late," he exclaimed. "Peter, no one will know what's happened to
you. What *will* your father think?"

"He won't be back yet," Peter answered, but Gran'papa insisted
that we should go.

Our way was through the sand-hills, and crossing a ridge we
came upon the same little group as we had encountered the day
after we met Procyon. The creatures were huddled close together,
in a hollow out of the wind, where they might absorb every ray
of sunlight. When they saw us they came to us, though now there
was only one toad instead of two. I don't know what had happened
to the other. Gran'papa sat down; all the creatures clambered over
him and the snakes curled away in his pockets. But Peter and I
were anxious to go to the jungle, because Peter had never seen the
strange plants that grew there.

So after a little while we went on, making our way up the valley
till we came to the place where the new lake had been formed by
the fallen rocks and earth which had blocked up the stream.

It had changed greatly since our first visit. There was no sign
now of the loose stones and rubble, which then had made the
place so ugly. All now was covered by foliage and flowers. The lake
was there still, but out of it were growing huge water plants, with
broad, flat leaves; on the bank were exotic creepers with massive,
trunk-like stalks—and all the creepers were pulsing, swelling,
moving . . . and the water plants moved too. Above the surface of
the lake, and through the leaves on the bank, appeared the heads
of peculiar creatures. Some—pale brown, with long necks like
swans and egg-shaped, green-eyed, heads—swam in the lake.
Others like crocodiles, but of many different colours, lay on the
bank or in the water near the edge. The plants and flowers were as
varied as the animals: but which *were* the plants, and which the
animals?

From a bare spot between jungle and heath we watched a creeper
and a tree involved in a deadly struggle. The tree, which stood at
the edge of the lake, was like one huge rhubarb leaf, growing alone.
The stem was a fleshy, pinky green, and round the stem twined a
thick and snake-like creeper. The creeper rose slowly, always turning higher and higher up the stem. As it ascended its grip grew
tighter. The colours of the stem seemed to separate; in places the

pink turned to red; in others the green faded and became very pale. A large, thick caterpillar fell suddenly from the top of the leaf, and was immediately devoured by a yellow spotted lizard on the ground beneath. Still the creeper went up and we could see it cutting into the stem of the tree. The leaf, the one huge leaf, began slowly to writhe and curl, and gradually the whole plant bent down. Below, though a little way from the foot of the stem, were thorny plants with dark, tough leaves, and bright red flowers. Across these, ever so slowly, the tree began to scrape itself, but only once. The movement grew slower and slower; the tree sank down, and from it there came a faint sigh.

Without a word we hurried away. We left Peter at the top of the hill, and he returned alone to the village.

CHAPTER XX

For a long time after this we saw none of the people from the village, except the children who left our food at the cairn. We spent the days on the shore or in improving our room in the cave. Gradually, and partly unconsciously, we were adapting ourselves to the life of the animals; and they too were changing, to suit the less brilliant surroundings into which they had come. The Dragon had faded like the others, and while he was marked with the same pattern as before, it was a little more difficult to make out. Yet he still had the power, if he wished, to shine like a huge glow-worm in the night.

Though we had no more human visitors we had others. We had not been very long away before we were discovered by Bran and Rory. They began to visit us now and then, often remaining for quite a long time. Once or twice they were followed by other dogs, and as there were usually enough scraps to feed them all, these other dogs came again. In fact it was not long before nearly all the dogs in the district, even the oldest and most decrepit, were visiting us frequently.

They usually came in the evening; and there were other visitors then too—surprising visitors—rabbits and foxes, weasels, and various kinds of birds—and when they were with us no animal ever attacked another: there were no fights. Huge caterpillars from the distant past, lizards and snakes, and stranger reptiles still, unknown and unimagined by the rest of mankind, lay down beside the dogs, the hares, the cats. . . . For there *were* cats; somehow that surprised us more than anything. Polyphemus was the first; he came one night, so stealthily and noiselessly that no one saw him arrive. In the same secret fashion there came others, gliding unperceived through the heather, so that when eventually they disclosed themselves, significant glances would pass between the mice, the birds, and the rabbits, and the more timid would shudder nervously. But there was no need to fear, for all were safe, even if enemies were not quite friends.

Thus we learned everything that went on in the village—the human part, in a curious, under-table sort of way, and the rest at first hand.

Of the animals of our own time, some were much easier to understand than others. The easiest were the rabbits. Their communicative senses—because rabbits are sociable animals who chatter away continually to one another—were very sharp indeed. The mice, also, were not difficult to comprehend, but most of their thoughts were too simple to be very interesting.

When we first came to the cave, it was the human news from the village that we were most anxious to learn. Yet gradually our interest in this waned, and we paid increasing attention to the doings of the many animals whom we knew. There was a bitter and ancient feud, involving all the dogs of the neighbourhood. We understood now why Bran and Rory had always fought Finnegan's collie, and why, when they themselves were attacked, Brennan's mongrel would come to their aid.

We were amused also by the high feeling between Polyphemus and the independent orange cat who lived at the harbour; and their mutual hatred for a certain nomad crow. It all arose over one small and rather smelly dead fish—at least I know it must have been smelly, for when the orange cat discovered it the boat in which it was found had not been out for a fortnight. The orange cat had had no meal for some time; so he took the fish to the roof of the boat-house to enjoy it in peace. He felt absolutely safe there, and decided to wash himself thoroughly before eating it. This was not his usual habit; he usually washed after eating, but it was what he did on this occasion. It happened that Polyphemus was passing the boat-house just at that moment, and attracted by the savoury smell he climbed to the roof with his customary lack of noise. The orange cat did not see him, and Polyphemus, though he had recently enjoyed a good meal, leapt forward, snatched the fish, and ran quickly along the roof. He had only taken a few paces when the most horrible snarl caused him to drop the fish hurriedly. He went on a step or two, and then, expecting an attack, turned round, with lowered ears. There, a few yards away, and in exactly the same attitude as his own, was the orange cat. Between them was the fish. For some time they glared at each other, with envenomed eyes. Suddenly the fish was caught up into the air, and the crow flapped slowly away.

We knew all about this, because the three of them always remained as far as possible from each other, and often thought about the matter—and the cats came and went by different routes.

These personal differences, however, were as nothing to the problems which troubled the rabbits. In the last few years their population had more than trebled. Where were they to go and what were they to eat?

One evening about three weeks after Peter's visit we were discussing the question. "And that's not all either," an elderly rabbit complained. "They won't even burrow—the young ones—they're too lazy."

"I'm thankful at any rate," said a kind-looking mother mouse, "that my children give me no cause for complaint."

"Don't they indeed?" sneered the orange cat. "Then you're the only one who hasn't cause, and plenty of it too—verminous little brutes. Every time I catch one I have to wash afterwards."

The mouse trembled violently and several of the rabbits looked at her sympathetically. "We know what it is, we understand," they comforted her.

"Don't be upset," Polyphemus interrupted sarcastically. "He never did catch a mouse—he's too slow. He's only a scavenger cat."

The orange cat arched his back and hissed. Then remembering

where he was, he sat down again quietly. "At least I'm not a thief," he retorted.

"Thief," repeated Polyphemus after a moment's hesitation. "I suppose you mean that wretched fish. Of course you never could see a joke."

"Hah! hah!" The crow laughed hoarsely. "*I* saw it anyhow. Haw haw."

The two cats glared at him and dug their claws into the ground. The crow continued to chuckle. "All right," he said, "all right—but even if we weren't *here* you know you couldn't catch me—you're not clever enough."

Polyphemus got up. "I think I'll go home," he murmured to us. "After all the company *is* rather mixed."

He slipped away, but not in time to escape the taunt of the orange cat. "Of course I never *could* see a joke."

"It's always that way," the mother mouse was saying with a sigh. "The things they like most are never really good for them. Cheese—they're all so fond of cheese—and it's really not good for their coats."

"Oh, I do agree," the elderly rabbit answered very seriously. "Take turnips for instance—my last family had a passion for turnip-tops, and they weren't at all good for them. They gave them the most terrible pains—at least I always ascribed it to that—and then the danger. . . ."

"Talking of danger," the mouse interrupted, "take cheese. Why, everyone knows how mice like cheese, and I think it most unfair the advantage that's taken of it."

Two of her children were talking together a few yards away. "And I burrowed, and I burrowed, and I burrowed—until I got right under the wall. Then I nibbled and I nibbled and I nibbled— till I came right out in the corner."

"And was there no one there?" asked the other, with breathless interest.

"Nobody at all."

Suddenly the Dragon shifted his tail and they had to scamper out of the way to escape being crushed. He was discussing something with Gran'papa, but I went on listening to the mice.

"So clumsy," said the smaller, "but as you were saying . . . ?"

"As I was saying?"

"As you were saying, the granary. . . . ?"

"Oh yes, as I was saying, the granary was empty—except for the sacks of corn of course." They both tittered and then the adventurous mouse went on with his story. "No, there was nobody there, nothing but the sacks of corn. So I went up to the first sack and at the thinnest place I could find I nibbled and I nibbled and I nibbled, until I had nibbled my way right through to the corn. It was delicious, but would you believe me—I had made the hole so big that the corn began to run out onto the floor. And the rattle it made! I tell you I popped down the hole again pretty quickly, simply trembling, but of course I soon went back."

"How brave you are," exclaimed his companion, "and so daring!"

The story-teller bowed. "What I intend to do," he went on, "when the time comes, is to make my nest there—a perfect situation and food for generations of mice."

The companion looked at him enviously. "Do you think I . . ." he began timidly. "Do you think I might make *my* nest there too?"

"Of course. There's room for everybody. I never was selfish."

There was a happy pause till suddenly they both spoke at once. "Look! Here's that horrible cat back again."

I looked too, and there was Polyphemus, and he was quite out of breath. He had returned specially to tell us that Father Binyon was on his way to the cave.

We were all very surprised, and wondered what he could want, but none of us could think of an explanation.

"What do *you* think he wants?" I asked Gran'papa.

"I don't know," he answered. "We'll just have to wait and see, but I expect there's something wrong."

So we waited, and presently we saw a black figure on the sky-line; but Father Binyon didn't know where the cave was and couldn't see us, because he was looking into the sun.

"Wolfe," Gran'papa said, "go and show him the way."

I went, and Father Binyon didn't see me till I was just beside him. "Well," he said, "where have *you* sprung from?"

"From the cave. Gran'papa sent me to show you the way."

"How did you know I was looking for you?" he asked.

I hesitated. "We were told you were coming," I answered guardedly.

"Who told you?" he said in surprise.

"Polyphemus."

"Polyphemus! How did *he* know?—and how did he tell you?"

"He just . . ." I was puzzled to explain. "It's just the way all the animals tell us things: they come, and sit there, and then we know."

He looked at me curiously, but only said: "All right; show me the way."

"It's down here;" I pointed. "This is the best way to come."

He seemed rather abstracted as he walked beside me, and for some time did not notice the animals. Indeed they were rather difficult to see, for they seemed to blend into the hillside. They remained absolutely still, but they were watching us, and their eyes glinted in the setting sun.

"Do you never feel homesick?" Father Binyon asked me.

"No," I answered. "I like living here better than at home."

"Do you not feel sometimes, at bedtime, a longing for your own room and your own bed?"

"I liked my room," I answered, "*and* my bed."

"I'm sure you think of it," he said, "and of your father and mother. You look out at the sea when the sun has set, and everything is grey. You feel sad, and you remember that winter will come, and you wonder what will happen."

"Sometimes," I replied reluctantly, "but we'll make big fires in the winter, and it'll be just as nice as home . . . perhaps."

"It may be," he said, "but will you have the Dragon to protect you? Or will he return to the nothingness from which he came?"

"We'll have him," I answered.

We were almost at the cave now, but still Father Binyon did not see the animals—not even a rabbit, which hopped slowly away from almost beneath his feet. We went another few paces. Suddenly he saw everything, and stopped dead.

For a moment he remained thus. Then he went forward, and shook hands with Gran'papa. "So the whole family's at home," he remarked quietly.

Gran'papa shook his head. "Only half of it. But sit down—we've actually got chairs, you see."

"Thank you." The priest sat down, then shifted his chair a little because of the slope of the ground. "I knew you'd everything," he said. "Indeed I'm responsible for a good deal of it—I arrange about the food."

"I know you do," Gran'papa answered, "and we're very grateful."

"Oh . . ." the priest jerked his head deprecatingly, "you're still part of my charge." He hesitated a moment. "I suppose you wonder why I've come."

"At one time I would have been surprised," Gran'papa told him. "Now we look on you as our only ally—our only human ally at least."

Father Binyon smiled without parting his lips. "If I am," he said, "it's a curious alliance—and only an alliance of convenience."

"It is very convenient for us," Gran'papa admitted, "but how does it benefit you?"

"It doesn't benefit me," the priest said. "It's just part of my duty to be the ally of everyone in trouble—and *you* are in trouble now."

"On the contrary," Gran'papa told him, "I have never been happier in my life."

"I knew this was going to be difficult," Father Binyon sighed, "but I want you to come back. It's safe now, and will be safe . . ."

"But we're much happier here," Gran'papa interrupted, "aren't we, Wolfe? If we'd never come, and hadn't experienced this, it might be different, but . . ."

"I know, I know. It attracts me too." He looked round thoughtfully. "It's curious," he went on, "—it is for spiritual reasons I want you to return, and yet I will use practical reasons to try and persuade you."

"Perhaps I mightn't understand the spiritual reasons," Gran'papa said, a little ironically.

Father Binyon laughed. "As a matter of fact," he answered, "you are the only person in my congregation to whom I *can* talk of spiritual things."

"I see," Gran'papa returned. "Nevertheless I think there are others who could understand if you did talk to them."

"Perhaps—perhaps," the priest conceded, raising his hands a little in a gesture of acquiescence. "But in a great many of them the spiritual side does not exist at all. It makes them much easier to deal with—to advise, and to persuade. You, on the contrary, are sometimes difficult. Yet I think I understand you very well."

Gran'papa looked at him. "Do you?" he said. "Sometimes I think I don't understand *you* at all—and never will."

"I wonder why," Father Binyon answered gravely, "for I don't think I have a very tortuous mind."

"Perhaps not; still, I should prefer you to be simpler."

"In some ways," Father Binyon went on, "I'll admit you are more simple than I am. And yet, at this moment, everything about you is complicated and confused. Do you know why you're here now? It's because all this *has* a spiritual appeal for you. That's why you are so difficult. You are attracted by things that seem pleasant, and away you go. The rest, the duller. . . ."

"You needn't say so much about my being difficult," Gran'papa interrupted him. "How long have I been in this parish, and when, before, did I ever give trouble?"

"Never here," the priest admitted, "but when you were a young man you once or twice expressed peculiar views, did you not?"

"Who told you that?" Gran'papa exclaimed.

"I was warned before I came. However, that's nothing to do with my visit to-night. I've come to try and persuade you to return." He looked round at the animals and then at me. Procyon, the dogs, and most of the smaller creatures had dropped to sleep. The Dragon, however, was wide awake, and the cats too watched us, with sparkling, attentive eyes. "I've all these against me," the priest said. "All the time they are exercising a silent, but none the less effective, influence."

"If they thought there was any danger," Gran'papa told him, "they'd be awake and quite ready to act."

"Well, my argument is this," Father Binyon said. "If you go back now you'll be quite safe, and everything will revert to the normal. They're tired of sending you supplies, and besides, I've spoken to some of them. I don't think you'll be able to stay on indefinitely—not after winter comes—and it's better to return when you can than to wait till you have to."

"I don't know that we'll have to," Gran'papa said.

"Not now, perhaps, but I think you will eventually, and by that time your chances may be much less favourable. They may not let you return."

For a moment or two Gran'papa did not reply: he sat thinking, with his chin upon his hand. All about us I heard a gentle stir. The giant caterpillar, who had been rolled up like a great green ball, slowly unwound himself, opened his eyes, raised his head, and looked sleepily about. Snakes did the same; a hornet stretched out his wings, and rubbed them together; the lizards blinked; the rabbits hopped a little closer; the mice scurried out from under stones—one ran up the leg of the table, and sat there, cleaning his whiskers; a fox yawned; dogs scratched themselves, or got up to walk in uneasy circles, with bristling backs. Only the cats remained motionless, attentive, and unblinking as before.

Father Binyon looked round, and half smiled. He noticed Polyphemus for the first time, and put out his hand, and called to him. Polyphemus ignored him. Father Binyon sighed. Gran'papa remained silent, his chin on his hand, his elbow on his knee, staring at the ground.

I whispered Bran's name, but all the other dogs came to me as well, and I patted them, and stroked them, and scratched behind their ears. There were so many that I was nearly overwhelmed, because they all nosed towards me, trying to lick my hands and face.

At last Gran'papa spoke. "Even if the people do not want us to return," he said, "the Dragon will still be our friend."

It was a threat of course, and the priest realized it. "If you still *have* the Dragon," he answered significantly.

"Who's going to kill him?" Gran'papa asked. "Saint George?"

"No—nobody. . . . But in the winter it is very cold."

Gran'papa started. "Nonsense," he exclaimed. Nevertheless I could see that a sudden fear had touched him. But he put it from him and the priest went on:

"Have you never thought that all this is unnatural, exceptional, and that the exceptional does not last. God has ordained it so. God is on the side of His Church."

"But we're not against His church," Gran'papa exclaimed, with some exasperation. "I know that you want to put me in the wrong and that it's useless to argue with you—on that subject at least. I'll only say, *Why* should we want to return? We can light fires in the winter, and the cave has all the advantages of home *without* my daughter-in-law."

"How will you get food?"

"In the same manner as at present."

"I don't think you will."

"Then the Dragon will know what to do."

All the animals looked hard at the priest. "And so will we," they thought.

Father Binyon put his hand to his forehead, and pressed it there for a moment. "We're back to the beginning," he said, but it seemed as if he spoke with some difficulty. "There won't—be—any—Dragon."

"Then I'll kill them all before I go," and the Dragon's eyes glared.

"We'll undermine their houses," thought the rabbits.

"We'll nibble their corn and their seeds," the mice resolved.

"We'll steal their ducks and their hens and their geese," planned the foxes.

"We'll chase away their sheep," growled the dogs.

"We'll bite them with poison," hissed the scorpions and snakes.

"We'll chase them, or sting them, or tear them," the other animals determined, according to their individual powers.

Only the gentle hare could think of no evil to do.

"Then there will be starvation and desolation," the cats purred. "We'll scratch their eyes out," and they began to wash their faces.

"There are evil spirits here," the priest muttered, crossing himself. "They take possession of my mind. I am not strong enough—Oh, Lord Christ Jesus, guide me."

He got up, and so did I, to accompany him for a short distance, and show him the path to the top of the hill. When I turned to go back it was quite dusk, and he grasped my hand. "Come with me, child," he murmured in a low voice. "It is better that you should."

"No," I answered, trying to pull my hand away, "I must go back to Gran'papa."

"That is a bad place," the priest said. "At one time I was uncertain whether it was good or bad, but to-night I felt the spirits of paganism communing with each other; they nearly overcame *me*, a priest of God."

"It was just the animals thinking," I told him.

"Those were no animals," he answered. "Come with me. I may save you yet." He tightened his grip on my hand, and walked on determinedly, dragging me with him.

"If you don't let go," I said, "I'll shout for help, and the Dragon will come."

He clapped his hand over my mouth, and held me, while he made a gag with his handkerchief. Then, twisting my arm, he forced me to walk very quickly. "I would rather," he said grimly, "that the whole village was wiped out by the powers of evil, than that one soul in it should be surrendered to the Devil."

I made no sound, because I couldn't, but with all my strength I wished and willed that the Dragon, and Gran'papa, and every animal, would come to my aid.

At first all was silent but for my hurrying, stumbling footsteps, and the priest's firmer tread. Then came a faint, whispering sound, like the slow sighing of trees before a storm. Then a noise like distant thunder; and soon it seemed as if the whole hill-side were awake and coming towards us.

Faster and faster the priest drove me on. My arm ached, and I could hear him panting. Closer and closer came the sounds of rescue. I could see faint colours, reflections. . . . .

Suddenly Father Binyon dropped my arm. "Go now," he said. "May God Almighty and the Lord Jesus Christ be with you and save you, where through weakness I have failed."

He went on, and I went back. In a moment I was among the animals, and a few minutes later Gran'papa had caught us up. The animals would have pursued Father Binyon, but Gran'papa forbade it, and we returned to the cave.

CHAPTER XXI

Father Binyon's warning did not trouble us much: neither did the continual stories which the animals brought of an intended attack by the villagers. They might come if they dared. We weren't afraid of them and we had no intention of leaving the Dragon; but the priest's words had reminded Gran'papa that though winter was still far away it might be wise to prepare. So we visited the bog and cut turf; later, when it had dried somewhat, Dobbin could carry it in, in panniers.

Meanwhile we endeavoured to make the cave as comfortable as possible, levelling the floor and smoothing away the rough places in the ceiling and walls. Soon it began to look quite cosy.

"If we'd only a well," Gran'papa remarked one evening, as I picked up the buckets to go and fill them at the stream, "then *every-thing* would be convenient."

"Yes," I said, "and the stream's so shallow too—unless you go away down to one of the pools—and then I always spill most of it, climbing up again."

"You can easily remedy that," he replied. "Make a dam across the stream and you'll have a pool where you want it."

"Would it be easy?" I wondered, and then an idea struck me. "The Dragon could do it," I said. "He likes burrowing. It wouldn't take him long either—just a minute or two."

But Gran'papa wasn't paying very much attention. "Do you know how the Romans brought water to their houses?" he asked.

Of course I didn't—I never did know things, he complained sometimes; but how could I, unless I learned them from him?

"In wooden pipes," he told me now. "They brought it from tanks outside the city."

"Couldn't we do that?" I asked immediately, "—from the stream?"

"We've no wood," he pointed out. "Besides, I'm afraid we're not clever enough."

"Then I'll get the Dragon to block the stream," I said, and I went off to ask him. For the time being I forgot about the Romans and their pipes.

The Dragon was quite willing and the next morning we set off together for the part of the stream nearest the cave. I showed him where to dig, and he began immediately, cutting into the earth with his fore-feet and showering it away with his hind ones. The soil flew in every direction—I was covered with it from head to foot—but only a small portion went into the stream. I got the Dragon to change his position; it was no good; whatever reached the water was immediately washed away.

Presently Gran'papa came to see how we were getting on. He

told me that I would have to make the dam myself, and he sat down on the bank to watch. The Dragon went to the jungle, and Procyon, who had come with Gran'papa, paddled about in the stream. I paddled too, carrying big stones, or rolling them along the bottom to the place where they were needed.

Gran'papa kept giving directions. "No, not that stone," he would say, "the other one. Yes, that's it, but the other way up—oh no, not like that. . . ." Eventually he pulled off his shoes and stockings and came into the stream himself. His legs struck me as curiously white and bony.

We worked hard all morning, piling the biggest stones together, one on top of another. When it was time to go to the cairn we had a little dyke stretching across the narrowest part of the stream. The top of it was above the level of the water; yet the water itself had not been raised perceptibly. The only difference that we noticed was in sound: instead of a smooth, low-toned flow, there was now something choked and irregular.

After dinner we returned and I looked at it despairingly. "It's no good," I said. "It all goes through."

"It *is* good," Gran'papa told me. "That's only the foundation."

"If we put in more earth," I answered, "it'll just be washed away like the rest—and if we fill it up with little stones it'll take ages and ages."

"Yes," Gran'papa agreed, "that's true. Now come and help me to gather some heather."

"Heather!" I said. "Will *that* stop the cracks?"

"It'll help to stop them—at least I hope so."

We pulled a great deal of heather, and soon we had quite a pile on the bank of the stream. Then we pushed it in, and it floated down and caught in the dam. Still the water flowed through, but not so fast: slowly it began to rise.

I watched, with a sort of fascination, till at one corner there burst forth a little trickle. Rapidly the trickle widened; the stream was beginning to cut a new course beside the old one. It was annoying, but we did not fill it up immediately. First we strengthened the rest of the structure, making it higher and broader, and lengthening it at the far end to prevent a similar accident there. We cut out sods too, and put them with the heather on the upper side of the dam.

We were not able to finish that day, but we returned in the morning, and blocked the new course with stones, more sods, and heather. Thus we made a little pool where we could fill the bucket without difficulty.

For some time I was satisfied. Then I remembered the Romans and their wooden pipes, and I wondered if I couldn't bring the water of the stream to the cave. Gran'papa said I was lazy, but it seems to me now that I was quite inventive and industrious. What I planned, was to change the course of the stream, so that part of it at least flowed beside the cave, returning to its original bed lower down. The Dragon was always ready to help, and he again was going to do the digging.

We started work at the bottom end, because we didn't want any water in the channel till all was finished. The other end was to be at a place some distance above our dam, where the bank was low.

There was more work to be done than I'd thought, but it was no good for *me* to dig, because, compared with the Dragon's, my efforts were infinitesimal. So I just stayed beside him and talked to him, and he got a little further every day. At the cave there was to be a small pool, but at first the Dragon only dug a plain course. I don't know how long it took him, but at last, one evening, he reached the top.

In the morning we intended to construct the pool; and make a breach in the bank to let through a quantity of water as a trial.

It was getting late when we returned to the cave, and we were surprised to see Peter there, with Gran'papa. He was very excited, and he was out of breath because he had been running.

"What's the matter?" I asked.

"They're coming to-night," he said. "They're coming to kill you —with guns and pitchforks and swords."

For a moment I was frightened, and then, with sudden relief, I answered, "But they can't: the Dragon will chase them."

"*I'll* chase them," the Dragon thought complacently, and Peter smiled.

"They're going to try anyhow," he said. "They meant to surprise you when you all were asleep."

He was very tired, for he had come all the way round by the point, so as not to be suspected. We would have liked him to remain with us, but Gran'papa thought it was too dangerous. He might be seen, or we might lose the battle. So Gran'papa made him go back by the same route as he had come, and lent him Dobbin to take him part of the way. I went with him, to bring Dobbin back.

I rode in front and Peter rode behind, and Dobbin's feet went ploppety-plop, down the hill.

"When are they going to come?" I asked.

"In the very early morning, not long after midnight, when they think you'll be sleeping the soundest."

Ploppety-plop, ploppety-plop.

"How did you find out they were coming?"

"Peadar Finnegan told me. He said: 'Your friends will have a grand sleep the night.' 'What d'you mean?' I asked him. 'Because they'll never wake up,' he says, and then I knowed what he meaned."

"It was clever of you to know," I said. "It was good that you did."

"Then me father heard two of them talking. They were talking of meeting at the churchyard after midnight, and he thought they were up to no good, though he didn't know what it was—but that's what it'll be sure enough."

Ploppety-plop, ploppety-plop.

We followed a path along the top of the cliffs, where, looking down, we could see the waves, like shadows, breaking on the shore. It was some time after sunset, and in the atmosphere was a peculiar whiteness, almost merging into grey. The landscape could be seen, though not perfectly distinctly. The rounded slopes and contours, cut off so suddenly by the edge of the cliff, gave the impression that they were not hard rock and earth, but vapours and evening mists. It was one of those times when nature enforces silence even on small boys, and Peter and I jogged along together without speaking.

Eventually we reached our place of parting. He slipped down without a word, and I thanked him again for what he had done.

I turned back, and found that while we had been watching the sea, night had stolen up behind us and taken possession of the land. I was lonely now, and the whole world seemed lonely too. I dug my heels into Dobbin, but though he was going towards a stable he would not hurry. I think that for some reason his stable at the cave did not satisfy him, and he pined for his own old stable at home.

When I left the cliffs and went upwards again, I noticed a curious thing. All around me in the heather were small noises, like the rustling of many creatures. I feared they were ghosts or goblins, or the little people, and I hardly dared to look down lest I should see them. Yet from time to time I did look, with hurried, frightened glances—and I saw nothing but a vague blackness. I wished the journey was over; but now I was bound, as if by a spell of terror. I sat quite still, and Dobbin plodded on at his own slow pace.

At last I came over a fold in the hill and saw a red glow in front of me. Gran'papa had lit a fire to guide me back. As I got nearer my terrors dissolved, and by the faint, reflected light of the flames I saw who my travelling companions had been. They were all sorts of animals—snakes, and foxes, and rabbits, and scorpions, and mice—with many other creatures besides, all scurrying and hopping and slinking, on their way to the great battle against the men of the village.

"I'm glad you're back," Gran'papa said. "Now warm yourself at the fire—and you'll have to keep awake. While you were away Procyon went out to tell some of the animals, and *they*'re going to tell the rest."

I was thankful enough to get warm, for it was the coldest night since we'd left the cottage. I stretched out my hands to the blaze, and looked round to see what animals had come. But, though there were a great many, I couldn't see more than a face here and there. The flickering circle enlarged and contracted, and sometimes the light was pale yellow, and sometimes red.

Gran'papa was rather restless, going in and out of the cave, and counting the fresh arrivals of animals. But in spite of what he had said I began to feel sleepy. Procyon lay with his head on my knees, and with my arms half round him I leaned drowsily against the Dragon, and blinked at the fire.

"Do you think they've started yet?" I asked Gran'papa, when, at the end of one of his tours of inspection, he came and stood beside us.

"No; there's still an hour to midnight, though I doubt if, after all, they'll wait till then."

The Dragon yawned, showing a mouth so big that both Peter and I could have got into it at once. It was like a cavern itself, with a double row of huge teeth on upper and lower jaws. "Could we not go to sleep now, and wake up again when they come?" he wondered heavily.

"No," Gran'papa answered. "We must keep on the alert—we should really post a sentry."

I jumped up. "Please Gran'papa, can I be sentry?"

Gran'papa shook his head. "No," he said, "you're not to get mixed up in this. You can watch from a distance—and remember, if anything goes wrong, go straight home to your mother."

"But Gran'papa . . ." I began. He gave me a sort of "no nonsense" look, and I didn't like to go on.

"Where's Procyon?" Gran'papa asked.

"He's gone," I said. "He was here a moment ago."

"He's at the top of the hill," the Dragon told us. "He's keeping watch."

"Perhaps, of course," Gran'papa reflected, "Father Binyon will get to hear of it and be able to stop them."

"*Would* he stop them?" I asked, "—after our not going with him when he came to get us back?"

"Oh yes, he would try. He doesn't want murder."

Something pressed against my legs, and I started. "Oh, Polyphemus, is it you?" I stroked him. "*He'll* know," I said.

We asked him.

"Father Binyon is sleeping soundly, and outside the churchyard wall the men are gathering—yeaow."

"*Poor puss,*" I exclaimed, "what's the matter?"

"There's nothing the matter," Gran'papa said. "He's just trying his voice," and he was right.

Every minute more and more animals would arrive. All the strange creatures from the jungle, all the wild animals who visited us in the evenings; bulls and rams—and every single goat in the neighbourhood, each with his queer eyes glinting in sour pleasure. Then, in a long single file, came the ganders, with their necks stretched out menacingly. At the same time came the remaining dogs and cats, but about half the dogs went away again quickly, because they could not fight against their masters. Among the cats there were no such scruples. Silently they sharpened their claws on an old log, which Gran'papa used as a seat.

"I think," Gran'papa said, "that our best plan is to pretend we suspect nothing. We'll hide, and then they'll go into the cave to kill us, and we'll have them trapped."

"How many will there be?" I wondered.

"All the men are coming," one of the animals answered, "except those who are too old, and Father Binyon and Michael Rymple."

"I've got another plan," I said. "We could wash them all away with water. There's only a little bit of bank left between the stream and my channel. If the Dragon dug that out at the right moment the water would gush down suddenly on top of them all."

"But we'll need the Dragon," Gran'papa objected. "We'll need him down here to fight."

I was disappointed, but the Dragon had an idea. "They won't all go into the cave," he said. "A great many of them will stand about outside, just where the water will flow."

"But in any case," Gran'papa interrupted, "we'll need you to make the attack."

"I know you will," the Dragon replied, "and I will be there to make it. Just as they have discovered that we are not in the cave the water will sweep down upon them and throw them into confusion. After the water I will come, then the rest of you—and we shall see how long they will stay."

"That's a good plan," Gran'papa agreed. "You can go up there now—and Wolfe, *you* must remain there. Meanwhile the rest of us will hide."

Suddenly Procyon reappeared. "There's somebody coming," he told us, "one single person."

"Hurry," Gran'papa said, "all to our places." The Dragon and I climbed the hill, and the others hid themselves near the cave.

It was tiresome waiting, and for a long time no one appeared. Procyon went by close to us, on his way up the hill, and I knew Gran'papa must have sent him to find out what was happening. A little later he showed on the sky-line, and at the same time there appeared, not far from him, a dark figure. Procyon avoided it: they both sank once more out of sight, and it was some time before we saw either. Then the moon shone for an instant and revealed a woman hurrying towards the cave. It was Mother.

It must have been she whom Procyon had noticed at first, though she had been too far off for him to recognize her. There followed an interval of darkness, and after it passed she was standing at the mouth of the cave, hesitant. Suddenly she plunged in, and when we saw her again she was looking in our direction; but before the dark background of the heather she could not see us. Her face was very white and haggard in the half shadow of the moonlight. "Wolfe," she called, "Wolfe, come to me."

Hearing her I felt almost compelled to go, and I might have, had I not remembered that it would mean deserting Gran'papa.

"Wolfe," she called again and again, each time a little louder, "Wolfe."

There was no answer. Slowly she looked round, but so well were we all hidden by the shadows and unevenness of the hillside that the whole place seemed bare and abandoned.

The moon went in and left her standing there, solitary and unanswered. None of us moved, and there was no sound but the faint far-away murmur of the waves, the rustling of the stream, and the occasional slight hiss of a breeze through the heather.

For a long time after that it was completely dark, and we began to fear that the villagers would reach the cave without our knowledge. Then once more the moon shone. Mother must have gone home. All looked still, and silent, and deserted. By this time the clouds had drifted away, and the moon had a clear path through the sky.

Presently we heard a faint sound of voices; the pale light glinted on metal; and we saw a body of men cross the summit of the hill. "Here they are," I muttered.

I was strung up now to the highest pitch, and so was the Dragon. It was with difficulty that I prevented him from letting loose the water when they were just over the top. "Not yet," I whispered. "Remember our plans."

The men came down the hill slowly, stopping every few minutes to look round, and to mutter among themselves. At last they formed a half circle round the entrance to the cave, and five or six, armed with guns and pistols and swords and knives, went in. Six more, with pitchforks pointing inwards, stood ready behind them.

"Now," I told the Dragon.

In a few seconds the bank was broken, and the stream began a surging, tumultuous course in its new channel.

For a moment we watched it splashing down, and then, with a thump of his feet, the Dragon went after it. It was the Dragon's feet which gave the first warning, but a moment later he unfolded his wings and swooped like a bird of prey. Immediately every kind of noise was let loose—cries of fear, hissings of snakes, barkings of dogs, meeyowings of cats, bellowings of bulls, and many other strange sounds—battle-cries of toads and lizards, and giant cater-pillars, and scorpions. . . .

The villagers who had been in the cave rushed out and gazed up in consternation. A minute later the water swept in among them, knocking over some and soaking many. Then, springing from their hiding-places, came the animals. Cats jumped on the men's backs and tore at their faces and ears. Round the legs of others the snakes curled, while scorpions darted at them and stung them. Some were bitten by dogs; others were nibbled by mice. I saw Cauley staring in horror at the Dragon, quite unaware of a bull who was approaching him from behind. Down went the bull's head; up went Cauley. He came to earth with a bang, but scram-bling to his feet he began to run. The others were doing the same. The villagers were defeated.

I no longer remembered Gran'papa's orders. I charged down the hill to join in the pursuit. I didn't know where Gran'papa was, but I discovered that he had told the animals that unless it was absolutely necessary no one was to be killed or seriously injured.

Now there were no sounds but the drumming of feet, my shouts, and the cries of the animals. The villagers, in their utter terror, were completely silent. Soon I was among pursuers and pursued. Cats bounded through the heather beside me at an incredible speed. Soon we left behind the wriggling snakes and the mice, and many other small animals as well. Some of the bigger ones, too, began to drop out, till only Procyon and I, and the cats and the dogs and the rabbits, were left pursuing—and really many of the dogs weren't pursuing, for they were in front of the men, going backwards, and jumping up and snapping at them.

Then a new misfortune befell the villagers. Suddenly a small party of giant caterpillars, arriving late for the fight, reared their heads out of the heather. To avoid them many turned to one side, and not looking where they were going, floundered into the bog.

I couldn't run any further, and I sank down exhausted in the heather. The animals, including the caterpillars, gathered round me, and when we had all rested we returned in triumph to the cave.

Gran'papa and the Dragon were together at the cave mouth, and I was afraid that Gran'papa would be angry with me for disobeying his orders and joining in the pursuit. But he was too elated to think of that. "Where were you?" he asked, "—fighting to the finish? Did you enjoy it?"

"Oh yes," I answered. "It was lovely—didn't the water do well? —and the Dragon? I wish they'd come every night."

"It was the Dragon who decided the battle," Gran'papa said.

"Actually," the Dragon told us, "I didn't do anything. After I let loose the water I flew down to the cave—and I haven't moved since. All the same, I think I was a great help."

It was perfectly true. It was he, not the scratching cats, nor biting dogs, nor hissing snakes, who had brought us the victory.

So we went on, talking excitedly, till the sun rose on the most extraordinary army the world has ever seen. Then I fell asleep, and when I awoke, late in the afternoon, they had all gone but Gran'-papa and Procyon and the Dragon. If the villagers had come then, when we were asleep, they could have killed us in a moment, for we had posted no sentries.

Without waking the others I went up to the cairn. There were our provisions, just as usual, except perhaps that there were rather more.

CHAPTER XXII

I returned to the cave. The fire had gone out long ago and to-day, for the first time, there was no sun: it was colder than it had been. Suddenly the Dragon coughed in his sleep, a huge, rusty cough. He awoke, and the sound woke Gran'papa also.

"Is it late?" he asked, looking round with an air of astonishment.

"It's nearly evening again," I answered.

"Good gracious!" He got up and stretched stiffly. "The air's very sharp. Don't you feel it?"

The Dragon sneezed. We all got splashed, and Procyon yelped and ran into the cave.

"Have you caught cold?" I asked the Dragon, but he didn't understand.

"I'm hungry," he thought, and lumbered off to the forest.

"I'm hungry too," Gran'papa said. "I wonder if there's any food at the cairn."

"I've brought it," I told him, and I began to unwrap the parcels. There were eggs, butter, and cream; a chicken and a duck; honey —and of course bread, and vegetables.

Gran'papa looked at them and smiled. "A peace offering," he said.

For two or three days the food continued to be better, but soon it relapsed to its former quality. I suppose they realized that we had no intentions of revenge.

Indeed everything was the same as it had been before the fight, except the weather. After several months, all extraordinarily dry and hot, it began to be rainy and cold. It did not rain all the time, but frequent gusty showers blew in from the sea. It was no longer a pleasure to visit the beach. Every night we lit a fire, and this attracted many more of the smaller creatures, who came to the cave for shelter and heat.

The Dragon went as little as possible to the jungle, and spent most of his time in the cave, dozing uncomfortably. The draughts made him shiver, his head was stuffed up, and however big we built the fire it did not warm him completely. Day by day the wind increased, till a week after the fight it became a gale.

When we awoke on the next Sunday morning it was quite fine, though there was no sun, and the wind was still blowing with tremendous force.

We wondered what had become of the Sea Serpent; and Gran'papa and I decided to go to the beach to see if there were any sign of him.

We left the Dragon at the cave, and it was only after some hesitation that Procyon, who I think was tougher than the other creatures, decided to accompany us. The air was filled with salt spray, and in it floated creamy gatherings of foam, which settled here and there on the heather.

We went to the shore by our usual path, down the gorge of the stream. The stream was thick and muddy, though being so short, it was no longer in flood.

For a time the sea was out of sight, but when we reached the bottom of the gorge it tossed before us, a wild, streaky grey, and rougher than I had ever seen except in the worst of the winter storms; nor had I ever been on this shore when the waves were breaking so high on the beach. They came thundering in like moving walls, hurling the big stones up the bed of the stream, and then, in their backwash, sucking them down again, with a dismal rumbling sound. I remembered how, when I was very small, Mother had told me that the angels made thunder by rolling big stones in heaven. I was always afraid that they might fall through on top of us.

The present scene was a little terrifying too, though thrilling and exhilarating as well.

We went along the shore at the foot of the sandhills and just out of reach of the waves. We looked across the water in every direction, and from end to end of the beach; but there was no sign of the Sea Serpent.

"He's very wise," Gran'papa said. "He's probably away out in some deep place, lying on the sea-bed in the sand, where all is calm and smooth and pleasant, and the storm is far away."

"I suppose it's always calm down there."

"Yes; the waves are only on the surface; down below it never changes."

I thought of this for a while. "I suppose the bed of the sea is like another country, all by itself. It must be strange when sunk ships drop onto it, filled with dead men. It'd be horrid."

"It would," Gran'papa agreed. "And what's that there?"

"It's like a plank of a boat."

On the shore were all sorts of rubbish and driftwood, and here and there we saw other planks as well.

"I wonder where they came from?" Gran'papa said. "Maybe some big ship has foundered; and this is one of the boats."

I looked at the planks closely; they were painted a bluish grey. "It's very like the *Cassie Donovan*," I said.

Gran'papa stopped and stared, "Michael's boat!" he exclaimed.
"Yes," I answered, "it was just that colour."

Gran'papa frowned. "I hope it's not," he muttered, and I hoped so too. We both liked Michael. I had often been out in that boat, if it *was* it. Besides, it would be terrible for Peter.

We didn't say any more about it. We left the beach by the path at the other end, and returned to the cave. Then I went to the cairn to see if our provisions had arrived.

At the cairn I found Teady McGeough. He had emptied his basket and was going away, but he turned when he saw me. "Did you hear about Michael?" he asked.

"Michael Rymple?" I said, though at once I felt quite certain of what had happened.

"Sure, what other Michael would it be? He was drownded out in the boat. The wee lad's cryin' his eyes out."

"How did it happen?"

"He went out for the lobster pots. He thought he'd get back before the storm was bad. That was on Friday—the foolishest day to do it."

"What's happened to Peter?" I asked.

"He's gone to live with his uncle."

"But Peter hates him," I exclaimed.

"Aye—an' the old man's mad too, at havin' to take him."

"Of course Michael *may* come back," I said, thinking for the moment that he might have been blown into some other harbour: then I remembered the planks.

"How'd he come back?" Teady asked, picking up his basket again, and turning round. "It's nonsense you're talkin'."

"You talk more nonsense yourself," I retorted, but he stalked off, pretending he hadn't heard.

I went back to Gran'papa and repeated what I had learned. "Why couldn't Peter live with *us*?" I suggested. "There's no danger now."

Gran'papa shook his head. "It'd be better not," he told me, though he wouldn't tell me the reason. I tried to persuade him to change his mind, but the most he would promise was to think it over.

Still, I hadn't much hope, and I felt very sorry for Peter when I saw him coming towards me next morning. I had gone to bring in turf, and I waited for him. He was looking very miserable.

"Hullo," he called, in a subdued voice.

"Hullo," I answered rather uncomfortably, because I didn't know whether to mention his father or not.

He drew closer. "Did you hear what happened?"

"Yes," I replied, "Teady told me."

"Wolfe," he said, "do you think your grandfather would let me come and live with you?"

I told him what Gran'papa had said the day before. "I'm afraid he won't. He was going to think it over, but that usually means he won't."

"He *might*," Peter exclaimed, and it sounded almost as if he were going to cry. "Didn't I warn him about the people, and them comin' to kill you?"

"You did, but I don't think it's like that. I think he'd like you to come—but. . . . I think he's got another reason. You'd be better to see him."

"And that's not all either," Peter went on. "I've something *else* to tell him." We went together to the cave.

Gran'papa was sitting in front of the fire, roasting a chicken on a pointed stick. The perspiration was showing on his forehead, and his face was red with the heat. "Come along," he said to Peter, "and help me to cook, and you can stay and help to eat it when it's ready. Wolfe, you go along to the cairn and see if the food's arrived."

"Don't let him go there," Peter said hurriedly. "Make him go somewhere else."

"But need I go at all?" I asked. "The food won't have arrived yet anyhow."

"Yes," Gran'papa answered, "go on—go down to the shore or somewhere, Peter and I want to have a talk together."

I didn't much like having to do what Peter ordered, but of course I went, though I wondered what was happening at the cairn. I stayed away a long time too, so that they could talk as much as they wanted, and it must have been nearly half-past twelve when I returned to the cave to get my share of the chicken.

"Is he going to live with us?" I asked Gran'papa, as soon as I was near enough to speak.

"No." Gran'papa shook his head, and Peter looked doleful: but I could see he'd known already, and that somehow or other Gran'papa had persuaded him it was better to live with his uncle.

"Did you tell him the other thing?"

"Yes," Peter said.

"What was it?" I asked.

Peter looked awkward, but Gran'papa answered for him. "Don't be so inquisitive," he told me. "It's a secret between Peter and me."

That was all he would tell, and after we had eaten our dinner he took me to one side, and made me promise I wouldn't question Peter. "Now," he said, "I'm going myself to see if the food has come. You and Peter had better stay here."

"I'll go and get it," I answered. "I always do."

"No," he replied. "You've had one journey already. I want to get it myself to-day."

So Peter and I remained. I kept my promise and did not ask any questions, though Gran'papa was away a long time.

The Dragon returned first, coughing a great deal, and when Gran'papa did come he brought no food. "I want you to come up the hill with me," he said to the Dragon. "It's for a special reason. Peter, you'd better go home—but mind nobody sees you. Wolfe, you stay in the cave till I come back."

So only Procyon and I were left, and I wondered more than ever what the mystery could be.

CHAPTER XXIII

It was to keep me from being frightened, of course, that Gran'-papa made such a secret of the whole matter. But it was no use, because when I was with the Dragon I couldn't help seeing what had taken place on the hill, every time it crossed his mind. So very soon I knew the whole story, except for one part which he managed to keep a secret.

Peter had learned, by overhearing a conversation between his uncle and aunt, that our food was to be poisoned, and that either Cauley or Finnegan would have something to do with it.

It was for this reason Gran'papa decided to go to the cairn, so that he could question the messenger when he arrived. He intended to ask him to taste the food, and if the child refused, he would know he had been warned not to eat it: but it might not be a child, it might be a man; then he would be additionally suspicious, because for a long time only children had come.

It was a boy who brought the basket, but as soon as Gran'papa saw him he knew that the plan he had made would not do. The boy was Patrick Creel.

He was an orphan, a little simple, and Gran'papa was sorry for him. He at once felt sure that the food *had* been poisoned, and that they had chosen this poor creature because he knew nothing about it, and because, if anything went wrong, no one would miss him. He was almost a beggar. He lived with a grandmother as poor as himself in a small cottage at the far end of the village. He worked at times for Cauley or Finnegan; but his wages were small. His father had been drowned years ago, when a curragh overturned, and his mother had died soon after.

Perhaps, however, he *did* know. If *he* refused the food it would be certain proof; and Gran'papa considered offering it. Yet, if he didn't know and accepted, Gran'papa would have to keep it from him—and to Patrick that would look very unkind.

Thus Gran'papa watched him approach, uncertain how he should act.

The boy seemed nervous, but that was natural enough. Doubtless many strange tales were told in the village.

"Don't be afraid, Patrick," Gran'papa said to him. "I'm not going to hurt you."

He was very thin, and ragged, and because he looked hungrily at the food Gran'papa felt convinced of his innocence.

Patrick stopped some yards from Gran'papa, and regarded him distrustfully. "They told me to leave it at the cairn, and make no mistake," he said.

"Where you are will do quite well," Gran'papa assured him, "but don't be so frightened."

"They say you can weave spells," Patrick answered, "and make a body dumb by just touching."

"Who says that?"

"Them ones down in the village."

"Well, I won't put any spells on *you*," Gran'papa promised him. "Now put down the basket."

"They say it was you as brought the storm."

"I hope you didn't believe them," Gran'papa replied quietly, and Patrick blushed.

"I didn't know, Master: sometimes they tell me what's not right; and sometimes they tell me true things so as I think they're not true; but they say Michael was drownded because he was your friend, and wouldn't hear a word against you."

"That had nothing to do with it," Gran'papa said, "and you can tell them so when you get back. Now it'll do if you leave the basket there. I can get it myself."

"I'm to leave it at the cairn, Master, and no mistake."

"You never brought the food before?" Gran'papa asked.

"No—only to-day."

"Why is that?"

Patrick looked puzzled. "Maybe they thought I'd break something," he replied, "and I was working for Cauley—I'm working out all the time now. He wouldn't let me off, except to-day. He always said to send some of the children as had nothing to do."

"So you have no idea why they sent you to-day?"

"No, Master, how would I?"

Gran'papa reflected. "Listen to this carefully," he said, "and remember it carefully. Go straight back to the village and find Father Binyon. Ask him to come here immediately with Cauley and Finnegan. Tell him that if he does not come I will be compelled to go to the village with the Dragon. Can you remember that?"

Patrick nodded, but did not move away. "I be to leave the basket," he said.

"All right," Gran'papa answered, "but first repeat what I have told you: then I will go, and you can leave the basket by the cairn."

Patrick obeyed. Gran'papa walked some distance away. Patrick put the basket beside the cairn, and turned and ran. "Don't be afraid," Gran'papa called to him. "Even if I do visit the village, I won't harm you or your grandmother."

After that Gran'papa came to the cave for the Dragon, and they returned together to the cairn.

For a long time there was no sign of anybody, and Gran'papa

began to wonder if his threat would be effective. Now that the corn was in stook they might be less frightened than they would have been a month earlier. If that were the case, he would take the Dragon to the village and see how great was their courage.

He had almost decided on this course, when he noticed three figures beginning the ascent of the hill. For a while he watched them, and they seemed to move very slowly. He turned to the Dragon, who was chewing a huge green plant he had brought from the jungle.

"You're not coughing now," Gran'papa said.

"I do not cough," the Dragon answered, "so long as I chew this plant."

Gran'papa examined it closely. It had a thick green stalk, covered with profuse clusters of deep purple flowers. The Dragon was eating the flowers: he squeezed them between his teeth, so that a treacly substance flowed into his mouth and squirted in small drops to the ground. Gran'papa took a flower and squeezed it himself. The extract was sticky and slightly sweet. After he had swallowed it he felt a tingling glow in his mouth and throat.

When next he glanced down the hill the three men were much closer, and soon he could make out the expressions on their faces. They were all hot—it *was* hot again to-day, and if only the weather stayed like this it would be more pleasant for the Dragon.

But it was not pleasant if you were climbing a steep hill-side, and Cauley and Father Binyon looked more and more angry the nearer they came: Finnegan was too frightened to be angry—and suddenly, when they were less than a hundred yards from Gran'papa, he stopped and pointed. The others stopped also. For the first time they saw the Dragon.

Gran'papa smiled to himself; then he too looked at the Dragon, motionless but ready, beside the cairn. His big head rested on the ground, and with steady unblinking eyes he grimly watched the approaching villagers. It was surprising that they hadn't noticed him before, but against certain backgrounds his mottled green skin was almost invisible. Besides, during the labour of the ascent their eyes had probably been set straight before them; they had no energy to spare for wandering glances.

After this short hesitation the three men advanced once more. Father Binyon was slightly in front of the others, and his eyebrows were contracted in a black frown. His face was damp with sweat, and nearly purple with anger and exertion.

"What's all this about?" he demanded fiercely. "Something important I hope, to bring me traipsing up a mountain in weather like this."

"It's very important," Gran'papa answered simply, "and I had several reasons for asking you to come."

The priest sat down on a boulder, and looked at Gran'papa. "I would like to hear them," he said.

"So you shall," Gran'papa replied. "First of all, I knew that without you these two would be afraid to come, and if they *hadn't* come the Dragon and I would have had to go to the village to find them. There might have been some damage. Chiefly, however, I brought you to hear a confession. No, not your last confession"— he glanced at the miserable conspirators, who at these words had turned pale—"but by rights it ought to be."

"It wasn't us," they exclaimed simultaneously. "It must be a mistake."

"They are lying," said the Dragon.

"You are lying," said Gran'papa—and then through the Dragon he saw what was going on in their minds. "Cauley," he went on, "last night you went out alone to search for a hemlock plant."

"*I* knew nothing about it," Finnegan interrupted almost in a scream. "I wasn't there."

"He is lying," said the Dragon.

"You are lying," said Gran'papa. "The day before yesterday you talked it over together in the boat-house. You planned that Cauley was to come with the plant to your barn, and that there you would compound it into a juice and put the juice into this little bottle of poteen."

"He thought of it all himself," stammered Finnegan. "I had nothing. . . ."

"He is lying," said the Dragon.

"You are lying," said Gran'papa.

Cauley looked at Finnegan contemptuously. "What's the good?" he asked. "It's magic, can't you see? Yes; we did it."

"And is it only in the poteen?"

"Only. . . ." Finnegan began.

"He is lying," said the Dragon.

"You are . . ."

But Cauley interrupted. "It's in everything," he said. "We were only going to put it in the poteen. Then we put it in everything to make sure." He had spoken the last few sentences with a sort of furious self-control, but now all of a sudden his temper burst out. "And I hope you break your neck," he shouted, "and that the Devil takes you—and he will too, and it won't be long either. There! Now you know what I think of you and you can do what you like."

He spat on the ground, but Gran'papa didn't pay any attention to him, though when he was telling me about it he said he liked Cauley better than Finnegan, because he was more straightforward.

Gran'papa turned now to Father Binyon. Father Binyon hadn't uttered a word the whole time. He had just listened in astonishment. "Well," Gran'papa asked, "what do you think of it?"

Before answering, Father Binyon spoke in a low voice to Cauley and Finnegan. "Go over there," he told them sternly. "I'll deal with *you* later." They shambled off a little way and looked round uncertainly. "Further," Father Binyon called, and not till they were quite out of earshot did he allow them to stop. Then he said to Gran'papa, "It's the first I knew of this, but I'm not so very much surprised."

"Nor am I," Gran'papa said, "but I don't want it to happen again—because if we hadn't been warned we'd have eaten that food."

"Oh!" the priest exclaimed, "so you *were* warned. Who warned you?"

"It was Peter Rymple as a matter of fact, but he doesn't want anyone to know, and I think he's very wise."

The priest nodded. "Very. I thought possibly one of the animals had warned you. Wolfe told me once that you got to know things through them." He looked searchingly at Gran'papa. "You do, don't you?"

Gran'papa smiled. "Oh, yes," he said.

"It all seems to me so strange," Father Binyon began. "I felt it that night I visited you, but differently then, perhaps, only because it *was* night." And suddenly he went on impulsively, "Why don't you tell me about it? I mean tell me everything."

So Gran'papa told him the whole story. He spoke hesitatingly at first, but gradually as he recalled our various adventures with the Dragon he forgot how unlikely they must seem, and spoke more easily. Besides, Father Binyon believed him. He could feel that, and that he was not unsympathetic. He listened very attentively and without once interrupting, and when the story was over it was nearly a minute before he spoke. Then he pointed to the Dragon. "Do you think he would talk to *me*?" he asked.

"If *you* talk to him," Gran'papa said. "Try and he'll answer you."

The priest hesitated. "But I don't know how," he began.

Then he looked up a little surprised, for the Dragon was moving closer. "What do you want to know?" the Dragon asked, but the priest did not reply.

"What do you want to know?" the Dragon repeated, but still the priest was silent and puzzled.

"What do you want to know?" the Dragon asked a third time, and suddenly Father Binyon understood.

"I've got it," he exclaimed. "I know what he's saying." But for a moment he couldn't think of any question to ask. Then he said, "Had they any religion. . . . Had the men when you lived before any religion? Did they worship . . . ? Did they bow down . . . ?"

"Oh yes," the Dragon replied. "They bowed down to the sun, to the moon, and to the stars. They killed animals, or sometimes one of themselves: they were always killing."

"And had they priests?"

"Oh, yes, they had priests too. They worked very little, but the other people gave them food and they grew fat. That I could not understand either."

"I believe all you've told me," Father Binyon said at last to Gran'papa, "but it doesn't really solve any of the problems. You see, the people are against you. I had great difficulty some weeks ago in preventing them from going to the cave at night to try and murder you."

"You didn't prevent them," Gran'papa said drily. "They came."

"Oh, and what happened?"

"Fortunately we were warned on that occasion also and we were able to deal with the situation." He told the story of the fight.

"Are you not afraid," Father Binyon asked when he had finished, "that there may be other situations and that perhaps you will not always be able to deal with them?"

"I don't see why there should be any more," Gran'papa answered; "they ought to have learned their lesson by this time, and if they think we have magic aid they should be all the more frightened of us."

The priest considered. "Of course they *are* frightened to a certain extent; but now they hate you, and hate as well as love, you know, can cast out fear."

"And do they hate us so much just because they have to feed us?"

"Oh, no, though of course they resent that too, I dare say. But it's your evil influence they're afraid of. In any community, as you know well enough, there are always mishaps of one kind and another. I don't really believe that this summer we have been any more unfortunate than usual, but whatever misfortunes there were have been blamed on you."

"I remember about the fishing of course," Gran'papa said. "That was ridiculous."

"Yes, and then there was the drought and now the storm, but that's not all by any means. Every little thing is remembered against you, from blight on an apple-tree to the death of old Flaherty, who was eighty-four. They are convinced that until you either die or give up your present way of life these disasters will continue."

"And Wolfe . . . ?"

"Well, naturally he isn't popular, though really I think they regard him more as your victim than anything else. I mean, if they had succeeded in their expedition to the cave they would have killed *you*, but Wolfe would have been brought home safely enough."

Gran'papa reflected. "Is there no hope of disillusioning them?"

The priest smiled and shook his head. "Not the slightest. You must remember that every priest of this parish has spent half his time fighting superstition, and never before has a superstition had such good foundation as this. If only you would come home. . . ."

"I won't go home," Gran'papa said stubbornly.

"It would be the only way. I believe I could get them to look on it as a sort of treaty. You would give up the Dragon. They would give up their revenge."

At this point Gran'papa got up and went over to the Dragon. They stood together and Gran'papa put his arm round the Dragon's neck and the Dragon rubbed his head against Gran'papa. "We'll never give each other up, will we?" Gran'papa said, and the Dragon said they wouldn't.

"So you see," Gran'papa told Father Binyon. "I'm going to stay here; and even if something did happen I wouldn't want to return. This life of the last few months has been so happy that I wouldn't want any other . . ."

"And what about Wolfe?" asked Father Binyon.

"I hadn't forgotten him," Gran'papa replied. "Wolfe . . ."

.   .   .   .

But the Dragon had stopped. His mind was a complete and impenetrable blank.

"What did they say about me?" I demanded anxiously.

"I don't know."

"You don't know? Didn't you hear?"

"No—just at that moment I fell asleep."

I looked at the Dragon suspiciously. Could he, could the Dragon be telling a lie?

As a matter of fact I eventually learned the rest, but at the time I knew nothing—only that Gran'papa and the Dragon had gone up the hill on some mysterious errand.

CHAPTER XXIV

At last they returned, and a little later I was sent to the cairn to see if fresh provisions had been brought. They had, and there was never another attempt to poison our food. From that day too the weather improved, and our life went on as it had done some weeks earlier.

The Dragon's cough had gone, and there was no longer an absolute need to light the fire. But because the animals liked it we lit it, and every night they came to the cave and we discussed together all the news of the day.

"The Sea Serpent's going to-morrow," a green lizard murmured one evening, in envious tones.

"To-morrow!" I exclaimed. "I never knew."

"Next week," the Dragon thought.

"Next week," the lizard repeated. To him time was a negligible thing. All the future was to-morrow, and the past was yesterday. This very moment was the present—and now that also had gone, slipping away unperceived, like the ticking of a clock.

"Where's he going to?" asked a fox. He had stolen up quietly, and was at the very outside of the circle, among the horses and donkeys and cows. None of *them* had ever seen the Sea Serpent. To them he was the most mysterious creature of all, existing only in the thoughts of others.

As soon as the dogs realized who had asked this question their hair bristled, and they growled low growls. The cats washed their faces and watched, but the Dragon, to whom these social differences seemed more remote than the age when he was born, answered: "He is going to the far southwest, travelling a great distance in the depths of the sea."

"How can he live in the sea?" a donkey thought, a mystified expression on his greyish brown face.

"He lives with the fish," a cat replied. "If only I too could swim like that—but the water's so wet."

"Does he catch the fish?" the fox wondered, but nobody answered.

Perhaps the Dragon knew, or the snakes, or the lizards, or the giant caterpillars, but it was early in the evening still, and most of them were comatose or asleep. It was always like that. When the fire was freshly lit the dogs and the cats, and all the more modern animals, took the chief parts in the conversation; but gradually, as the heat increased, their eyes, which at first had stared steadily into the flames, would begin to blink and grow heavy. The open periods would become shorter and shorter, till finally they would close their eyes completely, and curl up, and sleep. At the same time the others, the creatures from the ancient world, would begin to awake. Their dozing had been cold and shivery, and they needed the heat to enliven them. The Dragon's eyes would brighten and his thoughts come more quickly. Only his fore-paws and head could get near the fire, but now, with so many companions pressed round him, there were always furry animals and hairy animals to warm his huge body and tail.

It was in such a state they were happiest: then they would talk of the old time, while among them their remote descendants would snore in heavy sleep.

Not till we had reached this period in the evening did we learn much more of the Sea Serpent and his plans.

It was the same lizard, who awoke suddenly from a dream, and told us with a yawn, "He's asking everyone about his journey. He talks to seals and porpoises—even an old, mournful gull, who is supposed to have travelled once a long distance to a foreign land."

"Some believe," thought a snake, "that under the sea there is a great hot place. A wise fish, who finds himself swimming in warmer water, will turn back—because in the very middle there is nothing at all—just a great heat, and if you fell into it, it would burn you up. They say that it is near to this place the sea serpents live now, and that it will be quite easy for him to get there."

"I saw him this morning," the Dragon said. "He told me that that isn't true, or else it is far away, and also in the southern sea. He went to look where the porpoise thought it was, and he did find a huge mountain right under the water, and the sea was very hot; but nothing else was there—no fish, no crabs, no lobsters. He went away, and when he had travelled a little distance there was a great explosion; he knew that if he had been nearer he would have been killed. It was because of this danger there were no fish."

"Perhaps the sea serpents did live there," suggested the snake, "when it became too cold everywhere else, and they may all have been killed by some explosion."

"Very likely," the Dragon said, "—and there may be other dragons—if only I knew! Possibly there is some hidden forest on some hidden island, where it is still hot and everything is as it used to be. Yet even if that were so, how could I get there?"

"If you do go," I exclaimed, for it seemed that there must be a way, "you'll take us with you, won't you?"

"And us, and us, and us . . ." echoed snakes and scorpions and lizards, and every strange creature—but one.

He only, in the midst of this tropical dream, was homesick for snow and ice. I put out my hand and groped, till in the darkness I touched a stone, chill, and slightly damp. At the same moment the cold influence grew stronger. I realized that what I grasped was not a stone, but something awake and alive. An entirely new picture gradually clarified in my mind.

Here, too, was a sea, which emerged slowly from enshrouding mists of half-dead memory. It was bluish green and very deep. On it there floated huge sheets and blocks of ice. That part alone was clear. Round the edges, appearing fitfully, was a white land, with black rocks sticking through the snow. I saw a grey-white reptile on the ice.

"Where did *you* come from?" I asked the stony creature, in surprise.

"I too was uncovered," he answered, "at the time the earth moved."

"But you're not like the others. You don't think like them."

"No," he agreed sadly. "I am different. I come from an age more early still. Before these creatures were conceived, or their eggs laid, I lived my life and buried myself, still living, in the earth. Why I continued to live I do not know, but gradually I became encased in stone. Before I lived perhaps there were other periods, some hot, some cold, and there must have been many since. In every period there must have been living creatures who disappeared with their time."

"And you lived in a cold time?"

"All the world was ice and snow."

"Then," I said, "does the fire not trouble you?"

"I feel no fire," he answered.

"Why is that?"

"Because I am more than half turned to rock. The crust which formed round me grows thicker every year—inwards and out-wards. I feel neither heat nor cold, moisture nor drought."

"But how did you get up here?" I asked. "It was in the jungle the land slipped."

"Don't you remember," he thought, "that this afternoon you picked up stones, and threw them for the green creature?"

"For Procyon?"

"That was what you called him. I was under those stones, and he carried me here in his mouth."

"I'm sorry," I said, "but I didn't know."

"Don't be sorry," he answered. "I like the company."

After that I could see nothing more. The door was closed, and I felt only the faint outline of this old, encrusted relic.

I looked round. All the animals were sleepy or asleep. The Dragon stared solemnly into the fire. There only, in strange caves and recesses, could he see other dragons besides himself, and they changed to devils and mocked him spitefully.

CHAPTER XXV

The following Tuesday was the last day we spent with the Sea Serpent. When we set off for the shore, the dew was still thick upon the ground and half the hillside was in shadow. We went slowly, for the night had been a little cold and the Dragon was stiff. Gran'papa was on Dobbin, and Procyon, of course, was with us also. *He* was neither stiff nor cold, for we had made him a coat from an old blanket, and he wore it all the time. We had thought of trying to do the same for the Dragon, but all the clothes we pos-sessed would not have covered a quarter of him.

As for me, I enjoyed the cool freshness of the air. All was clear and bright, except the deep hollows and the shore and the sea below the cliff. These were still grey, though further out the sun was shining. Yet now, with the coming of autumn, all the colours seemed to thin and grow pale. The blue of the sea was less intense, the blue of the sky less intense, than in the height of summer.

Coming through the valley we did not see a single creature, and when we reached the shore it was cold and bleak. Sharp little breezes lifted the sand in clouds and blew it against my bare legs, stinging them unpleasantly.

"Let's go away," I said. "It's cold and horrid, and the Sea Serpent's not here." I tried to shelter behind the Dragon, but the sand blew under him and round him, and found my legs just the same. *He* didn't like it either, because it got into his eyes, and made them gritty and sore.

"Be patient," Gran'papa told us, turning up his coat collar, "we'll soon find a sheltered spot. Presently the sun will shine out, and the wind die down; and we won't have long to wait till the Sea Serpent comes."

"You don't know what it's like with bare legs," I answered. "It's quite sore."

"You'll have to put up with it," he said; but I knew that already.

Eventually we did find a comfortable position, and fixing our eyes on the sea, we watched for the Sea Serpent. Gradually the blue water came closer. Here and there were green patches in shallow places over sand; the dark streaks showed rocks and weed. At last, slowly, as if a grey curtain were being drawn back, the sunlight swept across the shore. Immediately everything became cheerful, and we knew that summer had not yet gone away. I peered up through my fingers, and the sun was staring down as if he were pleased to have discovered us, after searching every nook. When I looked at the shore again my eyes were caught by the glint of splashing water, and *there* was the Sea Serpent, shaking off the spray as he emerged from the waves. "Here he is," I cried, and I jumped up to go and meet him. The others followed more slowly.

"Are you really going?" I asked him. "Why won't you stay?"

"It's getting too cold," he answered. "Every day the sun is later, and when at last it appears it is further off. It is still bright, but not so warm. The evenings also come very quickly, and then the sun sinks down behind the sea."

"But *we* cannot go away," the Dragon thought.

"We have the cave," Gran'papa reminded him, "and in the winter we'll burn fires in the daytime as well as at night."

"It is because I have nothing like that I *have* to go," the Sea Serpent said.

"You are fortunate," the Dragon told him. "All the rest would go too if they could."

"You're quite sure now *where* you're going?" I asked.

"I am going to find the island where the other sea serpents live. It has a lagoon and a coral reef. The sea is always blue, and the sun shines all the time. On the beach the sea serpents bask, and behind there are waving trees."

"It was like that," the Dragon thought, and added doubtfully, "here—once."

"Yes," the Sea Serpent went on, "it's just like it used to be here—long, long ago."

"Do you think there'll be dragons there?" the Dragon asked.

The Sea Serpent hesitated. "The seals or the fish or the porpoises didn't tell me of any; but they wouldn't know. There might be dragons in the middle of the island, all hidden by the trees, and they would never see them."

The Dragon considered this for some time. "I don't believe there are any," he decided, "but *if* there are, tell them about *me*. And if—if you come back next summer, bring me some message from them; perhaps I'll be here."

"I will," the Sea Serpent promised, "but maybe I myself shall never get there."

"And if you do," the Dragon thought, "it's unlikely you'll come back."

"It'll be really warm there," the Sea Serpent continued dreamily, "so warm that even I, after lying for hours on the shore, listening to the turtles and the monkeys and the parrots, will swim out again, and dive down to the cool depths of the ocean. There I shall rest in the still water, staring at the pink coral, and watching the creatures who must stay for ever in those shadowy depths. Because, if they leave the sea bed, they swell out and become helpless. Gradually they float upwards, and when they reach the top, or before it, they burst. When I'm down there I shall think of you all, and if the way has not been too difficult I will return and tell you about it."

"Couldn't you try to take us with you?" I begged, "we could go on your back."

"Would you leave *me*?" the Dragon thought. "I couldn't stay on his back. I'd be all alone in a land of strangers."

"You could fly," I suggested. "You could look at us down below you—and *that* would show you the way."

"But I can't fly very far," the Dragon said, "—over the hill, or perhaps a little further." He sounded melancholy.

"All this is moonshine," Gran'papa interrupted, in a sharp, sensible voice. "None of us can go, or *would* go without you. Besides, how could we stay for days on the Sea Serpent's back? We'd be soaked to the skin, and frozen stiff."

"I'm sure *I* could do it," I said, "so that I wouldn't get wet."

"I'm sure you could do nothing of the sort," Gran'papa took me up quite sharply. "You've been grumbling and discontented all morning—first about the sand and now about this."

"But let me try, Gran'papa—just to show you. Anyway it may be my last ride."

So he let me try, and I pulled off my clothes and climbed onto the Serpent's back. He went down to the water and began to swim out. Very soon I was quite wet, and to make it worse I fell off. That was very annoying, for I hadn't fallen off for a long time.

I scrambled out, feeling rather humiliated, while Gran'papa and the Dragon watched me. Procyon kept jumping up on me and wriggling his stumpy tail. "I'm sorry," I said to Gran'papa.

Afterwards we had our lunch. We had brought food with us, and so had the Dragon. Procyon ate grass, but the Sea Serpent went away to feed by himself in the depths.

The tide had gone out, and a strange, subdued sound came from the wet beach. It was like the bursting of many tiny bubbles, and I had heard it before, at low tide on hot days. Now I wondered what caused it. Was it just the sand drying, or did the lug-worms make it as they burrowed deeper to avoid the sun? Perhaps it was a combination of sounds—the hum of the busy life of many creatures—barnacles, limpets, mussels—each individually too small to be heard by a human ear.

"What does the Sea Serpent eat?" I asked the Dragon with a sudden change of thought.

"Fish," Gran'papa said.

"No," the Dragon told us, "the fish are his friends. He only eats seaweed."

"But," I said, "if he opened his mouth while he was swimming, could he help catching fish—just by accident I mean?"

The Dragon yawned. He wasn't very interested. "Perhaps he does catch them, when he's sleepy," he thought. He gave another big yawn. "It's almost warm enough for a doze." He closed his eyes.

"It is indeed," Gran'papa answered and closed his too. Soon I was the only one awake, and though it was now boiling hot, I got up and walked along the shore.

I went by the water's edge, running up and down the beach before the waves. Sometimes I let them catch me, and the swirling sea rose to my knees.

Presently I passed the green valley, and waded through the brown water of the stream. After that the sand ended. The shore became rocky, and at last, scrambling over big boulders, I came to the southern point. From there, a chain of low rocks, uncovered by the tide, stretched further out to sea. They were close together, but disconnected, and between them the water ebbed and flowed with each succeeding wave.

I jumped onto the first and scrambled along for ten yards or so. Then there was a gap. The top of the next was high—and rather far away; but when the water went down, a small barnacled ledge was exposed. Three times it appeared and disappeared. The fourth time I jumped. I got there all right, and scrambled up quickly to avoid the next wave. One of my toes was bleeding slightly, but it didn't matter, and I went on from rock to rock till I could go no further. The rock I had reached was flat, and gradually, in getting to it, I had become quite wet. So again I took off my clothes, and spread them out to dry, and lay down in the sunshine and peered into the water. On the landward side I could not see very deep, because the rocks came close together below the surface, and the gap was obscured by masses of brown seaweed which swept backwards and forwards with the waves. On the other side the rock dropped down straight to a sandy bottom of yellowish green. Above this I settled, because it was most pleasant to look at. I saw three fish, one after the other. They were brown, with round, blunt noses. Far apart two crabs hurried across the sand, and then, from the rock just below me, a lobster emerged. He crawled very slowly, keeping close to a low outcrop of the rock. When he had gone a little way I noticed that on the far side of the same outcrop was another lobster, moving with equal caution. I wondered if they were aware of each other, and if they were going to a pre-arranged meeting.

They reached the point of the rock at the same moment and seemed to touch. For an instant they remained thus in apparent surprise. Then both turned tail and scuttled back to their particular crannies.

Why were they so frightened, I wondered. Did lobsters eat each other? I continued to watch to see if either would return. And gradually, as I stared down at the water, I lost sight of it. The rocks and stones disappeared, and I saw instead the wonderful islands where the Sea Serpent would live. They seemed to be enchanted golden places, where all was happy all the time, and there was no night. What an adventure it would be to go there—and if only the Dragon could come also he would never again cough or get ill. Gran'papa too would have no more rheumatism, and all the strange creatures from the jungle would be happy.

There was a ripple in the water. One of the lobsters, who was cautiously extending a feeler, drew it in again hastily. The long neck of the Sea Serpent glided to the surface, and he rested his head on the rock beside me. "Would you *really* like to go?" he asked.

"I'd love to," I said, "but how can I?"

"I can take *you*," he answered.

"And the others?"

"No, only you."

"Then I can't go," I said, "—not without the others."

"Think, Wolfe," he told me, "how happy we'd be—sunshine all day long, lovely fruits for you to eat, warm water where you could bathe and never grow cold. I would give you rides too, whenever you wanted; and brown native boys would teach you to dive for pearls and ride upon the surf."

"I couldn't go without Gran'papa," I answered, "and I wouldn't leave the Dragon, or the other animals either."

"If ever you got tired of bathing," he went on persuasively, "you would find . . ."

"I never would," I interrupted.

"Well, there would be the forest if you did. In the forest grow many beautiful flowers. Among the trees prowl wild animals— lions and tigers, and monkeys and leopards; and because you were *my* friend you would be theirs also, and they would be kind to you and protect you. There might even be other dragons. . . . You would always be happy."

"I'd *never* be happy," I told him, "if I left Gran'papa and the Dragon and all the other animals. You're just like the Serpent in the Bible, who tempted Adam and Eve, and look what happened to them."

He sniffed. "You'd soon forget Gran'papa and the Dragon."

"I would not; but why can't you take us all—Gran'papa and the Dragon and Procyon—and Dobbin too? I'd like Dobbin to come."

"*I couldn't* take them all," the Sea Serpent answered, a little testily. "Don't be so silly. Besides, I don't want them; they'd only be in the way."

"I can't," I repeated.

"You're the only one I want," he continued. "Why won't you come? I would save the others if I could, but it's impossible. By staying you won't do any good. They're doomed, and if you stay with them you are doomed also. Soon the Dragon will die of cold. Your grandfather will be unable to protect either you or himself, and if you go back the village people will kill you both."

I shook my head. He had scared me a little, but I was determined.

"If you come with *me*," he went on quietly, "I will only go a short distance every day. Then I will land you somewhere, so that you will not be troubled by the cold of the water—and in a day or two we'll reach a warmer climate, and there will be no more cold for you to feel."

Again I shook my head. "I can't," I said. "I like you very much, but I can't, I can't."

"What's the good of staying?" he persisted. "You'll not be able to save your grandfather: you will only increase his unhappiness, because he will worry about your safety."

He was very plausible, very persuasive, and I felt like putting my fingers in my ears.

"Even *I* would stay," he went on, "if it would do any good; but why should we all die together? Come with me to those happy islands."

"No, I must stay."

"As you like then," he said, giving it up, "but you are cut off by the tide. I'll help you back." He made himself into a bridge and I scrambled across.

"You'll be sorry in the end," he warned me.

"If I left the others I would always be sorry."

He was completely in the water again, except for his head. He looked up to where I stood on the rock. "I like you better than any of them; but because I have to live in the sea I couldn't meet you so often as the Dragon did. Now I'll have no friends."

He disappeared quite suddenly. For some moments a swirl remained in the water; then it was calm again. That was the last I saw of him.

CHAPTER XXVI

I went back to the others a little sadly. They had wakened up again, and immediately the Dragon knew what had taken place, for I couldn't prevent myself thinking about it. He was very much disappointed, and so was Gran'papa; they had both expected the Sea Serpent to come again in the afternoon, and say good-bye to all of us together.

Gradually, too, the Dragon learned of the forebodings the Sea Serpent had expressed, and he told them to Gran'papa. So it was in a very depressed state of mind that we returned to the cave.

That evening it grew cold, and the animals from the jungle pressed closer round the fire. Previously it had been their custom to return before it was very late to their own dens in the valley and near the shore. To-night the hours went by slowly, but they did not move. There was no conversation; one pressed against another, and shivered, and thought of the Sea Serpent, and the doom he had prophesied.

At last I went to bed, but though I was inside the cave, in our own room, I knew that the creatures had not gone away. When I awoke in the morning and looked out they were still huddled there, and Gran'papa had stayed up, to stoke the fire and keep them warm.

Then the Dragon awoke, and went off to the forest to feed. The cold had troubled him also, but not so much as the others, because he had been protected to some extent by the cave. So Gran'papa suggested that all the animals should dig caves close together and opening off the Dragon's, to preserve the general warmth. They were pleased with this idea, and at once began to work, while Gran'papa came inside to get a little sleep.

Presently the Dragon returned, and when he saw what was going on he began to help. As usual he worked very quickly, and by the evening there was room in the cave for every animal. It was an immense place now, with tunnels in every direction.

That night we brought the fire inside, and though it made the cave very stuffy, the animals found it comfortable.

Then they were all happy again, but the next day was colder still, and it was almost noon before any of them ventured out to search for food. Gradually it was growing colder, and when we awoke one morning the whole hillside was white with frost. Within the cave it still seemed warm enough to me, but beyond the fire the ground was hard as stone.

"I think you'd better stay in the cave to-day," Gran'papa told the Dragon and the other creatures. "It's too cold for you to come out. Wolfe and I will go to the jungle with Dobbin, and bring back leaves for you to eat."

The Dragon was grateful, but at the same time he seemed very despondent. "Will it always be as cold as this?" he asked.

"There will be some warm spells," Gran'papa answered.

"But it won't be hot?"

"Not till summer comes again—but that won't be so long. We'll bring you food every day, and keep you company in the cave."

"Will you make the cave warmer?" The Dragon was shivering.

"It's as hot as I *can* make it," Gran'papa answered, "—and even so, we're using more turf than we can spare." He looked worried.

We fixed the panniers on Dobbin's back, and set off through the brown, autumnal heather. Presently the sun came out and began to melt the frost. Everything was fresh and damp, and pleasant to me: it seemed almost like spring. "If it wasn't for the Dragon," I said, "wouldn't you like this weather best?"

Gran'papa shook his head. "No; I like the long, hot, summer days."

"Yes—but sometimes it's too hot."

"I never find that—and *you* won't when you get to my age. You'll want a hot, hot sun, and a windless corner. You'll sit by yourself, leaning on your stick, your chin upon your hands. You'll watch a bee in the foxgloves, swaying them slowly with his weight, and you'll remember a summer long ago when you lived with your grandfather and a dragon in a cave on the hill."

"I don't want to be like that," I said.

"Don't you want to grow up and be a man?"

"No. I want everything to stay just as it is now, and I want to go on living in the cave, with you and the Dragon and all the animals."

"I should like that too," he said, "but we can't; everything changes."

"Why should it change?"

"Because it must; it is part of the order of things. Old things wear out; new things are made: they too grow old in their turn: you cannot step twice into the same river."

I know now that he was quoting the Greek philosopher Heracleitus, but at the time of course I didn't, though what occurred immediately afterwards stamped the words upon my mind. For as Gran'papa spoke we came over the crest of the hill, and saw what had once been called the green valley before us. Hardly a trace of green remained. Instead, it was a rusty brown, the colour of an old anchor which has lain for years at the bottom of the sea.

"Oh, Gran'papa," I exclaimed, "what has happened?"

"It's the frost," he said, as if he were answering himself rather than me, "—just the frost."

For a moment we both stared, and then we descended into the valley. It was a scene of extraordinary desolation. The undergrowth was shrivelled and brittle, as if a sheet of fire had swept down from heaven to blast it. The huge, sensual plants lay twisted on the ground, and their thick fleshy leaves crumbled to dust at a touch of the finger. Eventually we reached the stream; it was choked with dead leaves and branches, and hushed to a fainter murmur by the general catastrophe.

We wandered slowly along the bank. Presently we came to the remains of the little grove where I had found the strange plant with the moving blue eye. There it was now, stretched on the ground, crumpled and twisted. Gran'papa touched it with his stick, and it seemed to draw back slightly, with a faint tremor.

I shuddered. "Please Gran'papa," I said, "can't we go away? I don't like it here."

"What about the Dragon?" Gran'papa asked, "—and the other animals? Aren't you going to feed them?"

"I forgot."

We went on, and reached a sheltered place where only the upper foliage had been blighted by the frost. The underneath leaves were still green, though not so fresh as in the summer. We tore them off and packed them in the panniers. Then we set out again for the cave.

"There aren't many leaves left," I said in a low voice.

"Not very many."

"What will the Dragon do when they're finished?"

"I don't know."

I saw that Gran'papa did not want to be questioned. So I was silent, and puzzled over it by myself.

When we reached the cave the Dragon was shivering violently, and he showed no interest in the food we had brought.

"Suddenly I became hot," he told us. "I went outside. Now I am very cold, but my head is still hot."

His eyes seemed to have grown larger and brighter. The back of the cave was lit by a phosphorescent glow, which emanated from his body and tail, and burned with an ardour that was dull yet strong. It was a long time now since I had seen that glow. In the early days it had shone frequently in the darkness, but gradually it had faded, reappearing only by a special effort of his will. Why now did it shine once more?

The other animals seemed unwell too. They were cold and dull, and would not touch the food. So when we had put Dobbin into his stable, we piled more turf on the fire, and told the Dragon that we must go to the cairn to fetch our own provisions.

"Wait a little," the Dragon begged us. "I want to speak to you."

We waited, and presently he went on: "All of *us* belong to the past. We have come into your world by a strange accident, and soon we shall leave it again. We have not been very happy here. It has been an uncomfortable, makeshift existence, and the proper inhabitants do not want us."

"*We* want you," Gran'papa assured him, and I murmured, "Yes, we do."

"I know you do," the Dragon answered, "and if we went back to our own world we should want to take you with us. We cannot go back; we cannot even do what the Sea Serpent has done—and we cannot continue here. There may be some place where we could live, but we don't know the way there, and if we did we should not have the power to go. Gradually it will grow colder. . . ."

"Not necessarily," Gran'papa interrupted. "It never gets very cold here. It's because it's near the sea."

Dobbin neighed, and strained at his halter; he seemed uneasy. I went over and rubbed his nose and patted his neck to soothe him.

"Even if it remains the same," the Dragon continued, "we shall all die quite soon. It is too cold for us to live. Before we die, while the people are still frightened of me, go back to them. Make peace before it is too late."

"And what will happen to you?" Gran'papa asked. "Who will bring you food?"

"We shall not need food," the Dragon answered. "What use is food to the dying?"

"Nevertheless we shall bring it to you," Gran'papa said. "Now we must go to the cairn." He grasped me by the arm, and I took a step away from Dobbin. Immediately the old horse became agitated, and began to neigh loudly.

"It's all right," I told him. "We're not going to leave you. We'll be back presently." He stopped neighing, yet his eyes were strangely troubled.

Procyon had been with us to the jungle, but when Gran'papa called to him now he seemed reluctant, and held back. "What's the matter?" I asked. "*You're* all right."

I received no reply. It was as if a blind had been drawn down, so that I could not see any longer into the minds of the animals. The means of communication had suddenly been cut off; they were dumb.

I felt miserable. "Procyon!" I shouted. He hesitated, looked at the Dragon, and came forward slowly.

We set off. Gran'papa walked very fast. I kept up with him, while Procyon came dejectedly at our heels. Then for some reason I looked round, and caught a last glimpse of Dobbin's melancholy face watching us. "I think Dobbin is unhappy," I said. "I think he wants to go back to the stable at home."

"He won't have long to wait," Gran'papa answered grimly.

"Are you going to make peace?" I asked.

"Yes. You will have to go back home." His face was very stern, and he shut his mouth tightly.

"But Gran'papa, I want to stay with *you*."

He did not answer, and when we had gone some distance I spoke again: "You're coming home, too, aren't you, Gran'papa?"

He put his hand on my shoulder and drew me closer to him. "Remember this: if you want me, and think about me, and wish for me, you can always bring me back, no matter where I am, or where you are." But I didn't understand what he meant.

CHAPTER XXVII

It was long after twelve when we reached the cairn, but there was nothing there and no sign of a messenger.

"Will we wait?" I asked Gran'papa.

"No," he said. "We've enough food to do us. We'll go back to the cave."

So we turned, and walked slowly down the hill. The last of the frost had melted now, and the afternoon sun was pleasant. "The animals could come out to-day," I suggested, "and even go down to the shore."

"Yes," Gran'papa agreed, "they'd be better there than in the cave, and they'd have time to get home before sunset."

"I expect the lizards will be outside at any rate," and I looked ahead and watched for them.

"Procyon's not well," Gran'papa said presently. "He's terribly listless."

"Perhaps he's eaten something that doesn't agree with him," I answered, but Gran'papa shook his head.

"I believe *he's* unhappy too."

"What about?" I asked, but Gran'papa didn't know.

We crossed the stream and climbed the opposite bank, but still there was no sign of the creatures from the cave. "They must have stayed inside," I said. "I can't see any of them."

"Nor can I," Gran'papa answered, "but that doesn't mean they're not there." He bent down. "Go on, Procyon. You bring them out. Tell them they'd be far warmer in the sunshine." I think Procyon understood, but he didn't obey. He gave one feeble twitch of his tail, then crouched down low against the ground. "What's the matter with him?" Gran'papa exclaimed, and he bent down and stroked him.

Then we went on again and Procyon followed us reluctantly. I continued to look towards the cave to see if any of the animals were in sight. Presently I began to realize that the hillside was different. "Gran'papa," I said, "something's wrong."

He didn't answer, and after a time I added, "There seem to be more stones."

In a few minutes we saw clearly what had happened. The cave had disappeared. In its place was a fresh slope of gravel and earth.

"They're gone," Gran'papa muttered. "He's pulled it down."

I stared, hardly able to believe. "Are they inside?" I asked at last, with a feeling of misery and horror.

"Yes."

For a long time I gazed at the ruin without speaking. Then I looked up at Gran'papa. He too was contemplating the desolation, and his face was hopeless.

"Poor Dobbin," I thought. "He never got back to his own stable after all."

I think now Gran'papa must have known for a considerable time that our paradise was doomed. I hadn't, in spite of the warnings of the Dragon and the Sea Serpent. Even to-day I hardly understood.

Gran'papa had constantly reassured me, but I think that all the time he must have seen the end approaching, and realized that at most there could only be a few more weeks. Now, like Samson, the Dragon had pulled down the roof on himself, and on all the other creatures as well.

"Wolfe," Gran'papa said, "you'll have to go back now—at once."

"Should we not try to dig them out?" I asked.

"No; they're better as they are."

"Could we not dig another cave, Gran'papa, and live in it together, with Procyon?"

"What could we live *on?*" he said.

"Won't they bring us food?"

"Not now."

"Then Procyon can get us food—the way he did the first day— don't you remember, Gran'papa?"

"I do; but he'll never do that again."

We continued to stand and stare till I asked, "How will they *know* in the village? They can't have seen this. They may bring the food still. Let us go to the cairn and wait."

I wasn't really very hopeful; nevertheless we went; and Procyon followed slowly. All afternoon we sat there, leaning against the grey stones, hungry and wretched; but nobody came. We looked down at the soft colours of the sea and the sky and the heather; but we hardly spoke a word.

At last, when the sun was very low, and it was beginning to get cool, Gran'papa said, "I don't expect they *do* know what has happened, but they guess that the Dragon is ill; they have tried this to see if he is still strong enough to protect us."

"What will we do now?" I asked.

He looked at me. "God seems to have forsaken us," he said, "or we, perhaps, have forsaken the Christian Church. Before the Church there were other gods—spirits of the earth and the rocks, of the streams and the trees. Maybe we should call *them* to our aid."

"How could you do that?" I wondered.

"I don't know," he answered.

"Are *they* sleeping too—like the Dragon before the earth slipped?"

"Perhaps."

The sun had nearly set now, and was shining close to the water. Gran'papa stood up; "I'll pray to them," he said.

I stood up too, and for a time we remained silent, wrapped in the golden splendour of the sun.

Was Gran'papa praying? I waited for some visual manifestation, but none came. The only change was in the sound. The breeze stirred faintly through the heather, and for a moment I heard the stream more loudly. Then all was as before.

We sat down again. The sun had disappeared completely, and in the twilight we still looked at the sea.

Presently Gran'papa got up. "Come," he said. "I'm going to take you to Father Binyon."

"Should we not go home?" I asked.

"No," he answered. "When they turned me out before, is it likely they would receive me now?—and I wouldn't feel *you* were safe there. I'll leave you with Father Binyon. He's the only man I trust: *he* can protect you."

"But won't you come too, Gran'papa?"

"No: I don't think he could protect *me*—besides, I don't want to ask him."

"But what will you do, Gran'papa?"

"I can look after myself," he said. "Now don't ask foolish questions." He smiled, and I tried to smile back, but I felt very uneasy.

As we descended the hillside we came down into an ever-deepening shadow. All was quiet in the village, but we didn't have to go into it, nor pass near any of the houses.

When we came to the priest's gate Gran'papa stopped, and I knew from the sound of his voice that he was very tired. "I'm not going any further," he said, "but I'll watch you from here." Procyon lay down on the grass by the roadside.

I stopped still, and looked. I was dazed, and everything seemed unreal; I felt sick too, for want of food. It was not till he bent down, and clasped me tightly in his arms, and kissed me, that I realized we were going to part, and I burst into tears.

For a long time we remained thus, and when he began to let me go I clung to him. "Wolfe dear," he said, "we'll have to leave each other now."

"Could we not stay together to-night?" I asked, "—just one more night."

"No," he said. He took my hand, and led me up the path. "Wait till I get back to the gate," he told me, "then knock. I will watch you from the bushes."

He returned down the path. I saw him pick up Procyon again, and step into the shadow.

Then I knocked.

Father Binyon himself came to the door. Above his head he held a candlestick, and he peered down at me. "Well, my child," he said, "you have returned at last. Come inside."

Dumbly I obeyed. He led me along the passage to his room, and made me sit before the fire. Then he went out, and spoke for a few minutes to his housekeeper.

Presently she brought in food, and the priest pressed me to eat, but I could not. "Would you like to go to bed?" he asked.

I nodded silently, and he led me upstairs to a little room under the roof. "Good night," he said, "and may God bless you."

He closed the door, and I went to the window and peered out. At first, after the light of the house, I could see nothing; then again my eyes grew accustomed to the gloom. I saw the mountain, and gradually, and carefully, I traced the white wavering line of the road.

There, climbing slowly upwards, was a dark figure. I watched intently the slow and painful progress, but at last the figure reached the cairn and seemed to disappear into the ground. I didn't know whether he had stopped there, or if he had gone on, and dropped out of sight beyond the summit.

"Good-bye, Gran'papa," I sobbed, "good-bye, good-bye, good-bye. . . ."

ALSO AVAILABLE FROM VALANCOURT BOOKS

Michael Arlen	Hell! said the Duchess
R. C. Ashby (Ruby Ferguson)	He Arrived at Dusk
Frank Baker	The Birds
Charles Beaumont	The Hunger and Other Stories
David Benedictus	The Fourth of June
Charles Birkin	The Smell of Evil
John Blackburn	A Scent of New-Mown Hay
	Broken Boy
	Blue Octavo
	The Flame and the Wind
	Nothing but the Night
	Bury Him Darkly
	The Face of the Lion
Thomas Blackburn	The Feast of the Wolf
John Braine	Room at the Top
	The Vodi
R. Chetwynd-Hayes	The Monster Club
Basil Copper	The Great White Space
	Necropolis
Hunter Davies	Body Charge
Jennifer Dawson	The Ha-Ha
Barry England	Figures in a Landscape
Ronald Fraser	Flower Phantoms
Gillian Freeman	The Liberty Man
	The Leather Boys
	The Leader
Stephen Gilbert	Bombardier
	Monkeyface
	The Burnaby Experiments
	Ratman's Notebooks
Martyn Goff	The Youngest Director
Stephen Gregory	The Cormorant
Thomas Hinde	Mr. Nicholas
	The Day the Call Came
Claude Houghton	I Am Jonathan Scrivener
	This Was Ivor Trent
Gerald Kersh	Nightshade and Damnations
	Fowlers End
Francis King	Never Again
	An Air That Kills
	The Dividing Stream
	The Dark Glasses

C.H.B. KITCHIN	Ten Pollitt Place
	The Book of Life
HILDA LEWIS	The Witch and the Priest
JOHN LODWICK	Brother Death
KENNETH MARTIN	Aubade
MICHAEL NELSON	Knock or Ring
	A Room in Chelsea Square
BEVERLEY NICHOLS	Crazy Pavements
OLIVER ONIONS	The Hand of Kornelius Voyt
J.B. PRIESTLEY	Benighted
	The Doomsday Men
	The Other Place
	The Magicians
	The Thirty-First of June
	The Shapes of Sleep
	Saturn Over the Water
PETER PRINCE	Play Things
PIERS PAUL READ	Monk Dawson
FORREST REID	Following Darkness
	The Spring Song
	Brian Westby
	The Tom Barber Trilogy
	Denis Bracknel
GEORGE SIMS	Sleep No More
	The Last Best Friend
ANDREW SINCLAIR	The Facts in the Case of E.A. Poe
	The Raker
COLIN SPENCER	Panic
DAVID STOREY	Radcliffe
	Pasmore
	Saville
RUSSELL THORNDIKE	The Slype
	The Master of the Macabre
JOHN WAIN	Hurry on Down
	The Smaller Sky
	Strike the Father Dead
	A Winter in the Hills
KEITH WATERHOUSE	There is a Happy Land
	Billy Liar
COLIN WILSON	Ritual in the Dark
	Man Without a Shadow
	The Philosopher's Stone
	The God of the Labyrinth